THE WALTZ OF WOLVES

THE COMPLETE COLLECTION

ESME CARMICHAEL

ISBN: 9781838327293

THE WALTZ OF WOLVES
THE COMPLETE COLLECTION

Thank you for purchasing *The Waltz of Wolves: The Complete Collection*! This paperback contains the entire Waltz of Wolves trilogy, as well an exclusive Bonus story that follows Campbell's journey after the events that occurred in Waterman's Quarry.

I wrote each Part of *The Waltz of Wolves* in conjunction with specific events and/or revelations in the main Connection Series. To avoid potential spoilers, I recommend reading Parts 2, 3 and the Bonus story after The Mover of Mountains (Book 2 in the main series). Part 1 can be enjoyed anytime, and does not contain any spoilers.

To download a free map of the New World, please consider signing up to my Newsletter by scanning the QR Code below:

* * *

Like the main series, The Waltz of Wolves is a dark fantasy. A full list of content warnings can be found on Page 241.

PART 1

1

MAELSTROM, YEAR 150

Campbell Anders stood at the side of his family's dining table, holding a silver tray of canapés. A selection of blinis, each topped with a flower of smoked salmon, taunted him. He stared at the curling chunks of chive, then the decorative blobs of orange caviar. He felt sick.

And angry. Yes, he was very angry.

"Now, Campbell," Gerald — his father — said, walking into the dining room and shrugging into his black dinner jacket. "I expect you to be on your best behaviour tonight. Aside from Lord Mason's presence being a great honour, it is imperative that this deal occurs seamlessly."

Campbell inaudibly huffed. Their family single-handedly owned ten percent of all the wealth in Maelstrom, so how much more money did they really need?

"Oh, don't you worry, father," Miranda said, parading into the room. "If anything is certain, it's that Campbell will find a way to screw this evening up."

Campbell curled his fist, lying low at his side. He openly glared at his sister, who – oblivious – paraded to the mirror over the marble fireplace and flicked the odd piece of mousy hair from her face. Next, she delicately dabbed the skin around her mouth, trying to smooth out whatever makeup she'd smeared on herself. As he watched, Campbell's glare lowered into a grimace. He knew the exact reason why Miranda fussed over her appearance, and his stomach lurched.

"Whore," he hissed meanly.

Miranda formed a tight smile and glared at him from the mirror, before she turned with a nasty smirk.

"Be careful, brother," she said, looking him up and down. "It's bad manners for a Slave, even a temporary one, to badmouth their Masters. I could have you whipped."

Campbell rolled his eyes. This charade — of him being a Slave — had gone on for long enough. After all, he'd already accepted that his foolish, if not brazen, attempt to leave Maelstrom had failed spectacularly, but using temporary Slavery as his punishment wouldn't make a blind bit of difference. His family were just trying to humiliate him, again. Did Campbell regret sneaking out of the house and trying to leave Maelstrom's black heart? Absolutely not. If anything, it made him even more determined to escape that shithole.

The doorbell rang, rattling his ears.

Miranda's eyes widened, her face both flushing and losing colour entirely. "He's here!" she gasped, and ran from the room, the trails of her long, salmon-coloured gown disappearing after her.

Campbell's heart rose inside his throat, anxiety twisting his gut. He'd seen Mason before, once, when he was younger. But never inside his own home. Mason's presence in the Anders' Residence was, to some, an incredible honour. To Campbell, it felt like a violation.

Even their grand abode, neatly crammed with expensive ornaments and polishing Slaves, creaked and complained as Mason's dinner shoes pounded on the wooden floorboards. His father's voice wafted throughout the air, followed by a laugh – forced, genuine? No one could quite tell with Gerald Anders. He was expertly capable of only showing what he wanted to show.

A talent that, Campbell had heard, Mason also shared.

Footsteps grew louder, the air thicker, and Campbell's parents appeared at the doorway to the dining room. His father, standing proudly with a poker down his spine, wore his black tuxedo like a man who was born for such events. His greying hair, neatly waxed into position, overshadowed an ageing face and intense blue eyes, the colour of glaciers.

Campbell huffed again, annoyed that he shared those same bright blue eyes. He despised the thought of his father's features presenting themselves so readily in his face.

His mother stood diligently beside his father, beaming. With rich blonde hair pulled into a bun atop her head, Gillian Anders was a beautiful, sublime woman. She was also over two decades younger than her husband.

Campbell once assumed that Gillian had only been interested in Gerald for his money and social status. Why else would she, a gorgeous young woman who must have had her selection of suitors, decide to wed Gerald Anders: the pot-bellied swine who sold innocent lives into a lifetime of Slavery?

But as Campbell grew older and observed the true atrocities his father committed, Campbell decided that his mother must have loved Gerald. Why else would she stay with him? Surely, even a gold-digger with limited morality would grow nauseous at what his father did? So, Campbell assumed that his mother was not a gold-digger after all, just a despicable human being, effortlessly able to turn a blind eye.

He despised them both.

"Please, after you," Miranda said, grinning, parading all over the place.

Campbell felt the urge to roll his eyes again, but the low, ominous pound of dinner shoes quickly shot manners down his spine.

Campbell didn't know where to look when Lord Mason – the man who quite literally destroyed the Old World one-hundred-and-fifty years prior – came marching into his family's dining room. At first, Campbell's stare darted to the floor, but Mason's polished black dinner shoes came into his vision and he panicked. Pulling his eyes up along the pressed black tuxedo, they fell, reluctantly, onto Mason's face.

For a short moment, Mason and Campbell stared at each other. Silently assessing, just taking each other in.

Campbell assumed that Mason must have been staring at the bruised, angry fifteen-year-old boy with a sense of amusement and pity – if the smirk tickling his lips was anything to go by.

But Campbell stared at Mason's handsome face, topped with inky black hair, and felt nothing but fear. Pure, numbing fear. Campbell glimpsed into his eyes – resembling diamonds, which could kill with a single stare – and immediately dropped his attention to the floorboards.

Mason chuckled softly to himself, perhaps realising the source of Campbell's agitation.

Fear swiftly deteriorated, replaced by anger. Yes, Campbell despised Mason, too.

"I didn't know you were enslaving members of your own family these days, Gerald?" Mason said, wandering around the table. His voice, so low and succulent, caressed Campbell's ears, and he wanted to scratch out his eardrums.

Gerald laughed loudly. "Oh, it is only temporary. My son tried to leave this family, just so he could aimlessly wander the five Territories. What do such people call themselves? *Roamers*, is it? Regardless, it seems he'd like to forget that he is an Aristocrat, so I found it fitting to place him in the duty he'd rather belong in."

"Indeed," Mason hummed, grinning. "Well, I admire your punishments."

They took their positions at the table: Gerald at the head, bordered by Mason on one side, Gillian on the other. Miranda sat next to Mason, grinning like a schoolgirl, her eyelashes constantly fluttering.

Fucking whore, Campbell reminded himself.

Oh, if only his father knew what Campbell knew! If only the great Gerald Anders had heard Miranda's moans coming from behind that thumping closet door. If he had, no doubt Miranda would be serving canapés, right beside Campbell. Who was with her that night? Campbell was too disgusted to care. But his older sister had clearly set her heart on Mason becoming her next *entertainer*. Judging by Mason's returned smirks, or the odd wink over his glass of champagne, he clearly liked the idea, too.

"I hear you've been making good progress with your investigations, Lord Mason," Gillian said, wiping the stain of lipstick from her champagne flute with the pad of her thumb.

Mason's smile dulled. "Unfortunately, that lead has dried up. The girl is dead."

"Oh." Gillian said, visibly startled. "I-I am so sorry to hear that, I had no idea."

"It's of no matter," Mason replied, before a delicate sip of his champagne. "She will be reborn in the next nine months or so."

Campbell's eyebrows knitted together. *How was that even possible?*

"Darling brother, I require salmon!" Miranda clicked her fingers at him. Campbell grit his teeth as he paraded around the table, offering canapés between the courses of food. When did Campbell last eat? He couldn't remember, and his stomach berated him for it.

As the idle dinner conversation continued, Campbell grew more agitated. Finally, the family reverted to one of the sitting rooms, cradling tumblers of whiskey that Campbell was forced to serve.

"I am very intrigued by your new wares, Gerald," Mason said, as Campbell diligently refilled his glass. His third already. Clearly, Mason liked whiskey.

"Oh, you will be not be disappointed!" Gerald grinned, boasting his yellowed teeth, and took a laboured drag on his cigar. The air, already heavy with smoke and intoxication, grew even thicker and Campbell's head throbbed.

Commotion sounded from the corridor. Campbell turned to see a boy, only a little older than him, being roughly dragged into the room by two sour-looking Masonians.

Campbell sadly observed the grey rags covering a bruised, muscular body, up to the floods of greasy brown hair. But, above everything, it was the boy's eyes that made Campbell feel sick. A glorious shade of green jade, they shone ever so hopelessly in the light from the chandelier.

"Ah, here he is." Gerald grinned again. He paraded towards the boy, who continued to struggle against the Masonians' grips. Campbell's eyes trailed down and noticed Mason's loyal stooges lacked their usual weapon belts, yet they still possessed wooden batons and were quick to strike the boy's torso. He collapsed onto his knees, groaning.

Gerald took a great handful of his hair and yanked the boy's head up. "Lord Mason, may I present to you Harrison Dagger, son of Iuila."

"Oh, the resemblance is most striking!" Mason grinned, skulking closer. "He has Iulia's eyes too, I see."

Harrison spat on the floor, just before Mason's polished shoes. He grunted as more batons collided with his flesh.

Mason chuckled to himself. "And her defiance!"

Gerald threw the boy away from him, like he was nothing but a soiled napkin. "Can I interest you in such wares?"

A low hum arose from Mason's throat. "I am uncertain. I would very much like to own Iulia Dagger's son – she was one of my most treasured Slaves, before she escaped, of course. But I feel he is too..."

"Young?"

"Rabid." Mason lifted his nose in evident disgust.

"We could offer training," Gerald said. They locked eyes – blue to diamond – as Gerald casually puffed away on his cigar. "No extra charge, of course. But perhaps we can instil a sense of obedience in young Mr Dagger before he enters your establishment."

Mason's evil smile reformed anew. "I find that somewhat agreeable."

"Excellent!" Gerald motioned to the corridor. "Shall we discuss details in my office?"

"Most certainly." Mason downed his tumbler of whiskey and deposited it on Campbell's tray. Campbell barely registered its existence: his stare remained focussed on Harrison and the blood trickling from his nose.

"Of course, I do have other wares, should you decide against purchasing Mr Dagger," Gerald said, as their footsteps sounded down the corridor. "I have another in my possession: a Mr Ira Bentley. He's a few years older than Mr Dagger and tenfold more obedient, so you may find him better suited for your establishment."

"In that case, I may well indeed buy both of them! You do sell the best merchandise, after all."

Both men laughed as they ascended the stairs.

2

———

Gerald's grip bruised the bone on Campbell's arm. It was almost a relief when he was thrown into the barred cell, deep in the bowels of the Anders' Residence.

Campbell landed on the dirty floor with a loud slam, inhaling dust and mould spores. He coughed around the cloying air, but quickly recovered to see his father standing in the cell's entrance, a sick smile on his face.

"You wish you were one of the rats, do you, boy? Fine then, you can sleep with them tonight."

The barred door slammed shut and Gerald wasted no time in locking Campbell in. The padlock waited for Campbell's affections, yet he admitted he just didn't have the energy to try and pick it open. As his father trudged up the stairs, another lit cigar hanging from his mouth, Campbell tenderly felt the bruised, swollen flesh around his eye, and admitted that it just wasn't worth defying his father anymore. At least when he was younger, his mother used to help him, to defend him.

But now? Well, now Gillian actively supported Campbell's punishments.

There was a time when Campbell would stick up for his parents. He would convince his young, innocent self that he'd been in the wrong, so he thought it only made sense that he was punished for it. He used to tell himself it was for his own good: he would rather his father beat obedience into his skinny body, than be left with the Masonians. If anything, Campbell was certain his father would be kinder when ordering him into submission.

Not anymore. Yes, Campbell still believed his father's fists would be preferred to a Masonian baton, but Campbell no longer tried to justify his parents' actions. Campbell knew they hated him. The feeling was mutual, after all.

As Campbell lay in that cold, musty cell beneath his family home, he realised with no uncertainty that he remained under their roof solely to *maintain appearances*. Indeed, how much would business suffer if the son of the most prominent Slaver in Maelstrom was himself sold into Slavery – or executed?

Curling himself into a ball, Campbell almost wished to be executed. At least the noose would hug him tighter than his parents ever had.

A cough rattled through the empty cells. Campbell startled, searching. The cellar was dark, but slivers of silver moonlight, from the small window, cast just enough light to make out the isolated being, located in the cell next to him.

"Hello?" Campbell edged closer, his borrowed Slave's uniform – a white shirt and black trousers – picking up fat rodent droppings from the floor. "Hello?"

"I think you're in the wrong room, Aristocrat."

Through the dark, curled in the corner of the neighbouring cell with his knees pressed up to his chest, a boy stared at him. Campbell narrowed his eyes and picked out the strands of greasy brown hair, and the dark trails of blood below his left nostril.

"You were Upstairs," Campbell said, edging closer to the bars. "You're being sold to Mason, aren't you?"

A bitter laugh erupted from the boy's lungs. "After they break me in a little."

Campbell nervously licked his upper lip, and startled at the taste of salt. Mason's visit had clearly rattled him more than he cared to admit.

"You're Harrison Dagger, right?"

"What's it to you?" he spat, and Campbell could feel – rather than see – the glare cutting into him.

"Well, we're here all night, aren't we?" Campbell leant against the bars.

His spine pressed against the cold metal and he relished the prickling chill. "Might as well introduce ourselves."

"But *we* haven't introduced anyone. My name was given to you, without my consent."

Campbell winced. "Then let me give you mine as recompense."

"Gods, do you hear yourself?" The boy laughed, and only then was Campbell aware of the slight Herdinese accent, trickling in the echo of his words. "Such a fucking Aristocrat."

"I can't help what I was born as," Campbell whispered, as if his very words were poisonous. "Same as you."

"What's that supposed to mean?"

"You're a Herder." Campbell often imagined the nomadic groups of people, who wandered the icy mountains of the north with their Herds of reindeer, with a sense of awed envy. He'd give anything to bask in such freedom.

Silence came from behind those bars. As it grew suffocating, Campbell turned, trying to detect the boy through the lingering darkness. Only shadows stared back.

"I didn't mean to offend," Campbell said sincerely. "I just noticed your accent."

Silence continued, and Campbell wished he could hide in those shadows, to be completely swallowed up by them. Social interaction had never been easy for him, but now Campbell's isolation threatened to reach unbearable levels. He felt that imaginary noose around his neck, slowly tightening.

Campbell was brutally wrenched back to reality as the boy leant his head back and gave a terrific roar of laughter. A small chuckle escaped Campbell's lips, simply from reflex, although he was perplexed at what was so funny.

Eventually, as the boy's laughter subsided, silence returned like a thundering avalanche, sucking all air from Campbell.

"You've got a fucking nerve," the boy spat, then mocked the posh, Aristocratic accent. "One can tell your heritage too, darling, so here I am taking the piss."

"I wasn't," Campbell said, bristling. This boy was beginning to annoy him. All Campbell was trying to do was to find some common ground. What did he ever do to deserve his aggression? Then again, what did Campbell do to be born into such a despicable family? He had known from an early age that life was inherently unfair.

"Like Hel you were," the boy snarled. "You're an Aristocrat. I'm a nothing more than a rat to you."

"Stop calling me a fucking Aristocrat!" Campbell shouted, all of his pent-up aggression and anger busting from the seams of his control. "All my life, I've been told what a *privilege* it is to be an Aristocrat. But Aristocracy isn't a privilege, it's a *disease* – it's the infected heart of this entire city. Heck, of the entire goddamned Fjord Territory! So no, I'm *not* an Aristocrat: I'm not going to sell innocent people into Slavery and I'm *not* going to beat them or torture them like the rest of my *fucking* family!" Campbell paused, breathless, and wiped the thick sheen of sweat from his brow. "I am *nothing* like them, do you hear me?"

The boy remained silent, just staring. If Campbell had been in better spirits, he may have wondered if the boy had heard him correctly. But, that night, Campbell just couldn't care less. He threw his back against those cold bars, unwilling to waste any more energy.

"Takes guts to go against your family," the boy said.

"They're not my family," Campbell snapped back, and he meant it. He would disown them just as easily as they would him.

"What's your name, mate?" There was a tone to the boy's voice: a slight gentleness that wasn't there before. It lowered Campbell's guard.

"Campbell," he replied, quietly.

Something shuffled across the floor, and Campbell turned just as the boy's face came into the moonlight. Jade eyes illuminated beneath swathes of silver.

"I'm Harrison," he said, presenting his hand through the bars. "Nice to meet you, Campbell."

In perhaps his first act of friendship, Campbell shook Harrison's hand. He startled at the warmth of Harrison's skin, despite the incessant chill of those cells.

"And you," Campbell whispered, a little overwhelmed.

"So, why you down with us rats anyway?" Harrison asked, slouching against the bars, mirroring Campbell. Heat flowed between the bars and Campbell relished being this close to another being.

"I disrespected my father," Campbell replied, and an easy smile stretched his lips. "I tried to run away."

Harrison chuckled. "Nice. How'd you get caught?"

Campbell huffed bitterly beneath his breath. "Masonians found me and thought I was an escaped Slave. I told them who I was to avoid a beating, only to be brought home to my father... And I still got a beating."

"Tough luck," Harrison mumbled. "Well, if it's any consolation, I was kidnapped because I'm the bastard son of Iulia Dagger – the only Slave who's ever escaped Mason's Palace."

Campbell's ears perked up. "Jeez, I didn't know that was possible."

"It ain't now." Harrison laughed, bitterly. "Bastard's got dogs and snipers at his Palace now, to ensure it doesn't happen again."

"Well, is... Is she still alive? Your mother, I mean."

A long pause weighed heavily on the room. "No, she died about five years ago. Consumption, would you believe."

"I'm sorry."

"Don't be. I consider it a blessing, otherwise she would've been plucked from the Snowlands with me."

"You're from the Snowlands?" Campbell turned to meet Harrison's sad smile. "I've never been that far north." Actually, Campbell had never been out of the Fjord Territory. The other four Territories of Mason's New World remained a perpetual mystery to him.

"Gods, it's beautiful," Harrison said tenderly, disappearing into his memories. His white teeth gleamed in the light, and for a moment Campbell startled at how clean they were, compared to his father's, stained from years of cigar use. "Want to see it?"

"More than anything." Campbell ached to leave Maelstrom, to run from its corrupted heart and spread his arms to the free, wintry world. "But that's impossible."

Harrison cocked his head to one side. "Why?"

Campbell gestured to the cells around him.

"Oh, these?" Harrison laughed again – this time with genuine amusement – although Campbell still didn't know what he found so funny. "Don't you worry about these. They can't keep us in here all the time, can they?"

Campbell disagreed.

Harrison smirked, a hopeful sparkle in his eye. "They're going to start *training* me tomorrow, so I'm getting outta these cells. As for you... Well, I'm sure daddy won't be able to resist an apology."

Campbell almost choked on his own breath. "I'm not apologising to that bastard!"

"No, I mean to maintain appearances. Get yourself outta here, then we enact the next part of our plan."

Campbell's nose scrunched up. "What plan?"

Harrison Dagger formed a wide, spectacular grin. "I'm getting out of Maelstrom, mate, and you're coming with me."

3

———————

Sunlight blared through the window, rousing Campbell from his slumber. He groaned as his muscles flexed, his entire body aching from sleeping on the cold, stone floor.

Harrison, it seemed, had no qualms about sleeping on the floor. He snored his head off quite happily throughout the night.

That all came crashing down when Gerald Anders came bounding down the stone stairs, three Masonians at his tail. Harrison woke up with a grunt, his eyes wide and concerned, and assessed the group of bloodthirsty men who opened the door to his cell.

"Time to learn some manners, Mr Dagger." Gerald smiled around the smoking cigar in his mouth, throwing his hands in the pockets of grey trousers just clinging to the tails of his blue shirt.

Campbell watched with a sense of admiration and utter, complete horror as Harrison Dagger flipped the finger and blew a loud raspberry through his lips.

Gerald sighed. "Alright, boys. Take him out."

The Masonians were not kind to Harrison and forced him to his feet with swinging batons. He struggled against their grip and groaned with each strike, but three grown men easily outmatched him. They dragged him, kicking and grunting, up the stone steps and out of view.

Campbell locked identical glacial-blue eyes with his father, and exchanged silent insults.

With a small, satisfied smirk, Gerald turned his back.

"Wait," Campbell said, though it knotted his gut to do it. "I-I need to talk to you. Please, Father," he added, when Gerald's back remained turned.

"*Father*." Gerald huffed and finally graced Campbell with his full attention. "I didn't think you acknowledged such a thing."

Campbell forced a swallow, his throat suddenly so dry.

"I apologise for my actions, Father." The words were so acidic on his tongue. He despised their taste. "I have disrespected you and Mother, and I have brought shame upon this family."

He was going to continue, to beg to be released from the cage, but he bit his tongue still. He was afraid his father might catch onto his ploy if he seemed too eager to please.

Gerald Anders manoeuvred his large body towards the padlock. A thick sheen of sweat prickled Campbell's spine.

"*Shame* would be a kind term for the utter disease you have inflicted upon this family." Gerald took a laboured drag of his cigar, silently assessing. "Tell me, *son*, what's changed your mind? No longer want to live down with the rats?"

Campbell swallowed the curses aching at his throat. "I was wrong," he said.

Gerald seemed pleased with his confession. "It takes courage to admit such a thing," he said, and Campbell thought he detected pride in his voice. It was a painful admission: that the only time Gerald would be proud of his son was because of a lie.

Despite everything Campbell had done – and was about to do – that was the truth that stung the most.

With a wide smile, Gerald opened the cage. "Welcome back to the family, son," he said. With a tight smile, Campbell followed him up the stairs.

The first thing Campbell did was rush to his bedroom. The large room, doused in ruby red wallpaper, felt colder than the cell he'd spent the night in, and he quickly changed into something to dispel the chill. A pair of trousers and a woollen jumper were the preferred choices, despite the warm summer afternoon. He pulled on his leather boots – the ones he used to trudge snow

– and pulled against the laces. One of them snapped, catapulting Campbell onto the silk rug.

Campbell swiftly grabbed a spare lace and continued tying up his boots. Pressed for time, he threw the snapped lace in his back pocket.

Campbell deftly rushed around the huge four-poster bed, opening mahogany furniture and collecting a section of clothes. Would they fit Harrison? Campbell sure hoped so.

He pushed the clothes in a duffel bag and ran to the window. Campbell's bedroom was situated at the back of the four-story terraced house, to the opposite side of the main road. Apparently, Campbell's parents had chosen that exact house because of the privacy the back garden produced. The wooden porch allowed Gillian to sunbathe in the summer, without onlookers, and the wooden shed, towards the back of the garden, allowed an enclosed place for new Slaves to be *broken in.*

Far easier, and quicker, to train new Slaves in the Anders' back garden. It reduced the travelling time between prisons, and allowed potential new Masters to be served tea and biscuits in the drawing room, before the final assessment of their held *wares.*

Mason would likely be returning that afternoon. Perhaps he would even join Harrison's *training.* Campbell's stomach turned quite sickly at the thought.

The summer sun fell softly on Campbell's face as he pushed the window open. There, looking down to the emerald green grass, he watched with a bitten tongue as Masonians dragged Harrison across his family's garden. Their blue coats made a stark contrast against the berry-red roses lining the verge.

Harrison yelled as he was manhandled towards the shed, the door pushed wide open to reveal the spill of shadows within. He dug his heels in, peeling the Anders' pristine grass away and revealing the stinking mud of Maelstrom's foundations. Campbell cringed; Gerald had been known to break Slaves' ankles for inflicting such damage to his beloved garden.

The door to the Training Shed slammed shut and Harrison's screams immediately died. The shed was soundproofed, so as not to disturb the neighbours.

Campbell took a strained look below him, checked the coast was clear, and dropped the duffel bag. It disappeared into the rose bush, hidden from view.

He rushed back to the corridor and immediately bumped into Miranda.

"Oh, it's you," she said with a nasty sneer, looking him up and down. "Father let you out, then?"

"He actually rather enjoyed it," Campbell replied, glaring.

"I highly doubt that. You're this family's biggest disappointment."

"And you're its biggest whore."

Miranda's smile sharply fell, but reformed brighter than ever. "Did you know Mason's coming this afternoon? Two visits in two days, how wonderful is that?"

"Yes." Campbell's tight smile barely reached his nose. "How wonderful indeed, to have the murderer of two billion people enjoying tea in the family drawing room."

"Oh, you're too uncivilised to understand." Miranda threw her long, glossy hair across her shoulder. "When I become Mason's new consort, you won't be welcome with Mother and Father in his Palace. I hope you realise that."

"You know, Miranda, that's the best thing you've ever said to me." Campbell forced his smile a little higher. "Now, if you'll excuse me, Father is asking for me."

He was about to turn but Miranda swiftly grabbed his arm, digging her long red nails through his jumper. "Father's breaking in Mason's new Slave," she said, with narrowing eyes. "Why would he ask for *you?*"

Campbell brutally ripped his arm away, glaring. "He wants me to *watch*. He believes it's going to be the biggest push for my docility."

"Ah, that makes sense." Miranda shrugged her narrow shoulders. "Well, for Mr Dagger's sake, I hope he's sufficiently broken in before Mason arrives, otherwise Mason will do far worse than Father ever could.

"Now," she continued, as Campbell's face lost all colour. "I'm going to Ms Eynesbury's for a lesson. I best not tarry, otherwise I'll be late for Mason's visit here."

"Yippie for you," Campbell grumbled, turning his back to her.

"You should come with me, now that you're back in Father's favour again.

Ms Eynesbury will push those silly colloquialisms far away from your daily vocabulary."

Campbell turned with a shameless grin. "Thanks, but I think it's in all our best interests to know where I stand with my *vocab.*"

Miranda's teeth ground together as Campbell raced down the stairs and out of sight. He leant against the wall at the bottom, his heart pounding inside his chest. The shed blared at him through the hall window, and although Campbell desperately knew what he needed to do, anxious fear rose up his gullet, threatening nausea. There was no going back from this. They only had one chance to make it out of the Anders' back garden – never mind Maelstrom.

And yet, as the shed's varnished exterior concealed the screams from within, Campbell admitted that he didn't have a choice. Harrison was his one ticket out of Maelstrom, and by God did Campbell ache to live that dream. So he puffed up his shoulders and marched to his father's office.

Gerald Anders' office was a dark, domineering space, full of bookcases and gun cabinets. One cabinet contained a selection of fine revolvers, collected from all corners of the New World. Many of the revolvers were family heirlooms, passed from one parent to another, and then confiscated as they were sold or captured into eternal Slavery – at the hands of Campbell's own father, no less. It was sick, what Gerald did to those people. Campbell was ashamed to be his son, and it filled him with such pleasure to pick out the biggest revolver from his father's *prized* collection: a huge, black thing, barely fitting in Campbell's palm.

Yet, Campbell felt comforted by its weight and the jingle of bullets in his pocket. With a heavy sigh, he went to save his only friend.

It was hot that afternoon, only adding to the layer of sweat beneath Campbell's jumper as he faced the shed door.

This is it, he thought. He gripped his father's revolver in his clammy hand and barged into the shed without a second thought.

The image that greeted him was difficult to describe. There was Harrison, chained to the shed's wooden panels, surrounded by three Masonians. Harrison's ragged shirt had been ripped open, revealing a spattering of bruises and fresh, bleeding cuts. One of the Masonians held a knife that dripped shining pearls of blood to the floor.

Campbell's eyes locked to Harrison's, and a glimmer of a smile tugged at his bloodless lips.

"About bloody time," he breathed.

"Drop it!" Campbell yelled, aiming the revolver high.

The Masonian huffed out amazed amusement. "You're going to regret this, kid," he snarled, and dropped the knife with a clank.

Campbell jolted the gun from one Masonian to another, his hand trembling. "Release him!"

The Masonians unlocked Harrison's shackled wrists, already bruised and discoloured. Harrison fell with a loud thump and stumbled towards Campbell, panting through his marred, bleeding torso.

"Nice one, mate," he whispered, once close. Campbell put an arm around his back, supporting his weak frame as they slowly backed out of the shed.

Sunlight warmed their backs as Harrison slammed the shed door shut, hiding the atrocities within.

"Where're the clothes?" Harrison asked. Campbell replied with a shaky tone, his gun still poised. "Keep your aim on that door, mate."

With a subdued groan, a limping Harrison turned to the house.

"Shit!"

Campbell spun, the revolver held firm, and his heart plummeted at the sight of Lord Mason, standing on the sunlit garden of the Anders' Residence with a smirk curling his lips. Standing next to him, with his face twisted into a disgusted, *infuriated* grimace, was Campbell's father.

"Well," Mason remarked, throwing his hands into his trouser pockets. "How exciting."

"Campbell," Gerald shouted, hands balled at his side. "Put my revolver down *at once!"*

Campbell's arm shook noticeably, uncontrollably, but his grip remained firm and alternated between Gerald and Mason. For the life of him, he didn't know which man terrified him the most.

While Gerald was clearly incensed at the display, Mason became nothing but amused. He even chuckled as he turned to Gerald, the sun gleaming against his opaque, round sunglasses. "Tell me, is this part of Mr Dagger's training?"

Gerald's cheeks turned a blotchy vermillion and his stare darkened. "I told you to drop the revolver, *son.*"

Campbell winced at the word, spat like a weapon, and for a short moment he considered doing exactly as his father said, if only to spare the mother of all beatings he was to endure. But Campbell remembered all the other times his father had hit him, or sneered at him, or insulted him. A lifetime of abuse had caused Campbell to sprint to that very moment, and like hell would he give his father the pleasure! Gritting his teeth, Campbell's rage warmed his chest more than the blaring sunlight ever could.

"I'll never be your *fucking* son!"

Campbell fired. Bullets erupted from the revolver with almighty, deafening bangs.

Gerald ducked and dived into the nearest rosebush in a cloud of scarlet petals. To Campbell's shock, Mason remained completely unfazed – even completely still – and observed the scene with mild amusement.

Harrison grabbed Campbell's free sweaty hand and pulled.

"Come on!"

Campbell didn't need to think twice. He charged behind Harrison, who hobbled at breakneck speed, and helped him to the tall fence that surrounded the Anders' garden.

Masonians bashed down the shed door and were in fast pursuit. Harrison grabbed the top of the fence as Campbell buried his shoulder beneath his knees, pushing him up. Harrison lifted himself up the fence, then lowered his hand for Campbell.

Harrison groaned through his injuries, his arm visibly shaking as he helped Campbell to the top. The Masonians were almost upon them. With a shriek, Campbell heaved himself up and dropped to the other side, pulling Harrison over with a rough yank that ripped off whatever remained of his grey shirt.

Both boys collapsed in a puddle on the other side and were greeted with confused stares from an elderly Aristocratic couple, lounging on their patio with glasses of pink lemonade.

"Let's go!" Harrison scrambled to his feet, grabbing Campbell along the way. They raced across the next garden just as Masonian boots pounded on the other side of the Anders' fence, sprinting after them.

Panic grew in Campbell's lungs, his burning feet already aching in his laced boots, as Harrison dragged him at alarming speed across those Aristocratic gardens. Campbell grabbed handfuls of ammunition and reloaded his father's gun, still gripped in his hand with white-knuckle force. He fired blindly at their pursuers and screams erupted from horrified onlookers.

The pounding of Masonian boots diminished, and hope rose strong and forceful inside Campbell, propelling him onwards. They were almost to the edge of the housing row: the tips of full trees loomed above the final Aristocratic fence.

Once they made it there, they could disappear within the trees or hide in the undergrowth. Once they made it to the trees, they were free!

Hope ballooned inside Campbell; an exhausted smile worked his lips. He dragged Harrison's injured, flagging form onwards; fired more shots behind him; forced his aching legs to keep moving because they *were so close...*

Campbell leapt to the fence and heaved Harrison up the final panes of wood. He tumbled to the other side. Campbell was quick to follow, landing on Harrison with a shared grunt.

Campbell grabbed Harrison's wrist and hurled him up. He placed his arm around his back and took the first step to the forest ahead —

"Good afternoon, boys."

Mason leant against his polished car, arms and legs crossed, a wide smile on his face.

Campbell froze, his entire body numb, unable to move. He remained staring, mindlessly, at the Destroyer of the Old World, leaning against a vintage car that glinted in the bright afternoon sunlight. Harrison groaned, too exhausted to talk, and stared sadly at the wall of Masonians appearing on either side.

With a toothless smile, Mason pushed himself from his car and wandered, slowly and all too triumphantly, towards Campbell and Harrison.

"Not a bad effort, considering," he said. His eyes were still concealed behind those sunglasses, yet Campbell already imagined the deadly diamonds beneath.

Numbness was brutally ripped away by panic — a startling, surprising, and forceful panic — that raised the black revolver to Mason's forehead and pulled the trigger...

Mason remained completely unfazed.

To Campbell's horror, a dull clink came. The clip had been emptied.

Terror clung to his muscles, freezing them once more. He was unable to lower his arm, his finger constantly convulsing against the useless trigger.

With a tiresome sigh, Mason removed his sunglasses. Diamond eyes blazed wildly in the bright, afternoon light, sparking a whirlwind of colour...

Against every ounce of his self-preservation, Campbell could do nothing but stare.

"A word of advice." Mason scowled, easily prizing the revolver from Campbell's rigid fingers. "When you're firing blind shots, remember to count the bullets."

Mason slammed the revolver into Campbell's skull, plunging him into blackness.

4

Campbell awoke to the sound of repetitive thumping. His eyes creaked open, taking in the flood of shadows that assaulted his senses. Cold stone shifted against his moving body, and he groaned through the slow wave of pain, rolling across his skull.

"Yeah, he hit you pretty hard."

Campbell spotted Harrison in the barred cell next to him. Lying on the ground, still shirtless, he had his legs suspended high in the air and used the bare sole of his foot to slap helplessly against the stone walls. It didn't look like he was trying to escape, and he certainly wasn't restrained. However absurd, it looked like he did it for fun.

Campbell forced himself into the sitting position and took a strained look around his cell. Barred doors, barred dividers from one cell to the next... No windows; just the golden light from a dim bulb in the narrow corridor straddling the cells.

Campbell brought his knees to his chin and caressed the layer of dried, sticky blood around his temple.

"Where are we?" he asked.

"The Masonian Barracks."

Campbell's stomach lurched. "That's almost an hour's drive from Maelstrom."

"Well, I did say I was going to get us out of there." Harrison's deep sigh inflated his lungs, stretching the scabbed cuts on his torso. He winced through the pain and continued to thump the wall with his foot.

Campbell didn't know how to process this information. Yes, Campbell's longstanding dream was to leave Maelstrom, but he envisaged it would end in a flurry of relief, and not in the mouldy dark bowels of a cell.

"What happened? I don't remember anything."

"Mason hit you with your Pa's revolver, then you blacked out."

"I mean... After that."

"Masonians grabbed us, chucked us in a black van, and then brought us here." Another large sigh decorated his cell. "That felt like hours ago now."

"Have you seen anyone?"

"Only the Masonians who killed poor Tony." Harrison pointed over Campbell's shoulder, upon the motionless body of a man. Grey and purple bruises wrecked his flabby, naked torso, his face an entire mess of blood and dirt. Lifeless brown eyes gazed at Campbell.

Though no stranger to brutality, this was the first time Campbell had ever seen a dead body. The sight shocked him – not because there was a corpse in the cell next to him, but the fact that he did, indeed, look very much... *dead.*

In his Aristocratic innocence, Campbell had always assumed the dead would look peaceful in their voyage to the afterlife: arms crossed upon their chests, relaxed expressions...

But not Tony. His face remained in a perpetual grimace, blood clotting the deep gashes carved into his cheeks. Bones stuck from arms that bent in unnatural ways. He looked far from peaceful.

"I was surprised you didn't wake up," Harrison said, his brows knitted together. "Tony's screams were loud enough to startle *Jörmungandr.*"

"Oh my God..." Campbell dry-heaved into his lap.

"Hey, if you're gonna throw-up, do it closer to poor Tony. He's going to whiff soon, and I'd sooner keep the smells to one side."

Campbell retched again and forced his eyes to meet Tony, if only out of respect. "Why did they do it?"

"I didn't hear it all, but the gist is that he intentionally set one of his Slaves loose. You're not supposed to do that, apparently? Slaves are to be recycled back into the system or something."

"Of course," Campbell said, because he thought it was obvious. "That's how they support the Bolton Square Slave Auctions, and it keeps obedience…"

"Fucking tools," Harrison grumbled. "Poor Tony got the rough end of the stick there."

Campbell personally thought that was an understatement. Fighting nausea, he brought his knees up to his chin again and startled as his bare feet touched the cold stone.

"Where're my boots?" he asked, frowning.

"With mine, wherever they are. Most likely down a Masonian shit-hole."

Campbell watched Harrison's bare feet repetitively slam against the wall.

"Why would they take our shoes?"

"Shoelaces. They can't risk us hanging ourselves."

"Yeah, I get that, but why take the entire shoe?"

"Because then it's easier to remove our toenails." Harrison turned to a paling Campbell, with a grin. "Or so I've been told."

"You jest, right?"

"I've no idea why they took our shoes, mate," he said, with a tiresome sigh. "All I know is that my feet are so fucking numb, I can't feel any part of 'em."

Campbell suddenly understood why he was kicking the wall.

"Jeez…" he groaned, throwing his hands through his hair, dragging them across a jaw prickling with his stubble's first shadow. Campbell rubbed his palms against the rough skin, finding small comforts in the sensation. "How're we going to get out of here?"

"I've no idea."

Campbell's heart sank. "Please don't say that…"

"You want me to lie?"

"I want you to think of a way to get us out of here."

Harrison slammed his foot harder. "I've been doing that, all the while you've been catching up on your beauty sleep."

Guilt flooded Campbell. He wished he could sink into the cold stone floor and disappear into another reality.

"I'm sorry," he whispered.

"Nothing to apologise for." Harrison turned to Campbell and produced a smile that disagreed with the surrounding darkness. "And try not to panic, I've seen worse."

A burst of doubtful laughter escaped Campbell's throat. "Really? When?"

"Ah, you wouldn't believe it, even if I told you." His eyes turned serious; impossibly vibrant. "But don't let them see your fear, Campbell. You hear me? They'll break you completely if they see you're starting to crumble."

With a hard swallow, Campbell nodded his head – almost too quickly. But he trusted Harrison and he wanted to take his advice, no matter how hard it was.

A metallic door clinked, somewhere in the shadows. Harrison startled, like a wild animal, and scrambled to his feet.

"Stand up, mate," he whispered through the cells.

Campbell's knees quaked as loud, ominous footsteps echoed through the shadows. His head, already throbbing, ached more from his chattering teeth, but he couldn't tell whether it was from the cold, or the fear, or both.

Harrison Dagger, on the other hand, remained a beacon of strength. Clearly cold, for prominent goosebumps raced across his marred chest, Harrison merely clamped his jaw shut, squeezed his fists, and remained entirely unmoved as Mason strolled before them.

He dressed differently to when Campbell saw him last. The casual suit and sunglasses had been replaced with a uniform, reminiscent of the Masonian one. His white shirt and black trousers were almost entirely concealed beneath a long royal blue coat, supporting a weapon belt with a silver revolver on one side, and a long sword on the other.

Campbell's knees numbed and he wondered if they'd collapse from under him. Somehow, he remained composed as Mason's bright diamond eyes wandered to Harrison's injured, half-naked body.

Mason's lips curled into a smirk. "This isn't the Slave Training I'd anticipated, but it'll suffice for now."

"Fuck you." Harrison spat the words with raw hatred, his eyes seething.

Mason's smile merely grew. "I can't wait to cut that disobedience out of you."

"It won't work. Do anything you want to me: cut out my tongue, remove my eyes – none of it will make a blind bit of difference. The only way you'll have my docility is if you enslave my corpse."

Mason smiled. "Oh, your mother said something rather similar, but she still gave in, in the end. All it takes, my dear boy, is the right pressure point. Hers was one of my footmen – your father, actually. Make no mistake, I'll find yours soon enough."

Mason skulked closer, until his breath floated between the bars. "If only you knew just how *good* she was to me near the end of our time together."

Harrison's fists clenched tighter, his knuckles whitening. Mason's eyes dropped to them, then flicked back up just as quickly. His smile turned into a full, sinister grin. He stepped closer to the bars.

"Even all these years later, I still remember her taste."

Harrison leapt forwards and threw his arms between those bars. Mason jumped back, well out of his way, but laughed at the grubby fingers trying, rather helplessly, to claw away his sick amusement.

Mason's grin persisted. "Oh yes, I think I'm close to discovering your breaking point, boy."

Above Harrison's grating shrieks, two Masonians arrived with their sleeves rolled up, and entered Harrison's cell. Campbell remained glued to his spot, frozen with fear, and hated himself for doing nothing as Masonians landed punch after punch...

Unable to support his weight, Harrison tumbled to his knees and grunted at each kick to his stomach. Campbell watched, his face twisting, and felt that familiar rise of heat inside his torso, sinking into his knees, eroding the numbness that lingered there.

Just as Harrison spat out blood, life shocked Campbell's muscles.

"Stop!" He lunged to the bars separating their cells, trying to grasp Harrison's trembling body. *"Just stop it!"*

With a lazy wave of Mason's arm, the Masonians lifted Harrison's limp body and dragged him from the cells, into the shadows. Tony's corpse flashed behind Campbell's eyelids as he watched Harrison, heart to his throat. Their pained expressions had looked so similar.

Silence descended: a dark and dangerous silence, only cut by Mason's boots as he wandered to Campbell's cell.

There, as Campbell came face to face with the Destroyer of the Old World, he thanked whatever Gods were up there – Old or otherwise – for the bars that separated them. The way Campbell was feeling at that moment, he would've wrangled Mason's neck.

"Well." Mason smiled again. "Aren't you a sorry excuse for an Aristocrat."

"I'm not an Aristocrat!"

"Clearly." Mason's smirk widened. "This situation amuses me to no end, Mr Anders. Here you are, the son of one of my oldest friends, on some suicidal escape mission with one of my Slaves."

"Harrison isn't your Slave!"

"He is, legally now – as of twelve minutes ago, in fact. I've just signed the paperwork."

Campbell shocked himself as he formed a nasty smirk of his own. "I didn't know you were that desperate."

"Yes, well." Mason's smile tugged tight. "I find Mr Dagger's disobedience rather intriguing. Besides, I'm owed seventeen years of his life. His mother was already pregnant when she escaped my establishment, so Mr Dagger has been my Slave since the moment he was conceived."

Campbell felt nothing but admiration for Iulia Dagger. It was an admiration that had clearly worked its way into Harrison.

"*You* are a different matter entirely, Mr Anders." Mason wandered towards Campbell's cell with both hands behind his back. "You are not a Slave, neither are you born from one. In fact, you are the heir to the largest Slave Distributor in the New World. And yet, here you are, imprisoned in these corpse-filled cells, for helping the bastard son of Iulia Dagger – of *all* people. My-oh-my, what a small world this is."

"What do you want me to say?" Campbell said, and he felt – rather than willed – his face twist into a nasty scowl. "Do you want me to apologise to you?"

"Oh, not at all. Your family deserves your apology, not I. You have brought incredible dishonour to them."

"I don't care," Campbell said, and he meant it. Bringing such high dishonour to his pompous fart of a father was perhaps the greatest thing he'd ever done.

"Oh, I know you don't, and that's the problem here, isn't it? I can't possibly release you back to your family, and neither can I enslave you – you'll just cause trouble. The only other option, it seems, is execution."

Campbell stilled. That word kept flying around his head, without mercy: *execution.*

Mason picked his bait well. "Of course, it would be a shame if it were to come to that. Your life's promise flushed out with the rest of the gutter rats? It would be a terrible way to end such a noble Bloodline."

Campbell dropped his gaze to Mason's boots. The weight of his future felt so goddamn crushing… He suddenly felt so young, so inexperienced with the cruel world he called home.

"Then again," Mason said, smiling. "We could come to some sort of arrangement."

Campbell's ears perked up. "What arrangement?"

"You can still be enslaved rather than executed, but I'll need your word."

"What word?"

"A simple promise of obedience, of docility. Forget Harrison Dagger, forget the absurd dream of living *free* from Aristocracy." Mason leant back against the wall, crossing his arms. Campbell suddenly felt back in school, being scolded by his teacher for being unable to *make friends*. "Aristocracy is a blessing – being an Anders is a *blessing*. To waste your family's name, to throw it all away, as you are doing, is a terrible shame."

"So, what do you propose?" Campbell breathed, unable to produce the power behind his glare. "To be a Slave for the rest of my life?"

"Surely that is better than the noose? I believe Jürgen Doncaster is making enquires about a new Slave. He told me he's looking for a boy – around your age – to help around the house." Mason's grin widened, although Campbell didn't know why. "You'd have a roof over your head, hot food in your stomach… If I were in your shoes, I'd accept without a second thought."

Campbell didn't believe that. Not at all.

But yet, against every instinct screaming how *wrong* this was, he found himself considering Mason's deal. Standing in a cold cell in the Masonian Barracks, surrounded by Destroyers and corpses, he wished to be anywhere else – to *do* anything else. His dreams of freedom were squished beneath Mason's boot. The thought of his future was suffocating and he craved the outside air.

"What about Harrison?"

Mason arched a black eyebrow. "As I said, he is mine. What I do with him is no longer your concern."

That boot worked its suffocating way down Campbell's body, and pressed into his stomach. *No, this isn't right.* Harrison Dagger was his *friend* – the only one he'd ever had! To leave him, gasping for air at the bottom of Mason's cesspit, filled Campbell with blind, writhing disgust.

Perhaps, had Campbell been alone, he would have accepted Mason's offer. He would have gone, albeit grudgingly, to the Doncaster Residence and no doubt lived a long and unhappy life.

But the few hours he'd spent with Harrison were the most exhilarating, the most hopeful he'd ever had. To linger on with the images – the mere ideas – of what the brave, admirable Harrison Dagger must be enduring beneath Mason's fingernail would have been a sharp, rusty nail slipping down his gullet. So, Campbell spat it out, before he had the chance to swallow.

"Fuck you, Mason. I'd rather hug a noose than agree to anything you say!"

Mason's smile dropped with a loud thud. Diamond eyes narrowed, sparkling intently, merely hinting at the anger that swarmed just below.

A new smile spread across Mason's handsome jaw. A different smile, this time: not amused, nor condescending. Just evil. Pure, unquestionable evil.

"Goodbye, Mr Anders," Mason said, and left Campbell with nothing but a corpse for company.

5

———————

Campbell paced, alone, in his cell. For a while he did it to keep himself occupied, or to stamp out the memories of his conversation with Mason. Now, he did it to keep warm. Outside, the sun had long since disappeared and it had only grown colder. Campbell could at least wrap his arms around himself, but his feet were difficult to keep warm. They had already become sore and scabbed from the cold floor. Campbell paused his infernal pacing, stepping from one foot to the other, and threw his fidgety hands in his back jean pockets.

His finger twisted with a forgotten object. Slowly, he brought out his hand and stared at the snapped, black shoelace dripping through his fingers. Essentially, he'd smuggled it into the Masonian cell.

Harrison's words echoed: *They can't risk us hanging ourselves.*

Campbell stuffed the shoelace back into his pocket and continued to pace, avoiding Tony's body, and wondered if he imagined the faint sound of screams.

But those screams were *real*, and they were growing louder...

A door slammed open. A Masonian marched inside, gripping the wrists of two girls. Blonde hair flailed wildly beneath the dim light as one girl was thrown into the neighbouring cell, and then the other. They collapsed to the ground in a flurry of wild hair and jumpers. The Masonian slammed the door behind him and skulked into the cell.

The girls whimpered as he held the wooden baton in his hand, scrambling to the far corner.

The Masonian stood close to the bars separating the cells, twirling the baton.

"I think you both need to learn some respect," he snarled. One of the girls sobbed loudly, hiding her face in grubby hands and greasy blonde locks.

The Masonian bashed the baton against the bars and inched forward.

Campbell wouldn't be able to recollect picking the shoelace from his pocket. Neither would he recall slipping his arms through the bars of the cell, or swinging the shoelace around the Masonian's neck, pulling sharply.

In fact, the only thing Campbell would recall – apart from the Masonian's muted, gurgling screams – was when that old shoelace snapped in his hand. Propelled back, he slammed against the bars and slid down the cold metal, mirroring the Masonian in the adjoining cell.

Campbell froze, his mindless stare fixed on the Masonian's blue coat. The Masonian's foot twitched sporadically, and stilled.

One of the girls – the younger one, about ten years of age – plodded towards the Masonian's body and kicked his foot. He remained still, so she kicked it again.

"Is he dead?" Campbell breathed, unable to control the question.

"Who cares?" the older girl said, struggling to her feet. Like Campbell, they were both shoeless. Her steps were silent as she rushed over and hastily searched the Masonian's pockets. She picked out a large ring of keys and rushed to the cell door. "Thank you," she said, just as the door swung open.

Her words fell on deaf ears. Campbell gazed at the Masonian and kept asking himself what he'd done. He'd saved those two girls, but that fact seemed completely lost on him. In fact, only when the girl unlocked his cell door and fell to her knees before him, peeling apart Campbell's stiff limbs, did Campbell drag his stare towards her face.

"You did good," she whispered, and her words were like a honey balm, soothing a wound. "He was a wicked man, don't feel bad for him."

She wiped away the wetness on Campbell's cheek, startling him. Was he crying?

"What's your name?" she asked gently.

"C-Ca..." He coughed out his paralysis. "Campbell Anders."

"Anders?" The girl's brows knitted together, contemplating. She shook away her confusion. "Come on, this is our chance to get out of here."

Warm, soft hands grabbed Campbell's and pulled him, rather unsteadily, to his feet.

"I'm Caroline," she said, then nodded to the small girl with whom she shared a startling resemblance. "This is my sister, Alice."

Alice came bounding over and grabbed their hands. "Come on, we need to go!"

She pulled Campbell and Caroline towards the open door.

"Harrison," Campbell breathed, pulling away his hand.

"What?"

"I need to find Harrison!"

Alice grabbed his hand again. "No time!"

"No!" Campbell easily ripped his arm away and stumbled, rather shakily, to the Masonian he'd... *killed?* He didn't bother to check for a pulse – he didn't want to know the answer. He took the Masonian's baton and startled at its weight. Harrison really survived several blows with those things? Campbell cringed.

"I'm not leaving him," he declared.

Caroline stared at him with large brown eyes, chewing the rosy swell of her lower lip. "Who is this guy?"

"My friend." Campbell relished the way that sounded on his tongue. "He saved me from Maelstrom and I can't just leave him to Mason."

"Mason's *here?*" Caroline's eyes widened. "You can't just go cavorting around the Masonian Barracks when *Mason's* lurking about!"

"But I'm not leaving him to be tortured!"

Caroline grasped his hand, filling Campbell's entire arm with her warmth. "I know," she replied, and cast a sad stare to the Masonian's still body. "You don't seem like the type of guy who stands idly by while others get hurt."

Her words cut through Campbell, reaching the soft marrow within him. No one had ever said something so... *kind* to him before. He stared into those large brown eyes, so multidimensional, and they reminded him of a stone in his mother's bracelet. *Tiger Eye*, if he remembered correctly.

"Come on," she whispered, pulling him towards the door. "Whatever happens, we can't stay here."

Campbell allowed himself to be led into another corridor. He stared blindly in either direction, noticing the stone walls devoid of windows. How would they get out?

"There's a storage room at the end of this corridor, at the other end of the interrogation cells," Caroline said, as if reading his mind. She had Campbell's arm in one hand and Alice's in another. The small girl's eyes flicked wildly in either direction, her cheeks paling with every second. "The butch Masonian stopped there to dump our shoes, and there's an unbarred window there, too."

"Can we get out of it?"

Caroline bobbed her head from side to side. "Me and Alice, definitely. It might be a bit of a squeeze for you, but yes, I think we can all get out."

Campbell recalled Harrison's muscular torso and hoped the window was sizeable.

"Right, you go there and hide. I'll get Harrison and join you." Campbell tried to pull his arm away but she gripped him tighter.

"What if you *don't* get Harrison?"

"Then just go," Campbell said, without hesitation. "If I don't return in fifteen minutes, get yourselves out of here and don't look back."

Campbell tried to pull away but she quickly yanked him back. "Please come back," she whispered, and from the slight glimmer of moisture on that Tiger Eye stare, she meant it. Campbell swallowed the ball of emotion that pushed against his throat.

"I'll try," he whispered. He finally pulled free and everything shivered.

"Go," Campbell said, because he needed to believe she and Alice would survive. "Please, *go.*"

Caroline knew the unspoken meaning behind his words. With a final, sad smile, Caroline pulled her sister down the corridor and soon disappeared in the shadows.

Campbell remained alone. His forlorn stare found the other side of the corridor, looking longingly into the shadows for an answer.

What the *hell* was he doing? How did he expect to get Harrison out of whatever shit-hole he was in?

In that moment, Campbell didn't care. Harrison was his *friend*, and he couldn't leave him. Even if he *did* have the strength to leave Harrison, visions of his fate would haunt him until the end of time. Campbell didn't want that fate. He didn't want to leave Harrison to his.

Really, did he even have a choice?

With a slow, controlled sigh, Campbell walked down the corridor. He held the baton tightly in his hand, his palm sweating. Was he trembling with fear? He couldn't tell from the cold.

Truth be told, he couldn't think about how cold he was, or how fearful, or how stupid. He could just focus on the present: on placing one bare foot in front of the other; of traversing that cold, desolate corridor and finding Harrison lurking somewhere within.

Screams echoed, bouncing across the stone walls, assaulting Campbell's ears. He stopped, heart in his throat, and listened. Eyes scrunched together, trying to block out the sounds that reminded him so much of Harrison...

Eyes popped open. *Harrison. Those are* Harrison's *screams...*

Campbell's fear dissolved beneath anger. A blistering, pure anger that, any other day, would have shocked him. Not anymore.

In that one moment, perhaps for the first time in his life, Campbell felt purpose: an uncontrollable drive to rush down that corridor, to *save* the only one who had ever given a flying fuck about him. Ahead, a closed door concealed the screams behind it...

Campbell gripped the baton, lifted it high and barged into –

A store cupboard.

Campbell startled at the mess of old chairs, boxes filled with paperwork marred with big red crosses, and old coats. Some of the garments were Masonian, others clearly weren't. Maybe they were taken from prisoners?

Loud, anguished screams poisoned the air. Campbell spun around with the baton raised, but he was alone. He frowned at the room, completely stark of life, and followed the sound of grunts and groans that, as it turned out, seeped from a barred grate near the ceiling.

Tucking the baton in his waistband, Campbell carefully placed one of the chairs beneath the grate and slowly, silently stood on it. The room on the other side of the grate came into view and Campbell's fists clenched.

Strapped to the wall, blood dribbling from his shackled wrists, Harrison Dagger lay limp. His legs lacked the energy to hold him upright. Bruises and cuts painted his torso, glimmering with sweat and blood. That same blood speckled the grey stone floor, the crimson pools spread by three pairs of black boots.

Mason's boots were one of these pairs. He had since removed his blue coat, revealing a white shirt with both sleeves rolled up forearms speckled with blood, and paced before Harrison's limp body.

No, not *limp*.

Lifeless.

He looked *lifeless*.

Campbell fought the tears in his eyes. *No, no* – he *had* to be alive. He just *had* to be!

Holding a curved knife that dripped fresh blood to the floor, Mason stopped pacing and observed Harrison.

"Oh, wake him up," he snapped to one of the two guarding Masonians.

Harrison spluttered as a bucket of icy water was thrown at his face. His entire body shivered as he coughed and gagged in equal measure.

"Ah, welcome back, Mr Dagger." The sound of that rich, crooning voice made Campbell nauseous – more so than the sight assaulting his eyeballs.

From Campbell's viewing angle, he spotted Harrison's exhausted form glare at Mason with a green eye.

"Oh, no words of defiance?" Mason smirked. "I do hope you're not getting tired. We've only just started."

Campbell ducked as Mason wandered to the wall where the grate was. He dropped the knife to a metallic surface – a table, perhaps? – and returned to Harrison with a pair of pliers, poised in hands caked with blood.

Harrison spluttered out a condescending laugh. "Don't throw stones at glass houses, old man. How old are you anyway? Shouldn't you be snuggling up with your teeth right about now?"

Mason laughed softly to the room, his grating glare reforming. "Be careful of that mouth, boy, otherwise I'll fuck you with it."

"Oh, please do…" Harrison forced a wide grin. "It's been a good while since I've had a man and variety *is* the spice of life."

For a priceless moment, Mason seemed dumbfounded at Harrison's audacity. But the moment was fleeting, disappearing as soon as it arose. Mason twirled the pliers in his hand. "Open his mouth."

Harrison struggled frantically against the shackles and thick rivers of blood dribbled down his forearms. Were there blades inside the metal?

It took one Masonian to hold Harrison's head still, and another to prize his jaw open.

Mason approached with the pliers and a sick smirk. "I think it's high time we removed that smile of yours, Mr Dagger…"

As Harrison's strained groans erupted from that cell, Campbell's grip around the baton intensified. He worked around a swallow, just about to call through the grate and spit profanity to Mason when –

"Sir!"

Another Masonian bounded into the room, startling Mason's concentration. He turned sharply, diamond eyes blazing.

"The prisoners have escaped!"

Upon Mason's face was written pure, seething fire. "How hard is it to keep track of three *fucking* adolescents!"

Campbell ducked as Mason threw his arms in his blue coat and stormed from the room, the Masonians in tow.

Harrison was left alone, bleeding, in the dark corner of a torture chamber.

"Hey," Campbell whispered hoarsely through the grate. "*Hey!*"

Harrison didn't seem to hear.

Grumbling to himself, Campbell tugged the grate. It budged, but only a little.

Mason's enraged shouts echoed down the corridor. Panic bubbled inside Campbell's chest: he didn't have much time.

He pulled at the grate again. It budged a little more. Hope sparked.

With a gigantic breath, Campbell pulled the grate once, twice. Finally, it shook loose and bits of grey powder rained to the floor.

Campbell scrambled through the opening and gently lowered himself to the metal table. He stared, horrified, at the instruments neatly laid around his bare feet: blades, pliers, syringes...

All were bloodstained.

Campbell rushed to Harrison and absorbed the blood and injuries with morbid horror. Cuts gouged into Harrison's torso, blood soaked his forearms... Toenails scattered the stone floor, like bloodied little jewels.

"Harrison..." he whispered, cradling a face streaked with bloody bits of hair. Campbell gently pushed it aside, one portion at a time, and turned Harrison's face to his.

Breath caught in his throat.

One jade eye creaked open and gazed utter relief at Campbell. Harrison's other *eye* – or at least, what it should have been – was nothing more than a bloodied hole, dribbling thick lines of red down his pale cheek.

Campbell fought the tears in his eyes. "What did he do to you...?"

"Hey, mate," Harrison croaked, and a glimmer of a smile teased bloodless lips. "Ain't you a sight for sore eyes."

Campbell forced a glare.

"Too soon?"

"For God's sake, Harrison..." Campbell inspected the bloodied shackles. "How am I going to get you out of here?"

Harrison weakly gestured to the table. "One of the Masonians dumped the keys there. I reckon they were too preoccupied with you escaped *adolescents* to worry about me, or the keys." Campbell rushed to the table, fighting his way through Mason's torture instruments.

Harrison groaned loudly as he forced his legs to support his weight, releasing the pressure from his wrists and shoulders. "How'd you escape?" he asked, his face twisting, as Campbell desperately searched the table.

"I..." Campbell wondered how to proceed. "I found my old shoelace..."

Harrison knew his hidden meaning. "Ah... Well, thanks for that, otherwise I'd have lost my lovely pearly whites."

"Jeez, Harrison..." Campbell grimaced.

"Who're the others?"

"Dunno, two girls. They've found a way out of here."

A pair of keys jumped out at Campbell, hidden within the mess of surgical instruments.

"Yes!" Campbell rushed to Harrison's arms and forced the key in the minuscule lock.

Harrison winced. "Ah, easy!"

The shackles opened and Harrison crumbled to the floor. His arms fell like two dead weights, a line of raw red speckling each wrist.

Campbell took a lone look to the door, leading to an unknown part of the Barracks. Mason was out there, as were an unknown number of Masonians.

The open grate winked in his corner vision. It would be so easy for him, to climb on the table and crawl through that opening. Caroline and Alice would be waiting for him, their hands beckoning through the unbarred window...

Harrison's deep, laboured breaths found his eardrums. Strength had left him, peeled away with the rest of his toenails. How the hell would he get Harrison to that opening?

Campbell shivered at the shackles, dripping Harrison's blood, and his own wrists ached. If they were discovered, would he survive such torture? Campbell doubted it. He wasn't as strong as Harrison. Not in the slightest.

"Come on!" Campbell bit out, thrusting his arm around Harrison's back, lifting him with a shared groan. "See that opening up there?"

Harrison's single eye followed his gaze and his heart audibly sank. "Ah, shit..."

"That's our way out of here."

"I..." Harrison suddenly seemed so lost. "I don't think I can make that..."

"Yes, you can!" Campbell supported his weight and dragged him to the table. "You *must*, otherwise Mason'll be back here and you're only going to wish you were through that grate!"

Harrison forced himself on the table with a pained grimace. His limbs were slow, like Mason had strapped weights onto each of his ten toes, so Campbell rushed to his aid. With a great heave, Campbell lifted Harrison, forcing his shoulders beneath his knees.

"Come on, you can do it!"

Harrison crawled up the wall. Dirty blood streaked the stone: the only evidence of Harrison's presence, for he fell to the other side of that open grate with an almighty crash.

Campbell quickly pulled himself through and hopped down beside Harrison, who had fallen on, and smashed, the wooden chair.

"Masonians would've heard that," Campbell said.

"Yeah, well..." Harrison pulled himself upright, grimacing, shaking off bits of broken wood. "Balls to them."

Campbell took a strained look at the contents of that storage cupboard, then to Harrison's bare torso. They'd never make it out there, in the wilderness, in their current states. Campbell rushed around the room and picked out one of the coats – a long, brown thing – and threw it to Harrison.

"Just my colour," he mumbled, shrugging his bloody arms through it.

A black leather jacket screamed at Campbell. He caressed its roughness, the tip of his finger following the faded lines carved into the material. It looked to be a good fit.

As Campbell shrugged on the faded black leather jacket, Harrison ripped up another coat and tied thick bands of material around both wrists, and another around his head, covering the bloody eye-socket.

"Any shoes in here?" Harrison asked, casting a sad stare to the state of his toes. He quickly bandaged them too.

"No, but I know where we can find some." Campbell pushed his arm beneath Harrison's. "Come on, it's not far..."

Campbell supported a limping, grunting Harrison down the corridor. Shadows loomed from every direction, moving against the dim lightbulbs. Were Masonians hiding in the shadows? Doubtful, yet Campbell's heart still jumped every time the light flickered.

Finally, they reached their destination. Campbell edged the door open, peeking his blue eyes through the gap.

An empty room stared back at him.

The girls had gone, having crawled out of an unbarred window that still remained slightly open. Fresh, beautiful air caressed Campbell's face and for a short moment, he basked in the freeing sensation.

"Found your shoes, mate." Harrison threw Campbell his old boots, shoelaces included.

Thanks, Campbell wanted to say, but his words were quickly pushed down when he saw Harrison struggling to force his feet into his own boots.

His teeth bared through the pain, his remaining eye glazing with a fresh layer of moisture.

"Can I help?" Campbell asked, because he didn't know what else to do.

Harrison's bandaged foot finally slid into the boot. Relief washed over him, as well as a small smile.

"Just buy me a drink when we get out of here," he said, smiling.

"I'll buy you two," Campbell added with a smirk.

Commotion sounded from outside the door. Yells, shouts – a flurry of angry, armed men running up and down the corridor.

Life sparked in Campbell and he dragged Harrison to his feet with enough force that he yelped in pain.

Campbell didn't care – he didn't have time to! Freedom was literally breathing over his face, fluttering the greasy black locks of his hair – and like hell was he going back in that cell! He wouldn't give Mason the pleasure.

With another great heave, Campbell lifted Harrison. It was easier this time: the window was lower and freedom strongly beckoned. That freedom whipped Campbell's face as Harrison crawled through the window and out into the open air.

Campbell jumped up and grabbed the ledge of the window. A Masonian burst in.

"In here!"

Hands grabbed Campbell's feet, pulling him sharply back. The corner of the window cut into Campbell's cheek and warm wetness spread his jaw. Was there any pain? Campbell didn't have time for pain, so he kicked the Masonian's nose. The man flew back and collided with a stack of boxes. A cascade of shoes fell upon him.

In the Masonian's stunned stupor, Campbell noticed the revolver on his weapon's belt. It looked rather familiar...

"That's *mine!*" he hissed, and quickly grabbed the black revolver. He tucked it into his jeans, next to the baton.

More yells erupted from the corridor. Campbell leapt to the window and escaped into the cold air just as a flood of blue coats suffocated the storage room.

6

———

Word of their escape reached receptive ears.

Floodlights swarmed the grounds of the Masonian Barracks; Masonians patrolled the scuffed grass, securing ominous dogs on tight leases... A metal fence roared around them, containing screams, barbarity, and Campbell and Harrison.

"Oh-okay, mate," Harrison breathed, his chest heaving. "What now?"

That was a good question.

Campbell stared at the massive fence and tried not to panic. He took a strained look in either direction, yet only dread stared back.

But then, Caroline and Alice must have made it – surely? How did they get out of the compound?

"Come on," Campbell whispered, and helped Harrison around the corner of the building. A small group of Masonians lay huddled together, lit cigarettes hanging from their mouths.

"Shit!" Campbell hissed, beneath his breath. He quickly backtracked, pulling Harrison with him. He took a laboured gaze around the corner, to the pack of waiting wolves. "There are too many of them..."

Hope deserted Campbell, no matter how hard he tried to cling to it. They had come this far and yet it still wasn't enough – *how was it never enough?*

"Hey!" A small voice cut through the floodlights. "Hey, over here!"

Narrowing his eyes, Campbell stared through the artificial white and into the darkness ahead. There, cowering in the tangle of bushes, a mess of blonde hair shone.

"Caroline?" Campbell could barely breathe the word, afraid that it was his imagination, or yet another of Mason's cruel games.

But no, there she was, cowering in the long vegetation. Beside her, Alice frantically beckoned them closer with her small hand.

They ducked as the floodlights washed over them. Breaths were held, small lungs poised… The white light casually strolled elsewhere.

In the clear, Caroline reappeared and gestured desperately to the portion of fence directly in front of them. Campbell and Harrison edged forwards, silently. Heart to his throat, Campbell continually stared from one side, then to the other, using the shadows to his advantage and praying to all Gods that those floodlights would not reappear in a hurry.

They made it to the fence.

"Thank God," Caroline said, and a glimmer of a smile lifted her entire face. "We were worried you'd never get out of there."

Harrison's abused chest worked around a small chuckle. "The other adolescents, I presume?"

"Huh?"

"Ignore him." Campbell edged closer, as if he was trying to become one with the metal fence topped with rolls of barbed wire. "How did you get out?"

Caroline moved the grass aside, revealing a small hole beneath the fence. "Dug it out."

Campbell assessed their escape route. Sharp bits of gravel and rock stuck at odd angles from the mud, as did bits of earthworm and the odd scurrying woodlouse. Yet it remained large enough and certainly sturdy enough for Campbell to squeeze through, though he still dug it out a little more, just to be sure.

"You first," Campbell said, pushing Harrison onwards. Perhaps too exhausted to argue, Harrison edged into the hole. On the other side, Caroline and Alice grabbed each of his arms and pulled. With a suppressed groan, only Harrison's legs stuck out when they became bathed in artificial white light…

They startled, staring mindlessly into that blinding white bulb.

Then a great alarm sounded.

"Go!" Campbell yelled, and shoved Harrison through by the soles of his feet. Harrison shrieked, pain erupting from his toes, but scrambled free just as dogs barked in the shadows. Campbell took large handfuls of dirt and pushed them into the hole, blocking it.

"Run!" he begged, meeting Caroline's shocked Tiger Eye stare.

"No..."

Dogs rounded the corner. Campbell jumped to his feet. *"Over here!"* he yelled, banked left and ran.

"Campbell, *no!*" Harrison screeched, but he was already running, dragging the dogs' drooling snarls and thundering footsteps. Masonians joined the dogs, grabbing their guns, shouting for reinforcements as Campbell's lungs burned.

What was he doing? *What was he doing?*

He didn't care. As the cold evening air whipped his face and light burned his retina, Campbell suddenly didn't care about the consequences. He'd saved Harrison. He'd saved the girls. Three innocent lives were destined to go on, to *live* on, to bathe in the freedom Campbell had gifted them.

Yes, Campbell was an Anders. Yes, he was born an Aristocrat. But he was far from such titles. He was not his father – he would *never* be his father.

Campbell wanted to free people, not enslave them. He wanted to *save* people.

Finally, after fifteen long years, he'd found his purpose. And there, sprinting through the bowels of the Masonian Barracks, Campbell smiled.

Masonians blocked his path with their batons poised and their swords unsheathed. Campbell forced his pace to slow and raised his palms high. Dogs were called back, secured on leather leashes so they didn't rip him limb from limb. Campbell needed to be alive and kicking after all. It was more fun that way.

Lungs burning, chest heaving, Campbell observed the group of callous, sneering men surrounding him from all angles. Though his retinas burned in the spotlights' gazes, shining from all directions, his glare remained and settled quite firmly upon Mason, parting the sea of Masonians to stroll towards him.

"You continue to amuse me, Mr Anders," he smirked, and Campbell clearly saw the gargoyle that lingered beneath Mason's handsome exterior. "Do you really believe you will keep Harrison Dagger from me?"

"Well, you never found Iulia, so avoidance evidently runs in the Dagger family."

Mason's eyes sparkled wildly, dangerously, in the same artificial light that highlighted the spots of blood, marring the apples of grinning cheeks.

"I always find those who are mine."

"Not this time," and Campbell relished those words; he relished their *defiance*. Too long had he sat back and let Mason's sadistic Aristocracy rule his life. Now, it felt good telling the Destroyer of Old World where to stick it. "You'll search for Harrison Dagger all you want, and you still won't find him."

"Is that a challenge, Mr Anders?"

"It's a promise."

"Such loyalty for a boy you barely know, whom you are so willing to sacrifice *everything* for..." Mason's eyes strayed down Campbell's skinny exterior, before trailing back up. "Why, it's almost admirable."

Mason took an ominous step closer, the damp mud squelching beneath his boots. "Do you seriously believe he'd show the same loyalty to *you*, boy?"

"He got me out of Maelstrom." Campbell's dry lips stretched into a wide smile. "So, he's already good in my book, *mate.*"

An almighty crash sounded. Darkness descended, preluding the rain of broken glass and a large, angular rock. The Masonians ducked as a second searchlight shattered, then a third. Sparks rained down with the broken glass, falling upon a stack of wooden boxes. The summer sun had dried the wood and despite the cold evening air, the boxes easily began to smoulder. Hungry flames quickly grew.

Masonians rushed to those boxes. What was inside of them? Ammunition?

Whatever it was, Campbell saw his opportunity. Adrenaline raced through his fingers and in one quick movement, Campbell grasped the hilt of Mason's sword, unsheathed it, and thrust the pristine blade right through his heart.

Pride bubbled inside of Campbell. He forced the blade down farther, deeper into Mason's chest...

For a moment, Campbell expected Mason to be startled, perhaps even angry. He hoped those diamond eyes would fill with horror, before the sparkle dulled from them completely.

But the sparkle did not diminish in Mason's eyes. Neither did they show surprise, hate, or even fear.

Instead, they showed amusement. Utter, complete amusement. Beyond anything he'd experience in that wretched place, that chilled Campbell to the core.

Numb with shock, Campbell watched Mason's mouth form a wide, satisfied grin. Bloodied fingers curled around the blade, his scarred knuckles gleaming in the flickering firelight. Diamond eyes swirled with colour as he dragged the sword from his own chest, one impossible inch at a time.

Campbell's lips parted, his jaw slack as Mason pulled the blade free entirely and just...dropped it to the floor. Like it was nothing.

"I'm confused." Mason laughed, that grin persisting. "Was that supposed to hurt me, boy?"

The boxes exploded in a sudden release of heat and fire. Campbell lurched back, Mason lurched forwards. They all landed on the ground with a sudden slam.

Flames licked away Masonian flesh. Dogs barked and whined, escaping the rush of angry heat with their leashes dragging behind them.

World spinning, ears ringing, Campbell tried to focus. Dazed, the ground convulsed beneath his hands as he crawled upon the cold mud. He felt an object beneath his fingers and he startled at the sharp blade of Mason's sword. For a moment, as the entire world spun around him, he realised with sudden, stark understanding that the blade was clean. The bastard didn't even shed a single drop of blood.

"Campbell..."

Was that his name? Was someone calling to him?

With a head stuffed full of cotton wool, Campbell turned to the source of the small voice. Alice's eyes were wide and pleading through the fence. She frantically waved her arms, pointing down the length of the fence, to where they had dug the hole.

Campbell's desperation to kill Mason swiftly changed into a desperation to just survive, to make it out of those Masonian Barracks unharmed. He clung to this hope as he stumbled to his feet, forcing his trembling limbs to sprint down the length of the fence. He didn't even realise he had Mason's sword in his hand until he was back in the hole, recently dug out again, as he tried to pull his limbs through the small opening. He altered his position and both he and the sword fit through, pulled into forested freedom by Harrison on one arm, and Caroline on the other.

"Let's go!" Who shrieked? Perhaps it all of them; perhaps it was simply a shared thought, passed from one survivor to the next.

Whatever the truth, their actions were swift. Caroline and Campbell clung to Harrison as they helped him sprint through the mass of trees. Alice paved the way ahead of them, painting their path through the darkness with her delicate breaths.

They swiftly banked left, darting between the trees and escaping the immediate area of the Barracks. Earth trembled behind them. Birds squawked and escaped trees; wolves howled through the shadows...

Animals of all kinds sprinted through the night, followed only by the echoing thunder of falling trees as an unknown force carved deep chasms in the earth.

7

———

When the early morning sunrise bled through the trees, they stopped running.

Alice's foot caught on a log, hiding in the mossy undergrowth. She tumbled and barely caught her fall. She remained on the forest's floor, unable to recover her strength. Caroline gently peeled away from Harrison's side and rushed to her sister, cradling her pale face with two muddy hands.

Campbell's pace soon slowed, dragged down by Harrison's pained exhaustion.

"Okay..." Campbell said, and carefully supported Harrison's body to the floor. "We can rest here. But only for a little, we can't face the Masonians –"

"We've been moving at a snail's pace for the last three miles," Caroline said, her hair shimmering beneath the young, golden light, punching through the trees. "If those Masonians were still after us, the dogs would have caught us by now."

Beside her, Alice's face twisted with fear. No doubt she imagined the same thing Campbell did: long, sharp teeth digging into their flesh, ripping away their sinew one agonising inch at a time...

Campbell hastily shook away the images.

"I told you the bloody rag would work." Harrison chuckled, then clutched his chest with a grimace. Bruises shadowed his pectorals, occasionally peeking from his coat. Each of his injuries inched closer to his skin's surface, spreading ugly purple and grey across his ridged torso.

Campbell thought back to the previous night – however many hours ago it was – and remembered the bloody rag Harrison untwisted from his wrist. They'd attached it to a log and set it skipping down a fast-moving stream. The scent of Harrison's blood was now far away from them, dragging those hungry, drooling mouths to a completely different corner of the forest.

Indeed, the forest was enormous. It stretched ahead, forever it seemed, without an end.

"Where are we?" Campbell asked, staring at the claustrophobic mass of trunks and leaves.

"Woodlands," Harrison grunted.

"How can you tell?"

"Look at the trees, mate."

Campbell absorbed their colour and height, then reminisced to the trees around Maelstrom. Those trees appeared fuller, more rotund. B But the trees currently surrounding them were much taller and far older than those in the Fjord Territory. Branches lay thick and heavy with emerald green leaves; some wide and bulbous, others nothing more than sage-green needles. The scent of fresh, green growth mixed heavily with mud and decay, and yet Campbell inhaled it all, wishing for that scent of freedom and forest to absorb into his very soul.

Yes, undoubtedly the Forest Territory, but Campbell didn't realise that from the trees. In all of his fifteen long years, the Fjordland air had never smelled so good.

"What now?" Alice asked. Her voice seemed so small, so innocent... Large brown eyes gazed at each of them, forever searching for an answer.

With a loud grunt, Harrison propped himself up onto his elbows. "We move north, to the Snowlands."

While Campbell's heart jumped in excited glee, Caroline's sank to the leaf mulch. "That's hundreds of miles away... How do you expect us to make that?"

"Ye of little faith." The corner of Harrison's lip curled into a smirk. "I've been Roaming the five Territories for many years. Hel, I've got contacts in every village from here to Erinton's Cavern."

Campbell had heard of the town carved into the icy belly of a glacier, way up at the top of the New World. Rumour had it, a giant also lived in those caves. Though such things were clearly just stories, he would one day like to see the town that inspired so many of his imaginary boyhood adventures.

"You're in no fit state to go Roaming about the New World, Harrison," Caroline said sadly.

Harrison chuckled again and tried to hide his grimace. "What, this?" He pointed to the bloody rag around his head, covering what remained of his left eye. "This ain't all bad."

"You're a walking wreck," she said, completely nonchalant. "I'm sorry to bruise your ego, but it's true."

Campbell expected Harrison to be offended, perhaps even angry. Instead, he simply leant back and released a burst of guffawing laughter, followed by a wince. Moisture coated his surviving eye as he clutched his ribs.

"You've got spunk, but bruising my ego is a little redundant right now. We *have* to go Roaming because what other choice do we have?"

Caroline released a long and laboured sigh. She cast a solemn stare to her sister, who shared her unspoken defeat.

As the sun grew higher, warm morning light fell upon Harrison's features. It highlighted the specks of blood, the ashen hue to his cheeks... Harrison, despite his bravado, looked like death itself.

"We need to clean your wounds," Campbell said.

Harrison looked like Campbell had slapped him. "Nonsense. My wounds are fine."

A large sigh brought Caroline into their line of vision. She limped over, her knees visibly trembling, and gently kneeled before Harrison.

"You don't want an infection," she said glumly. "Not out here."

Harrison, as stubborn as he was, deflated into the mud beneath him. He remained silent, biting the profanity on his tongue, as Caroline delicately lifted the bloody rag around his head. She assessed the damage with a hard swallow.

Campbell did all he could to follow Caroline's stare, but the growing sunlight cast an ever-ominous shine onto the flaked, red goo in Harrison's eye socket. Nausea bubbled hot and ripe inside his gullet, and he quickly averted his gaze.

Caroline quickly ushered Alice to scour the surrounding area, searching for specific vegetation – names spoken in a language Campbell had never heard before. *Herdinese, perhaps?* No, absolutely not. Herdinese, as beautiful a language as it was, had never sounded quite like it.

"Campbell," Caroline snapped, dragging his attention. "I need you to find some *Allium ursinum*."

"*What?*" Campbell's nose scrunched up.

"Erm..." Caroline inspected Harrison's wound like she was trying desperately not to panic. "Err... *Garlic. Wild garlic* – it should grow close to the ground with small, white flowers. You'll be able to smell it as soon you get near it."

Campbell hopped to his feet and disappeared into the forest. Noise surrounded him, rising with the day's sun: chirping birds; the faint rustle of trees; the low groan of deer, prancing ahead...

How different to Maelstrom, bursting with the laughter of people or the low hum of car engines. Campbell unwillingly reminisced to the catcalls, or wails of pure euphoria, as an innocent person was dragged onto the stage, erected in the middle of Bolton Square. The Slave Auctions were a ghastly and disgusting blemish that merely intensified Maelstrom's ugly heart. How many people had been sold, in the one-and-a-half centuries since Ragnarök occurred?

Ragnarök. Campbell recalled the sound of cracking earth and the tumble of trees only those few short hours beforehand. He shivered.

Mason caused Ragnarök – that was a truth he had long heard, and long accepted. Mason wasn't human, he was something else entirely. Evidently, given that Campbell had stabbed him straight through the heart and the bastard still stood.

But Mason's *powers?* The way he could manipulate the earth, as though it was clay... Only now, as Campbell felt the shock and pure, startling dread rise around his lungs, did he understand that only now did he truly believe such stories. They were entirely real. Mason could destroy the entire world if he wanted to, as though it was a mound of dirt beneath his boot.

Ahead of him, shining through the emerald vegetation, a pool of white flowers clung to the base of the forest. Campbell's senses confirmed the pungent, garlicky smell and he quickly grabbed a few handfuls and returned to Caroline.

Alice was already there, cradling a bunch of yellow flowers and a piece of bark.

"How do you know all this?" Campbell asked, watching her grind the flowers between two rocks.

"Our mother's a botanist." Her hands slowed, her stare meeting the trees. "I mean, she *was* a botanist."

"I'm sorry," Campbell whispered. "And your father?"

Alice spat on the floor. Caroline just huffed. "He found out our Ma was having an affair with his favourite Slave. So, he killed the Slave – he made our Ma watch as he killed her – and sold us to his best friend." As Campbell's face lost all colour, a mean little smirk worked its way through Caroline's lips. "But we got the last laugh. Morning tea doesn't taste so good when it's spiked with hemlock."

Campbell didn't know what else to say, so he didn't say anything at all. He just watched Caroline grind the flowers, releasing her anger on those unsuspecting petals.

Harrison accepted Caroline's tender care. She prepared the herbs, extracting oils from the flowers and heating the bark above a small fire they built. Harrison took the oils and ointments, begrudged docility, and grimaced around the taste of the bark, yet he seemed to relax surprisingly quickly. If Campbell didn't know any better, he'd say Harrison enjoyed the attention.

After a while, with some of Harrison's wounds tended and their limbs recovered, they continued on. Walking at a more manageable pace, Campbell relished the outside air. Despite the cold nights, summer days embraced the sun's warmth and thawed their tight muscles. By the time the noon sun rose high into the sky, Campbell was forced to remove his faded leather jacket, flinging it over his shoulder.

The weapons around his hips became noticeable: the Masonian baton, his father's black revolver, and Mason's sword, hanging through one of his belt hoops. Campbell could barely look at the pristine, gleaming blade. It wasn't bloodstained, and that stung.

"Nice sword," Harrison remarked, limping beside him. Caroline had fashioned a new rag from the bottom corner of her t-shirt, and Harrison wore its clean, black lustre with pride. Alice said he looked *badass* – whatever that meant.

"Ha, thanks," Campbell mumbled, sheepishly. He moved the sword a little to his side, trying to hide it from Harrison. As absurd as it seemed, it embarrassed him.

Harrison's single eye narrowed. "How'd you get it?"

Campbell chewed the dried skin on his lip. Thirst clung to his throat and he wished for a flowing stream of water. Or vodka. He would have accepted either at that point.

"You can tell me, mate," Harrison said. "Nothing to be ashamed of with me."

Campbell sighed, casting his glacial-blue gaze to the two girls ahead. Caroline's arm passed over Alice's shoulder, holding her close as they trudged through the forest's warm, green bowels. They seemed far enough ahead to be out of earshot...

"It's Mason's," Campbell admitted, in barely a breath.

Harrison's limping pace slowed, only minutely and only for a second. He hobbled quickly to Campbell's other side and meticulously inspected the blade with a spectacular grin. "You don't say?"

"Don't," Campbell said, bristling. He hopped to Harrison's other side, hiding the sword from his vision.

Harrison's curiosity narrowed. "Why are you ashamed of it?"

"Because it didn't make a blind bit of difference!" Campbell snapped, but he was hyperaware of the girls ahead and quickly dulled his tone. "I mean, I *stabbed* him, Harrison..."

The air suddenly felt so thick, so heavy. Harrison's eye widened, his tongue embraced by a rare silence.

A heavy sigh burdened Campbell's narrow chest. "I stabbed him with his own sword, right through his *fucking* heart... and he just..."

Blue eyes met jade beneath the flickering afternoon light. "He *laughed* at me, he just..." Campbell quickened his pace, anger heating his chest more than the sun ever could.

With a grunt and a groan, Harrison eventually caught him up. "I'm having trouble comprehending that you stabbed the bastard at all! Campbell, you should be proud of that and wear that sword like the proud battle-scar it is!"

"Why?" Campbell rounded on him, nostrils flared. "Why should I wear it when it's just a reminder of my failure?"

"Failure?" Harrison smirked, raising his visible eyebrow. "You think all of that was a *failure?*"

Harrison nodded to the girls ahead. "You got them out, Campbell. Hel, you got me out too – with all my teeth and all. So, should we consider all of that a *failure?*" A low laugh lifted Harrison's chest. "No, mate. What you did was certainly not a failure – it was the exact opposite, in fact."

Breath caught in Campbell's throat. He just stared, dumbfounded, at Harrison's soft smile. No one had said something so... *praising* to him before. Another warmth grew in Campbell's chest – a different one, this time. It filled his eyes with moisture.

Watching Campbell's reaction, Harrison's smile grew. "You are the bravest, most decent thing to have ever come out of Maelstrom, and I am *proud* to call you my friend."

With a parting slap on Campbell's shoulder, Harrison trudged ahead. Campbell followed behind him, glowing from the inside, and wiped a small tear from his cheek.

8

____

Darkness descended slowly that night.

First, the light dulled. The bright, yellow light cutting through the forest gradually turned golden, flooding the leafy ground. Insects buzzed lethargically through the air, hopping from one flower to the next.

As the end of the forest approached, the trees spread apart, allowing more of the dying sunlight to punch through. Shadows formed, thrusting the majority of the forest into darkness. But ahead, as the forest emptied out into the high plateau, red sunlight poured over them, erupting from a sky bathed in colour: red, orange, pink... It painted the sky with spectacular beauty, the clouds erupting with such vibrancy, they barely appeared real.

The sun continued to descend towards another field of trees, stretching ahead. Mountains loomed, far into the distance, flooded with murky, purple shadows.

"Is that the Snowlands?" Campbell asked. He imagined the field of lakes, the blankets of snow, the creak of glaciers slumping down towering mountains...

"Sure is," Harrison said, smiling.

Excitement bubbled inside Campbell's chest. He grinned at those mountains, so far away and yet still close enough to touch, just briefly, with an outstretched hand.

"Look!" Alice pointed to a speckled pool of orange light far below them, huddled within the trees at the base of the flat-bottomed valley.

"A town," Caroline realised. "We could get supplies there?"

"And a hot meal." Campbell's stomach grumbled loudly at the mere thought.

"Nah, ain't got time for food," Harrison said, and a cheeky grin stretched his lips. "I'm gonna get laid."

Caroline laughed out loud, trudging back to the edge of the forest. "Yeah, good luck with that."

"What are you talking about?" Harrison chuckled, wandering to her with his arms spread wide. "Apparently I'm *badass* now. Who *wouldn't* want a piece of this action?"

They set up camp at the edge of the forest, a fire burning quite happily. Campbell's worry peaked at this, for he imagined Masonians or hungry animals perusing the scene, attracted to the fire's light like fluttering moths. But the others flushed away such concerns: apparently it was normal to see a firelit camp in the wilderness, and animals actively avoided fire. Nevertheless, it took a long time to relax beneath the fire's comforting light.

Away from the artificial light of Maelstrom, the night's sky erupted in a sheet of flickering light. *Billions* of stars smothered the sky – twinkling, sparkling... It was a sheet of glitter, erupting in a suite of colour and pastel glows.

Campbell had always assumed that a night's sky without the seasonal aurora's glow was black. Dead, almost lifeless.

Never before had he considered the night looking so bright, so *alive*. Why did nobody tell him each star twinkled differently, or shone with different colours, or formed such beguiling patterns in the sky?

Campbell soon understood how ignorant Aristocrats really were.

Thoughts suddenly took a downward turn. Slaves – hundreds of them – screamed behind his eyelids. How many innocent people were still trapped in Maelstrom's stinking, mouldy interior? How many people did his own father sell just *that day?*

Campbell couldn't throw away his heritage. No matter how hard it was to admit, he was born an Anders and that label – that *ancestry* – would follow him until the end of time. But the *Anders* name was just that: a *name*. It did not define his personality, and it certainly did not define his actions.

But he felt some responsibility for the people trapped in Maelstrom. He wanted to help them, just like he had helped Harrison, and Caroline, and Alice.

With his father's revolver on one side, and Mason's sword on the other, why *couldn't* he help them?

"I want to free Slaves," Campbell blurted out. Five eyes immediately jumped to him.

Campbell avoided their stares, throwing his into the fire. The flickering orange flames were... enchanting.

"I want to free them," he said, quieter this time.

Harrison took a deep breath. "I know you do," he said, following Campbell's gaze. "I do too."

Beneath the glittering night's sky, jade and blue fell into the orange firelight and emerged determined.

"So," Harrison exclaimed, as though it was obvious, "let's get them out."

"Oh, don't be ridiculous!" Caroline rolled her eyes. "What are you going to do? Form a Rebellion or something?"

"Why not?"

Caroline huffed around such incredulity. "Jeez, Harrison – are you trying to lose your other eye?"

"If that is what it takes to save innocent people, then yes. Let him take it!" A wide smile stretched Harrison's lips, his surviving eye shining ever so powerfully. "After all, if you decide to waltz with wolves, you're likely to be bitten."

Caroline rolled her eyes. "You're going to get yourselves killed."

"They're going to try and kill us anyway," Campbell said, and he believed every word of it. Mason himself implied just that. "But I'll be damned to just sit back and relax while innocent people are killed, tortured, and assaulted every fucking day..."

Campbell's glacial-blue eyes sank into Caroline's, and tears quickly formed. "I couldn't live with myself if I just sat back and did nothing..."

A glimmer of a smile worked its scheming way across Caroline's mouth.

"I know," she whispered, proudly. "I've already said that you don't seem like the type of guy to stand by while others get hurt."

Caroline's smile widened and a curious sensation rose deep in Campbell's gut. A fluttering warmth – a sort of glowing apprehension for the future. He couldn't explain it, yet it felt good. He sank into it, relished it, until Harrison's awkward cough.

"You in, Caroline?" he asked, then peeked around her arm to see Alice. "And what about you, girl?"

Alice snuggled into Caroline's side, relaxing into her embrace. It took her very little effort to nod.

"Oh, *fine*," Caroline eventually conceded, though excitement pulsed from her hidden smile. "Someone needs to be there to patch you guys up, after all."

"Oh, I'm sure you'll do us proud, girl," Harrison said, with a wink. Caroline rolled her eyes again, and Campbell was certain she'd be doing that almost constantly in the years to come.

"What is it called?" Alice asked. Questioning stares flocked to her. "I mean, all the Rebellions have names, right? So, what's this one going to be called?"

Harrison blinked. "I hadn't even thought about that."

They remained silent, gazing into the fire, like the answer would flicker between the flames.

In this quiescence, Campbell thought about all that had transpired over the last few days. All the stories he had heard, the new people he had met... He wondered how his life would have played out if Harrison Dagger had never entered his family's home, or if Iulia Dagger had never escaped Mason's.

"What about the *Dagger Rebellion*," Campbell offered, meeting stunned stares.

Harrison turned bright red and forced a nervous chuckle. "I'm flattered, mate, but – "

"No, I mean, *Dagger* as in *Iulia Dagger*."

Harrison's words flew back down his throat. He remained staring at Campbell, with nothing short of respect.

"I mean, if our goal is to free Slaves, it makes so much sense to name our

Rebellion after the one Slave who managed to escape Mason's Palace." Campbell formed a wide, toothy grin. "Don't you agree?"

Campbell never expected to see a tender tear trickle down Harrison's cheek. But there it was, shimmering in the fire's warmth.

"Yes, mate." Harrison smiled, softly. "I like that a lot."

And there, as four friends sat below the sparkling Woodland sky, the Dagger Rebellion was born.

PART 2

9

GAINSTORN, YEAR 162

Mason's screams poisoned the air.

They ricocheted through the forest, bouncing off the soaked, cracked bark. Ground trembled, the low rumbling of threatening destruction surpassed only by the howls of wolves, the screech of fluttering birds, and Mason's pure, unrelenting agony.

Campbell Anders listened to those screams, his feet stumbling beneath him. Echoing through the darkness, Mason's screams sounded so torturous, so harrowing.

As he lumbered through the shadows, Campbell realised Mason's torture was just the outward expression of his own.

Campbell's legs finally gave way. He collapsed to his knees, his hands sinking into the cold leaf mulch. The cloying stench of decay gagged his throat and Campbell finally vomited. Bile steamed in the frigid Fjordland air.

Campbell saw the blood speckling his firing arm, marring his faded black leather jacket. Bloodstains reached his shoulder.

A small, bruised cry escaped his burning gullet. It echoed through the forest, but was just a mere whisper compared to Mason's screams, spewing from the burning remains of the small village behind them.

Campbell almost looked back to Gainstorn. He imagined he was there, that those vengeful flames were licking the flesh clean off his murdering, despicable bones. But he couldn't look back. He couldn't bear to see the dead, diamond eyes behind that angry, orange glow.

Those haunting eyes had been so different to Mason's.

Another cry escaped Campbell's throat. Tears finally left him, along with the last of his strength, his resolve. He didn't stop his flood of emotion. He didn't deserve to be free from pain.

He didn't deserve to live.

"Campbell!" Harrison Dagger lunged through the shadows, following the sounds of Campbell's despair.

Campbell didn't have the energy to lift his head, to see the judgement and utter disgust that must have lived behind Harrison's singular green eye. As Harrison's dirty hand gripped Campbell's arm and dragged him to his feet, Campbell wished he'd drop him. To save himself and leave Campbell to be torn apart by whatever horrors lurked within the shadows. Harrison needed to leave him, to let him sink into that leaf litter and decompose.

Just like she was doing. But she wasn't cocooned by mushy leaves. Her coffin was a bloodstained cot.

A strained whimper burst from Campbell. Emotion built inside his empty stomach, the events of Gainstorn finally settling upon his soul. Memories assaulted his vision. Trembling knees failed to support his shaking frame.

"On your feet!" Harrison yelled. He thrust Campbell's numb arm around his shoulders, dragging him upright. "*On your feet, Anders!*"

Campbell didn't want to be on his feet. He wanted to die.

Physical numbness spread into his toes and he could no longer feel himself placing one foot in front of the other. But that numbness didn't reach his gut, or his heart. In fact, as life deserted his limbs, he realised he *felt* more then, in that one moment, than in his entire life. He felt it all.

What have I done? The question kept racing around his head. As Harrison's desperate orders to keep going—to keep moving—cut through the air, all Campbell heard was his own inner voice, his own last dribbles of warped humanity.

What have I done?

"Come on, mate," Harrison said as they rushed through the darkness. His voice was cracking, as was Campbell's. As was Mason's, still echoing through the trees.

A sob burst from Campbell's chest.

"It's okay," Harrison whispered, holding him close. "I've got you..."

And despite what Campbell had just done, Harrison never let him go.

10

———

Mason's audible agony had dispersed, soaking into the ground with the rest of the rainwater. In the dark silence of the forest, Harrison's strained grunts intensified, his steps and strength faltering. Campbell's arm gradually slipped from around his shoulder, and they both fell to the forest's stinking floor.

Campbell's fingers curled, sinking into the mess of soggy leaves and blankets of cold, wet moss. He felt that same moss flowing up his fingers, spreading through his arms, settling in his nauseous gut. Visions kept flashing before his eyes: the pouring rain that wrecked visibility; the collapsing huts, bursting with Rebels and Masonians; the baby girl, her diamond eyes sparkling in the flickering light from her burning home...

Her small limbs had wriggled so frantically as raindrops soaked her delicate—*perfect*—features. Campbell remembered her small lips turning blue, the icy rain completely saturating her clothes, her blanket, her bedding...

Campbell remembered the barrel of his father's old, black revolver pointing inside the crib... He remembered the excruciating *bang*.

Another spasm crunched his insides, leaving him heaving and gagging. His empty stomach gave little to vomit, but a large dribble of spit hung from his bloodless bottom lip. Campbell watched it lengthen, swinging in the delicate breeze as it hit the mossy ground beneath him, but he just didn't have the energy to wipe it away. He was shaking so much, he doubted he physically could.

"Hey, Campbell..." Harrison scrambled over and wiped away that long string of spittle with his coat sleeve. "C'mon, mate, look at me..."

Cold, dirty hands cradled Campbell's face, shadowed with stubble, and brought their eyes to meet. Harrison's brow furrowed, emphasising his surviving green eye and his black eye patch.

"You did what you had to do..." he whispered desperately.

Campbell's features scrunched around such falsehoods. No, he didn't do what he *had* to do. He did it because he was a coward, because the thought of Mason's unbridled power scared the shit out of him.

But, more than anything, he did it because he was *told* to.

Campbell retched again. Nothing came up, but Harrison's hold slipped.

In the absence of Harrison's warm reassurance, more visions flashed before Campbell's bloodshot, glacial-blue eyes.

Campbell remembered Mason gradually appearing through the rain. He remembered the bloody blade of Mason's sword glimmering in the firelight; he'd unsheathed it, then just threw it away from him, like it was nothing. Mason's steps were slow, careful, both his palms clearly shown in surrender.

"Please, don't do this," he had said.

For the longest time, Campbell didn't believe that he was hearing such words. That Lord Mason—the immortal, sadistic slaughterer of two billion people—was... *begging* him? Campbell doubted such a scenario could ever exist.

But when Campbell's aim remained true, and as the baby screamed inside the cot, Mason's diamond stare grew desperate. He'd dropped to his knees before Campbell, who, shocked at a such a display, remained silent and unmoved.

"You can have anything you wish," Mason had said. "Wealth—is that what you want? I can give you wealth—I can give you everything! Please, j-just let me take her, just lower the gun..."

Campbell remembered how odd those words had been. He never thought Mason knew how to... *beg.*

And yet, there he was, begging for the life of this baby. His future *mate. Alira.*

Mason must have seen Campbell's resolve, for he edged forwards, carving deep gutters in the mud beneath his knees. Rain flattened his black hair against his scalp, water dripping from his nose and jaw.

"You want freedom, isn't that right? You've always wanted freedom—that's why you chose Harrison Dagger over your Bloodline. I can give you that freedom, Campbell! I can let you—let *all* of you—live freely in the northern Territories. I won't seek to harm or to punish you. You will be free to live, to grow old, to have children of your own!"

Campbell felt, rather than heard, the sincerity in Mason's voice. Indeed, as Campbell stared at his heaving breaths, at the paleness of his slightly parted lips and the glaring whites of his eyes, Campbell realised that Mason seldom spoke about such things. Perhaps, for the first time in his long and wretched existence, Mason was telling the truth?

"Just lower the gun!" Mason's words echoed loudly between them. He edged closer. "*Please*, I am *begging* you!"

Yes, he had begged. For a fleeting moment, Campbell had relished such knowledge. To know, with no uncertainty, that he'd reduced the Destroyer of the Old World to *begging*.

But such satisfaction had been quickly lost. The baby's cries grew louder, her lips bluer, and Campbell heard the inalterable finality of Svenja Svellec's words ring inside his head...

"*You must kill her. If Mason finds her—if you are unable to bring her to me—then you must kill her.*"

So, he did what he was told.

"*Campbell!*" Harrison's harsh, grating yell brought Campbell's mind back to the present, and to the hands cradling his face again. "I need you to walk with me, okay?"

"I killed her..." The words felt alien on his tongue and coated his gums with acid. "I *killed* a baby..."

Harrison's throat convulsed on a large swallow, his eye looking impossibly green and vibrant. "You didn't have a choice," he whispered, but the words seemed broken, almost inaudible. Harrison's bottom lip trembled around such a vocal strain. "You did it because Mason found her—try to understand that you didn't have a choice..."

Emotion rose inside Campbell, replacing the nausea with pure, unrelenting pain. His spine curved, his chest caved, and suppressed cries shook his entire body. Harrison threw his arms around him, holding him close, running his fingers through Campbell's matted black hair.

Despite Harrison's comfort, and his warmth, Campbell remained cold and disorientated. He stared blindly to the leaf mulch and saw that baby's blue lips. He closed his eyes, but he just saw her blood.

And he heard her screams everywhere, suffocating him with one impossible, deafening *bang* at a time.

Unable to escape, Campbell pushed his face into Harrison's chest and wailed.

11

They reached camp when the dawn sun sat low in the sky. It cast a red glow on them both, illuminating them with ominous foreboding.

Yet, despite their aura, their fellow Rebels rushed to them immediately.

Caroline sprinted at breakneck speed towards them, her blonde hair flying in every direction. She thrust her body beneath Campbell's limp arm, supporting him, so both she and Harrison could carry his numb, catatonic state to the safety of the camp. The wooden doors of the barricade opened, welcoming them into the camp's tender embrace like an old friend.

Campbell realised he'd have no friends. Not anymore. Not after they knew what he'd done, what sort of *monster* he really was.

The camp was modest for its size. Just a few wooden cabins, interspersed with tents smothered with leathers to keep out the worst of the Fjordland rain. Fires burned brightly, even in the daytime, and the tall pillar of black smoke merged into the dull sky. Several fires burned in the rural Fjordland hills, created by the isolated communities, or the small groups that Roamed the New World, so it was more suspicious if the Rebel camp didn't have a fire. As a result, their supply of firewood never faltered. Caroline even had wood-chips buried in her hair, no doubt from her early morning chores.

"Easy now," she said gently, as they led Campbell further into the camp.

As they set Campbell down on a wooden stump, Caroline snapped to the nearest Rebel, "You! Water, now!"

People scurried and crowded the small space. "Back up, give them some room!"

The crowd edged back, their eyes wide and concerned.

"Campbell..." Caroline gently took Campbell's cheeks. For a brief moment, he startled at the warmth of her calloused hands, but the sensation vanished just as quickly. He remained numb.

"Can you help him?" Harrison asked with a grave expression.

Caroline shrugged her narrow shoulders. "There's nothing physically wrong with him, I..." Her voice trailed off, her eyes lost inside her own memories. "Harrison, did you hear the way Mason screamed?"

Harrison licked the rough skin peeking from his lower lip. He just nodded.

Caroline dropped her stare to the mud. "I've never heard someone sound like that. It... It sounded like he was being tortured."

"Not even that..." Harrison rearranged the elastic band from his eye patch. "I never want to feel what Mason felt. Whatever it was, whatever... *force* or magic made him experience that much... *pain.* By the Gods, I hope none of us experience that."

Campbell recalled the sheer *agony* spewing from Mason's throat. Any other day, he would smile at such a thought. Not then. He didn't deserve to smile. Not anymore.

"Campbell..." Harrison's soft voice didn't make a dent in Campbell's stare, which remained fixed on the trodden leaves. "C'mon, mate, try to look at me..."

He didn't.

"He needs time," Caroline said, so only Harrison could hear. "Don't force it."

Harrison agreed, but with a dejected huff.

Somewhere in the distance, a door slammed shut with a rattling bang. Scuffling boots sounded, growing louder, and Harrison jumped to his feet to meet the flurry of people.

"Thank the Gods..." He threw his arms around a handsome man, lingering in his mid-twenties and only a few years younger than Harrison.

They embraced each other desperately, as though their very souls nestled in each other's hearts. Campbell often thought they were.

Eventually, Harrison peeled himself away and held the man's bearded face delicately between his hands.

"Are you alright, Dan?" he whispered.

Daniel's lips curled into a sad smile, his nose wrinkling. Tear-tracks glimmered against flawless black skin. "Shouldn't I be asking you that?"

Harrison's jade-green eye turned incredibly glassy, a helpless tear trickling as he tenderly pressed his lips to Daniel's.

"Harrison." A woman paraded into the space, strikingly beautiful, with a small girl held in her arms. Harrison pulled himself away from Daniel, his eye finding the child's small body. A hurt, despairing breath escaped his lungs as he rushed to her, grasping the child in his thick arms. He cradled her like her precious creature she was, burying his nose in her silky black hair and inhaling deeply.

"Gods, forgive us…" he said.

An old woman hobbled into the mass of people, her limping gait supported by a wooden walking stick. Silver hair fluttered in the breeze, her thin lips twisted into a smirk. Loose skin pushed its way up, bunching into the apples of her cheeks, resting below golden eyes that gleamed like metal in the morning light.

"I didn't expect you to be so squeamish, Harrison," Svenja Svellec said.

"How dare you," he hissed, glaring at the woman, being sure to protect the child's delicate features—and her eyes, identical to Harrison's—away from Svenja's butchering stare. "You told us what needed to be done, but *only* if Mason found her. But you knew he'd already found her, didn't you? You knew what we'd have to do before we even left for Gainstorn!"

Svenja's lips curled up, revealing her golden teeth. "I had a hunch. But you knew what the stakes were the moment you stepped foot there."

"You should have told us," he said, gritting his teeth. "You should have *warned* us!"

"And then what? You would all fight me, wouldn't you? *Oh please, Svenja, there must be another way…*" She smiled again, but no amusement spat from the motion. "There *was* no other way, Harrison. A death of one child to save countless lives—like that of your daughter's."

Harrison's stare turned homicidal. "You leave Isla out of this."

"One life to save all the others. That's the reality, but I never expected you to like it, only to accept it."

Harrison and Svenja stared each other down, then Harrison gently passed his daughter back to her mother.

"Kat, take her inside."

Katarina smiled tightly, for she disliked taking orders from Harrison, but as she saw his seething *rage*, she grudgingly accepted. She returned to the wooden cabin, Isla's small body tucked neatly against her.

"Don't tell me that Mason's pain wasn't of immense enjoyment to you all," Svenja said. She leant on her walking stick with both hands, her small nose raised. Pure power seeped from her skin, shimmering in the surrounding air. Normally, Campbell was mesmerised by such a sight. It seemed so unusual, so *magical,* for a woman of her immense age and fragility to exude such visible power. More than once, Campbell had wondered *what* Svenja Svellec was—because she sure as hell wasn't human.

But not that day. Perhaps Campbell had just accepted there were things he would never understand: why Svenja Svellec exuded power, or why he'd shot a helpless baby in her cot. At any rate, Campbell remained still and silent, unable to accept anything. All he could do was listen, using Harrison's voice to cling to his sordid reality.

"And what happens when he recovers, hm?" Harrison skulked towards her, his surviving eye seething. "Because he *will* recover, won't he?"

Harrison threw his hands through his shoulder length hair, glowing a dirty caramel in the dull morning light. "Fuck's sake, Svenja—why didn't you warn us?"

"Would you have agreed? Would you have gone to Gainstorn—done what was necessary—knowing you'd risk Mason's retribution?"

"That is beside the point, woman! Do you know the position you've put us in?"

"What position? The way I see it, you have a golden opportunity to free Slaves. When else will you have such a lengthy window?"

Harrison threw agitated hands in his matted hair. "And when he returns to his full strength?"

"You better make sure you stay out of his way."

Harrison's jaw clenched, a muscle ticking beneath his cheek. His shoulders hunched, then trembled, and only when Daniel squeezed his arm did his tension disperse, like delicate snow flurries blown away by the wind.

"Be that as it may," Harrison said. "Whatever your reasons, Mason's wrath is on your hands."

"So is his entire existence." Svenja grinned, forced and bitter. "Mason will be incapacitated until the next Alira is born. Until then, I suggest you make good use of the time Campbell has given you."

12

After the last retch had rolled up his body, Campbell collapsed on the floor. A Rebel removed the steaming bucket, gently clicking the door shut behind him. Campbell was left alone.

He craved the solitude.

Before, he'd drink downstairs with the others, clanking his tankard of mead against the little ruts in the table, laughing as Alice danced with everything that moved, spinning and drinking so fast she'd fall to the floor. Harrison's guffaw would rattle his lungs, but Dan would steal silence from his lips, throwing his arms around his neck and kissing him into oblivion.

Then, there would be Caroline, sitting next to Campbell, a small smile tucked into her lips. Her eyes—resembling a polished Tiger Eye stone—would shimmer in the flickering light from the burning hearth, and Campbell would hold that stare for as long as he could. His stomach would flutter with delicate bits of warmth—from Caroline's presence, or the mead? He could never be sure. But he enjoyed it, sank into it. He wanted to bathe in that feeling, to be consumed by it.

That warmth had gone now, as had the comfort. Now, sinking into the deepest pit of his belly, only ice remained. Dank and heavy, like that ball of stinking, slimy moss. And no matter how much he puked, how much his stomach rolled and screeched, that ball of moss would always be there, always linger inside of him.

It had become a part of him, like the cold blood that ran through his veins, or the glacial-blue hue that coloured his eyes.

Campbell likened it to a disease. An infection that had poisoned his blood—his very soul—and left him permanently soiled, like a dirty, bloodied bandage.

But the more he realised—and he *felt*—the pit of despair and the terrible, inconsolable guilt inside his stomach, he understood the blemish upon his soul was more than a disease, more than a measly bacterium that had putrefied his insides.

It was a cage. An empty, suffocating cage, surrounded by metal bars, reaching higher and higher through the ceiling of his room. Campbell imagined—no, he *felt*—those bars rise, punching through the clouds, finally merging with the colourful, ethereal bursts of colour in the night's sky.

Would the aurora still be there, when Mason screamed inside his Palace?

Regardless, Campbell had trapped himself inside his own cage. And he deserved to stay there. He deserved to rot inside the cold, unending bars of the cell, erected the moment his revolver's bang echoed between those soaked tree trunks.

Then, with no uncertainty, Campbell realised he was already rotting. Though no one could see it yet, they must have smelt it, seeping from the clogged pores in his skin. Campbell felt it too.

Just like that ball of slimy moss, soaking inside his stomach.

The door creaked open. Campbell's sore eyes raised long enough to spot Caroline's lithe form, tentatively entering. She offered a small, comforting smile. Campbell shot his stare to the cracked floorboards.

Caroline delicately closed the door behind her, her heeled boots clanking against the hollow floor. Those same footsteps muffled as she stepped onto the sheepskin rug, lying at the foot of a bed doused in blankets and furs. She walked straight past Campbell to close the red velvet curtains, hiding the busy Rebel camp outside, and placed something on the wooden dresser.

Campbell didn't have the energy to lift his head and see what it was. Knowing Caroline, it was some form of herbal medicine.

As expected, the delicate scents of lavender and camomile permeated the air, following the soothing rush of pouring water. Clearly, Caroline had come prepared.

She knelt before him. Wood creaked beneath the leather patches on her knees.

"Drink this," she said, and her voice was like an ointment, soothing Campbell's soul. He closed his eyes, sinking into that voice and her presence, and the scent of *calm* that wafted up from the ceramic cup held delicately in her fingers.

Campbell heard her reshuffle her position, so he opened his eyes to her sitting cross-legged before him. Her long blonde hair framed her beautiful face, only slightly scarred from the Rebellion, and rosy lips that tilted into a comforting smile. How was it, that everything about this woman screamed *comfort?* Campbell would never understand, but he loved her for it.

His heart always sang in her comforting presence and screamed whenever she left. She'd smile, her face lifting with pure elation, and the warmth inside his belly would reach almost unbearable levels. Campbell's chest would tighten when she walked into the room, the very air thinning beneath her smooth skin and calm demeanour, and Campbell felt like he was gasping for air. And yet, he wanted to drown in her presence. He craved it.

Even now, after everything he'd done, he wanted Caroline there. He wanted her to rub her hand between his shoulder blades. No lies, however kind they might be. Caroline would never lie to him, and Campbell loved her even more for that.

Yes, he did love her. More than he could ever show or understand.

When in Caroline's presence, her warmth dived into his chest, then his stomach. It even trickled into his legs, reached the tip of his extremities until his toes tingled.

But the *usual* sensations he knew he should feel—the rampant desire, or the carnal sparkle that usually donned Harrison's eye when he looked at Daniel—remained elusive to Campbell. He *knew* he should feel it, *knew* that warmth should not be contained everywhere else in his body but in the one place he'd heard so much about. But he felt nothing, and he had no... *desire.* At least, not the desires Harrison usually went on about.

He didn't understand it, and as the years went on, he grew more frustrated at its absence. One night, after far too much to drink and with Caroline's laughter radiating a bright golden glow, Campbell had dragged Harrison to a secluded corner and confided in him. Surely, Harrison could help him, to make him understand why he didn't feel what everyone else did…

"What's wrong with me?" Campbell had said, a tear in his eye.

Harrison had listened to Campbell's grave concerns with a raised eyebrow, and a tender, knowing smile.

"Nothing at all, mate," he had replied, with a gentle squeeze of his shoulder. "Nothing at all."

So, Campbell had remained impartial to the desire that spread through everyone else. But the warmth never left him, nor did the glowing sparkle inside his heart that lifted with Caroline's laugh, and her smile, and her mere presence.

Did Caroline know how much Campbell loved her? It was unclear. Maybe, one day, Campbell would tell her. He'd always hoped he would. He'd hoped that, one day, he'd have the confidence to explain *what* he felt, and what he didn't.

But those hopes had now been squashed, crushed beyond recognition, merging into the ball of rot that sang deep inside his soul. How could Caroline love him after what he'd done? How could she bear to be in the same *room* as such a despicable *monster*?

Campbell despised himself. Caroline must have done too.

"Drink," she said, startling him. She hovered the steaming mug of tea further into Campbell's vision.

Campbell released a steady stream of air through parted lips. He could smell the lavender, and while it didn't dull the pain, it helped him bear it. It was another warmth he needed.

With trembling hands, Campbell took the mug inside his palms. Heat merged into his skin, so hot against the numbness, and Caroline watched with a soft focus as Campbell took his first, tentative sip.

Strange, how he could smell the lavender, but not taste it. He might as well be swallowing hot water. But it cleared the acidic stench of vomit from his mouth, at least. As he concentrated on the line of heat trickling down inside his chest, Campbell's sigh of utter, complete defeat filled the space between them.

"I'm so sorry," he whispered to the air.

Caroline's warm hands grasped his shoulder, trying to squeeze away the tension. "You did what you had to do, Campbell."

Campbell took another sip of the tasteless hot water, letting it coat the inside of his mouth. "I killed... I-I killed..." He couldn't bring himself to say it.

Tears burned behind his eyes, but he didn't have the energy—or the internal resources—to allow them to fall. Maybe he would feel better if they had.

"She was the End of Everything..." she whispered. Another gentle squeeze of his shoulder, the soothing pressure rippling down Campbell's entire arm. "If Mason found her, she would have destroyed the world—and yes, maybe not tomorrow, or the day after that, or the day after that... But one day, twenty or thirty years from now, she would birth Mason's child and then..."

A large, defeated sigh passed between her lips. "Well, she'd have lived up to her title."

"Her lips were turning blue..." Campbell said, so quietly. "She must have been so, so cold..."

"You put her out of her misery." Warm hands—clammy from the mug of hot tea—cradled Campbell's cheeks, forced his sore eyes to meet hers. A thick layer of moisture held onto her lower lashes, somehow resisting the long fall. "And not just her misery in Gainstorn, but the years of torture beneath Mason's fingernail. She would have grown up in his Palace, and as soon as she Came of Age, he would have..."

Tears finally punched through Caroline's resolve, trickling down her cheek. "You saved her from that, Campbell. You saved her from an *eternity* of pain."

Campbell shook his head, his lower lip trembling. How could he possibly believe such a thing? How could his act of pure, wretched barbarity be *justified*?

"Hey," Caroline said, compressing her grip, forcing his shaking head to still. "You saved all of our lives—and the lives of so many others too... Even if you don't realise it yet."

Campbell forced his eyes to lift again, and their stares met. A sparkle of hope reappeared between them, fleetingly, like a forgotten caress.

"Come with me," she said.

Lacking the energy to argue, Campbell obliged, pulling his creaking limbs from the wooden floor.

The Rebels had occupied an old Aristocratic hunting lodge. A holiday home, once booked out for long weekends, where Aristocrats could hunt large game in the forest during the daytime, then return in the evenings for excessive food, drink, and gossip. No doubt congratulating each other on the blood spilled that afternoon, as they devoured the animal's carcass. Indeed, as Campbell descended the winding wooden stairs, he gazed at the mess of stuffed heads lining the walls: bears, elk, moose, rabbit, snow leopard... A whole manner of marble, lifeless eyes gazed back at him—*judged him*—as he followed Caroline into the main dining room.

A hefty oak table loomed in the centre of the room. Once full of flickering candelabras and golden cutlery, now it was a mess of maps and little tokens, snatched from the chess and backgammon boards from the adjoining games room.

Campbell had tried to teach Harrison chess earlier that week. They'd played one full game before Harrison got bored and went to clean his guns.

Clearly, guns were the only thing on Harrison's mind as he leant two muscly arms on the table before him, scouring the maps with his surviving eye, occasionally nodding at whatever the Rebel beside him said. Indeed, the room was full of Rebels. Men and women studded the floor, rigid and immobile. Like metal spikes. One wrong movement, and Campbell would fall and impale himself on them.

The room swiftly became suffocating as all those eyes burned into him, almost forcing him back up those stairs. Some Rebels met him with nothing but respect, others with indifference. Others, like Harrison, produced a small smile.

Perhaps realising Campbell just wasn't in the mood to talk, Rebels mercifully averted their gazes and returned to the table, and the plans and plots scattered across it. Svenja Svellec, however, was nowhere to be seen. Campbell considered this a blessing, but a forgotten part of himself remembered his near-constant frustration at how she always popped in—or out—whenever it suited her, and without a moment's notice. Clearly, the woman worked on her own timetable and answered to no one.

Yet, everyone was expected to answer to her.

"We should hold two weeks in contingency," Harrison declared.

"Bullshit!" Alice piped up, marching forward with her greasy blonde hair shining beneath a chandelier constructed from elk antlers. "Think of all the people we could free in those two weeks!"

"If Mason will regain his strength at the beginning of the *Twelfth Month*, then we need to ensure we're sufficiently scattered before then."

Alice produced one of the most vicious sneers Campbell had ever seen. "Running with your tail between your legs, Harrison?"

"Hardly," he replied with an equally vicious glare. "But I'm not risking all of your lives for the sake of two insignificant weeks."

"Two weeks for a Slave is a lifetime," Dan said from the outskirts. He remained encased in shadow, yet his dark brown eyes surveyed the scene with hope and plenty of determination. "We should leave at the last minute, to ensure we get as many people out as we can."

"Agreed!"

More agreements fluttered.

Harrison leant both fists on the table and hunched his shoulders, a deep sigh inflating his lungs. "Do you all realise the danger we're in?" he said, as an aura of tense quiet rippled through the crowd. "We killed Mason's future mate—*in front of him*. If that wasn't enough, Mason is being tortured—right now, as we speak—and will continue to be until the next Alira is born, in *nine months*. Can any of you imagine the scale of his retribution when he recovers?"

That ominous quiet turned into a hiss of fear.

"We need to ensure we are sufficiently far away from him, scattered across the New World, for our safety and for those we love."

Harrison's eye slid to Daniel, then to Kat on the other side of the room, stood with a poker down her spine and Isla's small body in her arms.

"We need to get the children out," Harrison said.

A roar of disagreements rose from the crowd. Parents snarled, insisting their children would be safer within their clutches, rather than out of them.

"Then go with them!" Harrison yelled, standing tall, allowing the entire Dagger Rebellion to see the resolve—the pure, unwavering determination—spewing from his jade eye. "I'm not keeping you here—I will *never* force you to stay, to fight for a cause that could cost you your lives—but I *can* send the children away, and so I am."

Kat's voice filled with venom, her red lips twisting into a cruel sneer that Harrison was quick to return. "I'm not leaving Isla."

"Then, by all means, go with her! But I'm not risking Isla's life by keeping her here." His stare briefly flicked to a couple: tall and lean, both with sandy blonde hair and narrow, sour expressions. Laura Isenhaur and Hamish Ashworth, if Campbell remembered correctly. Laura held a small, mewling bundle in her arms, gently rocking it back and forth. *Mikael.*

"Mason's wrath will be utterly merciless," Harrison continued, and that layer of silence sank to the crowd, crushing their retorts. "I seldom give such indisputable orders, and you know I don't like to do it, but this isn't open for any further discussion."

Harrison pushed himself from the desk, tapping his knuckle against the wood as a murmur of nervous dread trickled between teary parents.

Clearly incensed, Kat marched forwards, still carrying Isla. *"Harrison!"* She barked so loudly that Isla winced. "Isla stays here, with me."

Harrison rarely allowed himself to show such fiery, vicious rage. But if anyone was going to drag it out of him, it would be Katarina. "Don't you *dare* argue with me on this," he said, snarling.

"I have been waiting *years* to smite Mason. Do you think I'm going to walk out on the opportunity to make him hurt?"

"For *once*, in your godforsaken life, will you drag your finger out your arse and see the bigger picture!" Harrison pointed a sharp finger to Isla, sucking her small thumb in Kat's arms. "This isn't about your revenge, this is about our daughter's protection—her *life!* Now, you can stay here and help us free Slaves, or you can go with Isla. The choice is yours, Kat, but Odin himself walks in Maelstrom's gutters before I allow Isla to stay within one-*hundred* miles of this Rebellion, whether you're in it or not!"

Kat, always so fiery and quick to argue, became speechless.

A snide smile worked its way across Harrison's chapped lips. "Now, if you'll excuse me, I have a Rebellion to manage and children to evacuate."

If Campbell was in better spirits, he would have smiled at the affront on Kat's pale, porcelain cheeks. She was always a thorn in Harrison's side, whether she actively pushed her way in or not. Kat's one role, it seemed, was to disagree with everything Harrison said. Campbell often wondered why. Her arguments were often too brazen or too inconsequential to be taken seriously, and they'd only multiplied since Isla's surprise entrance.

Was it a coincidence that, just before Kat's comments grew particularly annoying, Harrison noticed Dan for the first time? Impossible to say. But clearly Kat's one-time night of passion with the leader of the Dagger Rebellion had left a lingering impression on her psyche. Her eyes practically glowed green when she realised Dan had been the *only* person to keep Harrison's attention. Did Kat's heart genuinely ache as Harrison found love with another? Campbell doubted it: she was far too high up her own backside to care for anyone but herself. Yet, she believed every man in the Rebellion should bow to her desires, then got pissed if they refused or rebutted her. Campbell and Harrison used to joke about it—usually around their fifth or sixth tankard of mead.

But at least one good thing had come out of Harrison and Kat's union: the little girl snuggling in her mother's arms, perusing the scene with Harrison's eyes.

The room gradually dispersed, ebbing away with tension and hushed whispers. With a sigh, Harrison meandered over to Campbell and Caroline, scrubbing the frown on his forehead.

"Do you think they'll go?" Caroline asked, once he was in earshot.

Harrison shrugged broad shoulders and leant against the wooden wall, before the only portrait in the room. They had removed most of the artefacts from the lodge, yet a few remained, such as the portrait of three hunting Aristocrats. Campbell stared at the painted shotguns and immediately forced aside his gaze.

"You mean the parents?" Harrison cocked an eyebrow. "Up to them, I won't force them either way."

Caroline licked her lips and stared solemnly at Kat, carrying Isla into an adjoining room. "And the children?"

"They're going." Harrison's jade eye contained nothing but pure, relentless determination. "Like Hel am I going to keep them with us."

A soft breath passed between Caroline's lips. "You're acting like our blood's already been spilt."

"It has." Harrison met her widening stare with that hard eye. Yes, exactly like green jade. "Why does no one understand the depth of the shit we're in? Our names—our faces—are being printed on every wanted poster in the New World. We *killed* an *Alira*."

Campbell did not ignore Harrison's choice of words.

"No," he whispered, and he shocked himself at the sound of his own voice. So weak, so feeble. Like someone had shoved the sound through a cheese grater.

Slowly, he met Harrison's eye. "*I* pulled the trigger. *I* was the one Mason begged. There is no *we* in this, Harrison. *I* killed her."

Silence weighed on them all. It crushed Campbell, pushing his shoulders down one excruciating inch at a time. He slid down the wall, his legs bunching before him, and forced his frantic breaths into the space between his thighs and stomach.

Slowly—with visible effort—Harrison crouched before Campbell's trembling frame. "You are not alone in this," he whispered. "*I* marched us into Gainstorn, knowing full well the consequences."

"You didn't pull the trigger..."

"But I put the gun in your hand."

Harrison's words seeped into Campbell, fighting through the seams in his leather jacket. Slowly, he lifted his bloodshot gaze to see a single tear trickle down Harrison's muddy cheek. "If you're a monster, mate, then I am too—and don't stick that label on us, *please...*"

Campbell jumped at Caroline's slender hand, slipping across his shoulder. "We're in this together," she whispered, and Campbell lost himself inside her Tiger Eye stare. "We always have been, we always will be."

Harrison's lips curled into a small, sad smile. "*We* are the Dagger Rebellion, to the end."

13

NINE-AND-A-HALF MONTHS LATER

Gunshots peppered the air, disappearing into the teal light dancing on the stars.

How strange, to hear those bangs rejoice. Leaning against a rock, Campbell perused the scene before him: the roaring bonfires, the barrels of mead, the drunk and dancing Rebels...

The air, thick with alcohol fumes and merriment, weighed upon his heart. Yet, he managed a small smile and brought the tankard to his chapped lips. Mead soothed his throat, slipping down his gullet. Gradually, that ball of anxiety eroded away, only a little, yet it made some welcome space inside his gut.

"Enjoying the party?" Daniel asked, wandering up to him. A tankard in his hand, he was one of the few Rebels who still had a shotgun slung around his shoulder. He clearly didn't consider the small, isolated town of Snow's Breath—nestled deep within the Glassland mountains—to be quite as hidden as everyone else.

In response to his question, Campbell just shrugged.

"Hmm." Dan took another small sip of his mead, the marble in his throat bobbing up and down. Firelight trickled down his flawless skin, catching the first shadow of stubble against his jawline. Campbell couldn't help but stare at the odd sight: Dan was usually so meticulous about a clean shave.

"It feels rather presumptuous, doesn't it?" Dan continued, casting dark brown eyes across the revellers. "To be celebrating this soon after Mason's uprising?"

Yes, it did. Though Campbell didn't dare say anything. Rebels still viewed him with an unsettling mix of dread and disgust, and none of them wanted his concern mixed into their tankards. All except Harrison, that is. But although Harrison agreed with Campbell's every concern, there was very little he could do. After all, the Rebels had followed his every order, no matter what. They'd forsaken hundreds of Slaves so the Rebels had ample time to scatter across the New World, hiding in other isolated towns like Snow's Breath, without attracting Masonian patrols.

For all intents and purposes, it looked like they had escaped Mason's retribution. The new *Alira* would have been born at the beginning of the *Twelfth Month*, and even three weeks later, they hadn't detected a tremor (literal or otherwise) of Mason's vengeance. Now, as the New Year steadily approached, the Rebels filled with a sense of hope and exhilaration.

They had made it.

They had smote Mason and plucked almost two-hundred people from slavery, across the New World. Those freed Slaves, along with most of the fighting Rebels, danced around the bonfires, cheering to the undulating lights above.

All except Campbell. And Harrison, of course. In fact, the one-eyed bastard remained rather elusive.

Campbell quickly swallowed his mouthful of mead, remembering how to speak. "Dan, where is he?"

Dan threw a lazy nod over his shoulder, towards the town's longhouse. "In there, brooding."

Brooding, of course. That's all Harrison seemed to do those days.

Finishing the last dregs of his mead, Campbell wandered towards the longhouse. A thatched roof glistened with frost, the only tell of any occupancy spewing serene golden light from the snow-crusted windows. Sighing, Campbell stared at the carved wood, surrounding a plain wooden door, and could clearly pick out the runes of the Old Gods. Newly graffitied, likely by one of the Rebels. Yet another sign of their presence; infesting the sleepy town like a swarm of ants.

A wave of heat hit Campbell as he stepped inside, warming his chapped cheeks, stinging life through his numb fingers. The air, choked with smoke and the charred remnants of rosemary, caressed his shivery body and carried him towards the bar, where he quickly ordered another refill.

"On the house," the scrawny bartender said, with a wink.

Hiding an awkward smile, Campbell perused the scene. A long table hugged the centre of the room, resting on an enormous bearskin rug. No head was attached, thank God, yet Campbell couldn't imagine the size of the animal that unwillingly gifted its skin. It was either something of legend, or multiple animals had been stitched together.

Campbell pushed forward, sincerely hoping for the former.

Around him, the space was littered with empty tankards, threads of material, and pieces of paper. Like a bunch of bratty, Aristocratic teenagers had trashed the place following a party. Campbell's older sister flashed before him, along with all her suitors. Memories of her angular face, her snotty glare, and hurtful comments immediately rose to mind, no matter how hard he tried to push them out.

Campbell rarely thought about his family. Truth be told, they didn't deserve any spared second. Yet, after this latest bout of disgrace, Campbell wondered what had happened to them. Maybe Mason had punished *them* for Gainstorn. A sharp pang of guilt threatened to burst. Campbell hastily pushed it aside, just like the rest of his wretched family.

"You're looking a little lost there, mate."

Slurred words were hardly customary of Harrison, so when Campbell followed their path and saw him sprawled before the blazing hearth, Campbell knew Harrison needed a friend. Someone who shared his concerns, his *guilt*. Not just of Gainstorn, but the months afterwards: the Rebel martyrs, or the executed Slaves who didn't make it in time. How many lives had been lost because the train couldn't bear to wait much longer, or because Harrison had chosen children to fill the vans, instead of adults?

Such choices pushed Harrison down, chipping away his personality. It pained Campbell to see Harrison disintegrate before his eyes. Gone was the cocky, charming boy he met all those years ago. Now, a broken man remained. Yes, he was the leader of the most successful (*infamous*) Rebellion in the New World's entire history, but such a title did not come without a price.

That same price dragged on the skin below Harrison's eye, which was barely able to focus as Campbell pulled out a neighbouring chair.

"Shouldn't you be joining the party?" Harrison asked, and downed the remaining mead inside his tankard. Probably only drips at that point, yet he was sure to guzzle every last one.

"I might ask the same of you," Campbell retorted, with a raised eyebrow.

Harrison's lip quirked upwards, and he threw the tankard to that monstrous rug with a dull *thud*. "I don't like to test fate."

"It's been three weeks since she was born." Campbell replayed the math inside his head: thirty-nine weeks following Gainstorn, give or take a few days, had this new Alira being birthed at the beginning of the *Twelfth Month*. Given such facts, Mason should have been walking around his Palace by now, murdering and raping to his heart's content.

Such a thought was sobering. Campbell recalled Harrison's parents, and all the torment they had endured in that same Palace, trapped beneath Mason's unrelenting fist. He hastily pushed aside the images.

Harrison's leg bobbed frantically, drawing Campbell's gaze towards it. Harrison had always been unable to sit still, but his fidgeting had worsened of late. As had his anxiety. A quick look at Harrison's gaunt cheeks made Campbell wonder when he last ate.

"Do you think he's given up?" Campbell asked in a hushed tone, as though Mason himself was listening through the walls.

"Huh? You think the Destroyer of the Old World would so readily forgive us for murdering his mate, and subjecting him to nine months of torture?" Harrison snorted. "I doubt it, but I just don't know why we haven't heard anything."

"No more news from the Palace?"

"None." Harrison huffed beneath his breath. "As though the entire Fjord-lands are still hibernating."

Campbell replayed the math inside his head again, just to be sure. No, it was indisputable: the beginning of the *Twelfth Month*, for certain.

What did that little girl look like? Were her lips tinged blue, or did her parents coddle her in blankets and pretend her eyes didn't resemble diamonds?

A shiver ran the entire length of Campbell's spine. He shook it away, quickly, before the nausea returned.

"Kat keeps nagging me," Harrison whispered, both hands tightly tucked beneath his arms, a sour expression on his face.

"About the children?"

Harrison snorted again, louder this time, and stared at the roaring hearth. "She doesn't care about the other kids. It's Isla she's after." A weighted pause, Harrison losing himself inside the flames. "She says that since Mason clearly isn't coming after us here, then there's no danger in bringing the kids back."

A broken, shattered laugh erupted from Campbell's gullet. "You're kidding me, right?"

Harrison bobbed his eyebrow. "I told her to go fuck herself."

"Subtle, Harrison."

"You don't get it, mate," he snapped, but there was no hurt or insult in his words, merely truth. How could Campbell understand? He wasn't a father.

"I want Isla back too," Harrison said, speaking softly to the warm air. "I miss her, more than anything. She'll be five years old now. I've missed almost a year of her life, and I can't even contact her, to tell her how much I love her."

Tears glimmered in the firelight. "But I can't allow her to come back here. We're walking targets, Campbell. We could be for the rest of our lives."

Harrison thrust his spine back in his chair, as though wrestling with the truth. The truth that, to save her, he might never see his daughter again.

Such a fact stung Campbell, so God knows how Harrison and Kat must have felt.

Harrison huffed out a frustrated breath. "So, yes, I get why Kat wants her back. But I won't allow it. I'll put Kat on the next train out of here in a heartbeat, but that's the only way she'll see her again."

Her daughter, or the Rebellion. Kat could only choose one.

To Campbell, the choice was obvious. But then, he wasn't a father.

"You should tell Caroline," Harrison said.

Campbell's stare shot back to him, meeting the compassion in his eye. "What?"

"Caroline," Harrison repeated. "You should tell her."

Tell her that you love her.

Campbell shook the thought away, his gut crunching. He didn't want to talk about this. Unlike Harrison, he hadn't consumed nearly enough mead.

"She wouldn't understand," he whispered.

The pause weighed on them both.

"Sexual desire doesn't equal love, mate," Harrison said softly.

Liquid distress flooded Campbell's intestines.

"Is it about Gainstorn?" Harrison asked. "Because you know she doesn't—"

"I don't want to talk about this." Campbell's tone was harsher than he meant, but he needed to stop the conversation. Harrison's words shot back down his gullet. He gazed sadly at the fire.

"Sorry," Harrison said, eventually.

Campbell sighed, angry at the entire New World; for his lack of desire, for Gainstorn, or for Mason's empty retribution? Probably all three.

Campbell rose to his feet. "Try not to drink yourself into oblivion," he said, patting Harrison on his shoulder.

Harrison smirked. "Ah, but oblivion's so much fun."

Upstairs, where the merriment dispersed beneath the howling wind, Campbell rolled his shoulders and exhaled a long breath. He fell to the lumpy mattress, cradling his pounding head.

Rebels would be celebrating far into the night, of that he was certain. But how could he join them? Despite Gainstorn, and Campbell's abominable actions, Mason's lack of reprisal didn't sit well with him. But to say the Rebels' actions were foolish was perhaps a little unfair. They had waited silently for weeks, the entire town holding its breath. Their children had been scattered across the New World, saved from any retribution, and although no one had wanted to be separated from their loved ones, they had all agreed. They had also agreed to forsake the lives of over twenty Slaves, simply because their only window to save them was too close to Alira's birth date.

Guilt didn't sit well with any of them. Many wanted to rush to the

Masonian convoy and save them anyway. Harrison had demanded those two weeks be held in contingency, lest they attract attention to their sleepy town, and—for the most part—the Rebels had agreed, albeit grudgingly.

So yes, they deserved to party. They deserved to laugh, dance, and to drink themselves into a stupor. Would Campbell join them, had that putrid ball of moss not be sitting on his soul? Impossible to say. Caroline would be there, of course, but Campbell had lost the energy to interact with her, outside of discussing the Rebellion. Why should he, when it was just so painful?

Campbell forced himself up and manoeuvred to the rickety chest of drawers, standing lopsidedly at the far side of the room. His jacket fell to his feet in a clump of faded black leather, then he kicked off his boots. His jumper, riddled with holes, was a miraculously still holding together, as was the t-shirt underneath. Bare-chested, Campbell ignored the sight of his visible ribcage (eating had become such a chore) and dived into the drawer.

Cool metal teased his fingers, hidden within his limited mess of clothes.

Campbell's breath stuttered. His father's black revolver had not seen the light of day—or even a candle—since that fateful night over nine months ago, when the barrel had gazed hungrily at a baby girl.

His head twitched to the side, forcing away the images.

Why did he insist on keeping the revolver there? He didn't know. Perhaps it was a reminder: he could never forget what happened—*what he did*—at Gainstorn, and so the revolver remained a punishment. A watching spirit, constantly judging him for his decisions, both past and future. Campbell hated that such a thing existed—that the weapon stolen from his awful father's office, the gun that had saved so many innocent lives over the years, had been twisted into an instrument of death.

The moss that resided in Campbell's soul had also smeared across the gun, soaking it in a slimy, stinking layer of green, insofar that Campbell refused to touch it. Not that he could: it would probably just slip from his fingers, rattling to the hollow floorboards.

Yet, the image of that gun refused to leave him. Even as he crawled his lanky body into the damp bed, or forced himself to sink into that meditative state of calm, Campbell saw that revolver flashing gold. It highlighted her small, blue lips.

That excruciating bang rattled around his memories, and Campbell finally surrendered to his sleep.

* * *

CAMPBELL AWOKE to the sound of shouting.

He bolted upright, fearing danger. With a pounding heart, he forced himself to listen.

Shouts seeped from the gaps in the floorboards, percolating down the corridors.

A vicious argument occurred downstairs, filled with... How many people? He didn't know, but it sounded like the place was packed.

Out of curiosity more than anything else, he quickly dressed and wandered downstairs. Alice's voice, or at least the sneer behind it, almost forced him back to bed.

"Since when did your spine crumble, Harrison?"

Harrison, who cradled his head like he had the hangover from hell, leant against the wall and just about forced a glare. "I'm not risking any more lives."

Campbell heard the pain behind those words, even if Alice didn't.

"You don't get to make decisions for us! These are *our* lives and if we want to go, then we shall!"

A cacophony of cheers rose from the crowd. Campbell edged around the perimeter until he found Caroline huddled in the corner, quietly observing the developing scene.

"What's happening?" he asked, once close.

"A Masonian convoy is transporting a group of prisoners to a nearby stronghold. Scouts say they're taking the south-eastern road."

Campbell quickly visualised an accurate map of the Glasslands. "That'll put them within three miles of here."

Far too close for comfort. Caroline's raised eyebrow suggested she agreed.

Clearly, the most obvious tactic would be to batten down the hatches. To remove all stench of Rebellion, each flickering glimpse of campfire, and pretend the village of Snow's Breath was just as isolated, just as unimportant as their early assessments indicated. Needless to say, a Masonian convoy realising Snow's Breath was a secret nest of Rebels would not bode well, for any of them.

Campbell knew the difficult choice had already been made: to leave the prisoners to their fates, lest the whole town crumble. A difficult choice indeed. Campbell didn't envy Harrison. Not in the slightest.

Although, the other Rebels clearly held a stronger, more violent opinion.

At Alice's evident rebuttal, Harrison's eye darkened. "It *is* my decision, Alice, because if a *single* Masonian catches a whiff of you and—Gods forbid —they follow you here, *all* of our lives are at risk."

"Mason isn't coming after us!" A grating shriek rang from Alice's gullet, sounding far too loud to be from her petite structure. "He's mourning his *beloved* mate—the monster who deserved *far* more than a bullet in her brain!"

Campbell winced.

"Alice!" Caroline's muscles pushed forwards, her face twisting. "She was a *baby!*"

"She was the End of Everything!" Alice's brown eyes, swirling with all the violence and hatred of a childhood spent soaked in revenge, rounded on her sister, and then Campbell. "And I'm sorry that neither of you see it that way, but it's true."

"What happened at Gainstorn is beside the point," Harrison said quickly, noticing the perspiration beading Campbell's brow. "Mason wants revenge, he—"

A voice emerged from the black, melding into all the others who were sneering, grinning at the promise of Masonian blood. "We can't stay cooped up here when there are *thirty* prisoners within our reach! We haven't heard anything for over three weeks now—*he's not coming!*"

Or he doesn't know where we are, Campbell wanted to say. But then he recalled the reports from the Fjordlands: the eerie silence that seeped through the border. If Campbell didn't know any better, it was as though Mason *was* mourning. Isolating himself from his New World, so he might shed his tears in peace.

Even the thought was disturbing.

Alice chewed on the inside of her cheek, her ashen complexion only emphasising the alcohol still in her blood. Campbell wondered if that was why she was being so brazen—more so than usual. She hadn't even reached her hangover yet; she was still drunk.

"It isn't open for discussion," Harrison snapped, waving the notion away. He pushed himself from the wall and headed for the door, as if the fresh air could blow away his headache.

A bitter huff rose from Alice's chest. "I didn't know the Dagger Rebellion took away freedom."

Harrison stopped. The very air seemed to pause, waiting.

Excruciatingly slowly, he turned. "What did you say?"

Alice's lips quirked up. "You're acting like our prison marshal. We want to make a difference, to *save* people, and what are you doing, huh? Keeping us locked up while you drink yourself into a stupor?" Her nasty laugh grated the air. "I didn't sign up to be your prisoner."

Harrison deflated. "I have *never* treated you like prisoners."

"Haven't you?" Alice crossed two defiant arms, her hip jutting out. A smirk crawled across her lips as a murmur of agreement rose behind her. "I'm beginning to think Mason removed your balls all those years ago, as well as your eye."

Harrison marched forwards, his face twisting with exquisite rage. Campbell jumped in and placed a stern palm against his shoulder, halting his advance. "Do you think I've forgiven Mason for what he did? To me, my mother, and to all those other, innocent people? What do you know about his rage, girl? *Nothing.* You don't know what it feels like to be strapped up on the wall, forced to wait for the *agony* you just know is coming!"

A single tear slipped down Harrison's cheek, catching the light from the hearth. Campbell pressed his palm against his shoulder and felt the tremors aching beneath his coat.

Alice remained still, her pointed nose held high, looking to Harrison with staunch defiance.

"Do what you like, all of you," Harrison said, pushing himself away from Campbell, from Alice—from the entire room. "Go and get us all killed, for all I care. I've sacrificed enough for you people."

Weighed down by over a decade of leadership—and all the epic victories and painful defeats such a title promised—Harrison stomped his way up the stairs, refusing to look at anyone. Observing from the outskirts, Daniel pushed himself from the wall and followed him, glaring at Alice as he went. "What the *fuck* is wrong with you?" he hissed.

Alice held that defiant pose and glared at Campbell. "You in, or out?"

Is she serious? Campbell didn't try to hide his grimace. "Oh, *grow up.*"

Without a backward glimpse, he ascended the stairs. Arguments continued in his absence, mostly between Caroline and Alice. Their voices swiftly loudened, then grew hoarse as Campbell scurried out of their echo.

A horrible feeling of unease settled in his gut. Yes, he understood Alice's desire for vengeance, and to save as many people as possible. That was why they created the Dagger Rebellion in the first place. Campbell thought back to that night, sat below a glittering Woodland sky. They were all just kids back then. Dreamers. Fools with an impossible notion to free the New World.

And they had succeeded. Or, at least, they had tried their damn best. Their numbers of freed Slaves in Snow's Breath added to almost two hundred, and while such a number didn't put bullets into guns or drop Masonian corpses to the floor, the trickle of hope could not be stopped. It was like a calming scent, spreading across the New World. Even Slaves who were still imprisoned could smell it, inhale it, and it gave them hope. *We're coming for you*, the scent relayed.

Because they did want to come for them, to save them. But how could they save innocent people if they were rotting in the dirt?

Harrison knew that. He knew the value of patience, even if such knowledge killed him.

Why didn't Alice see that?

Campbell didn't realise he wanted to speak to Harrison until he was outside his bedroom door. Was it too early to share a drink together? To toast their victories, to commiserate their defeats?

Time would tell.

Without knocking, Campbell opened the door.

Harrison's sobs immediately greeted him. Huge cries, filled with a plethora of anger and regret. Writhing on the floor, Harrison's contorted face was buried in Daniel's chest. Dan tried to calm him by whispering soothing words in his ear, or by tenderly stroking long fingers through his matted hair, but it made no difference. Harrison broke completely, grasping at Dan's clothes, pulling the fabric towards him, as though he couldn't get close enough.

Rigid legs bent at uncomfortable angles, his muddy boot pushing his discarded eye patch along the floor. Without it, Harrison's scarred face shone in painful, agonising detail. The empty eye socket created a basin for the mess of white, violent scar tissue. No tears trickled from that eye: Mason had removed the tear duct, as well as the eyeball.

But even without the wetness on his cheek, Harrison's pain was evident.

Campbell's own eyes rapidly filled at the sight. Harrison Dagger—always so powerful and defiant, a beacon of strength and courage—crumbled before his very eyes.

Daniel's watery eyes met Campbell's. So many unspoken words passed between them. With a shy nod, Campbell removed himself from the room, gently shutting the door behind him.

14

If there was one person Campbell did not expect to see on the morning of the *Shortest Day*, especially when he was naked from the waist up, it was Caroline.

"Oh, erm... Shit, hang on..." His cheeks blushed wildly as he plucked his jumper from the floor.

"Campbell..."

He finally met her Tiger Eye stare, and the fear that lay beneath it. "What's happened?"

Caroline almost choked on her words. "They're gone."

"Who?"

"Alice..." Tears raced down her cheeks and disappeared into her russet jumper. "She's leading a party to intercept the convoy."

Campbell's strength faltered, settling at the very base of his gut. *"What?"*

After *everything*, all those lives ignored and cast aside for the sake of secrecy, Alice's ridiculous venture would damn them all!

Harrison. "We need Harrison."

Pushing past Caroline, he ran to the end of the corridor and burst into Harrison's bedroom.

A tangle of bare, sleeping limbs spread across the bed, modesty only covered by a thin red sheet.

"Harrison!"

He woke with a grunting snore and pushed onto his elbows. A snoozing Dan still draped his arm across Harrison's torso, riddled with old scars from both battle and torture.

Harrison blinked a sleepy eye. "What is it, mate?"

"Alice is leading an extraction."

Sleep deserted Harrison's features. "The convoy?"

Caroline jumped to Campbell's side. "They've just left, I-I tried to stop them but..." Her words choked on a suppressed sob. She cradled her skinny waist.

"It wasn't your fault," Campbell said, and he begged her eyes to meet his, so she could see the truth behind them. "Did you hear me, Caroline?"

Biting her lip, she remained silent but forced a shaky nod.

Harrison gently removed Dan's arm from his torso. Dan stirred, blinking at the early morning visitors, and quickly pulled the sheet up to his neck. "Jeez, quite the crowd."

Campbell's cheeks blushed again. He quickly ushered Caroline out, closing the door behind them.

Her chest frantically rose and fell. Hands gripped her hips for dear life.

"Hey..." Campbell placed heavy hands upon her shoulders, turning her to meet him. The sadness inside her eyes crumpled his chest. He wanted to hug her, to squeeze away the agonising fear that ate away her hope, one delicious piece at a time. "She's going to be okay."

"I just can't believe she..." Caroline scraped delicate, trembling fingers through greasy locks. "What a *fucking* idiot!"

Campbell wetted his dry lips, wondering what else to say. "She did it because she wants to help people."

Caroline's stare hardened, sharp enough to slice his chest. "No," she said, her face twisting into a despairing, hating scowl. "She did it because she can't follow a fucking order! She's always been the same, even when we were kids!"

She thrust herself away from Campbell and marched up and down the corridor. "You want to know why we were in the Masonian Barracks that day, huh? I told her to wait. We knew they were on to us—that we poisoned our abuser's fucking tea—and I told her to hide in the hole in the dry wall, behind the dresser." A bitter laugh escaped her paling lips. "I dug it out, soon after our father dropped us off there. At the time, I didn't realise how much we would need it."

Campbell's fists scrunched. Although he knew the pervert was dead, he still wanted to strangle his corpse.

Caroline continued to pace. "I was waiting until the coast was clear, then I'd go back for her and we'd *finally* be free! But no, she didn't wait, did she? She wandered out, convinced that she could *help*—and got herself captured! I gave myself up so they wouldn't cut out her tongue."

Anger burned. Not for Alice's brave act of stupidity, but for the fact that Masonians *would* mutilate a nine-year-old girl like that.

Blue lips and wet diamond eyes speckled Campbell's vision. His head cranked to the side, forcibly expelling the memory.

Harrison appeared, fully dressed and fiddling with his eye patch, and marched them down the corridor. "How many left with her?"

"Err, around ten, I think."

"To intercept a convoy transporting thirty Slaves?" Harrison grumbled beneath his breath. "There'll be around twenty Masonians for that."

Two-to-one. The odds looked increasingly bleak.

"Shit!" Caroline shrieked. "I'm so sorry she did this, Harrison."

He swatted away her worry like it was a buzzing fly. "Not your fault, girl."

Something deflated inside Caroline, as though just hearing Harrison's reassurance suddenly made it real.

Downstairs, where the air was still thick with tension, Harrison unrolled a map of the area across the table. "They'd be planning to intercept the Masonian convoy around here."

He pointed to a bend in the road, where the drawn contour lines sharply narrowed and grouped together.

Caroline leant closer to the map. "They're going to form a bottleneck in that mountain pass."

Harrison nodded. "They're going to cut them off from either side, force them into a small space, and gun them down. The steep cliffs make for ample protection too."

Like birds of prey, roosting in the mountains, waiting to swoop down for the kill. Only these birds had shotguns instead of talons.

"Do you think they'll do it?" Campbell asked.

Harrison gave him a wary sidelong glance. "It's not whether they can succeed or not, it's whether they manage to take out every Masonian before one runs off. The last thing we need is one rabid dog, crawling back to its master with its tail between its legs."

"So, no survivors," Caroline said, her voice having lowered a few octaves. Of course, she'd happily kill every Masonian she saw, but this time the bloodshed carried a lot of pressure.

Should one of those Masonians escape, the entire village would crumble, with everyone in it.

"Should we evacuate?" Campbell hated suggesting such a thing, but it was a path they'd be foolish not to consider.

Harrison's pause thickened the air. "No. We don't have time."

He drew his finger along the map again, following the road. It was startling to realise just how close the road was to Snow's Breath, and Campbell cursed to himself. They'd chosen this town for the sole reason that no one used the south-eastern road. They couldn't: it was too treacherous, riddled with snow and bordered with tall cliffs that threatened rockfalls. And what good were expensive Slaves when their skulls were crushed?

Why had this convoy decided to use the road? Guesses were everywhere, pushing truth further out of reach. Had this occurred three days earlier, the town would be put into lockdown. Complete hibernation, so those Masonians would pass by, completely unaware of their presence.

But tempers had frayed too thin. Guns weighed too heavy. Bullets ached.

And one missed mark was all it would take to turn the tide on their good fortune.

Daniel suddenly scurried down the staircase, falling into the huddle beside Harrison. "I heard gunshots."

Spines straightened, eyes taking on an experienced sharpness.

"Where?" Harrison asked.

Dan scratched clipped fingernails through his morning stubble. "Up the mountain. It sounded like it was coming from the road."

Breath left them all like a roaring avalanche.

"*Shit!*" Caroline's chest pulsed with each panicked breath. "We have to help them!"

Harrison pressed his tongue in his cheek, no doubt remembering the vicious argument the previous day. *I've sacrificed enough for you.* The words rounding Campbell's skull were just as bitter, just as venomous as when they originally left Harrison's throat.

"I'm going after them," Harrison said, marching towards the gun cabinet. "At the very least, I can stick my boot up Alice's arse."

Caroline couldn't help but chuckle, relieved tears trickling down her cheeks. "I'm coming with you."

Harrison knew better than to refuse her, or Dan. Campbell's involvement was a downright certainty, even before he plucked the shotgun from the munition cupboard.

The four of them marched from the inn and into the bitter Glassland air. Campbell inhaled it deep, soaking himself with the dim light and the blood-thirsty glow that seeped from the horizon. It created a red tinge behind the mountains, a halo of crimson. An omen, or so some would believe. A message from the Old Gods: blood would be spilled on this day, the shortest of the year.

But Campbell didn't believe those stories, and he didn't consider the glow to be bloodthirsty, or even ominous. To him, as the snow held a delicate red flush and the stars sparkled with vehement lustre, he considered the world beautiful.

Green and pink light undulated across the sky, merging into the stars behind wispy clouds, only just deigning to hold the same ethereal glow. As they ascended higher into the mountains, the bustle of the town dispersed. The warm glow from the huts, as well as the burning braziers, sank into the majesty of the Glassland mountains.

Rocky teeth surrounded him, gazed at him, encompassing him in a myriad of ice and stone. Further into the hike, as his heart thumped and blood raced past his ears, Campbell could still detect the delicate creak of moving ice, the vibrations jutting the air like a struggling fly stuck in a spider's web.

How different it was to his upbringing: the stink of Aristocracy, the prison of golden wallpaper, and the suffocating embrace of stuffy, cigar-choked air.

Campbell inhaled deeper, willed his tired limbs to keep climbing the tough incline. Boots slipped against the frosty gravel, the frigid wind cooling the sheen of sweat upon his brow and back, but he kept moving, even if it killed him. But even if he died that night, he would gladly gift his body to the mountains. He'd give anything to sink into that same majesty, to be entombed within the rock that had dragged many gasps from his lips.

Those same lips tilted into a sad smile.

Yes, he was ready to die.

"Over there!" Dan ducked low, the tip of his shotgun peeking from his coat, and found a viewing point behind a large rock. Campbell scurried to Dan's side, lying low on his front with the others following. Sharp cold bit through his jumper, sinking into his ribs. A sudden inhale shocked him, as he tried to acclimatise to the snow.

"What do you see, Dan?" Harrison whispered, nestling in close. His one eye, while fully functional, made depth perception difficult for him.

Dan poked his head above the rock. "Three Rebels, about forty metres from here."

Campbell chanced a peek and saw them kneeling in the snow, their hands forced behind their heads as Masonian guns waved in their faces.

They didn't even last twenty minutes! Campbell bit his tongue, determined to keep his anger subdued.

In the middle of the captured trio, Alice's pale face shone beneath the aurora's light, her blonde hair fluttering in the breeze.

"Alice is there," Campbell said.

Caroline tensed. She inched her head up but ducked just as quickly. "Where?"

"The middle."

Caroline shot a disgusted stare to the bodies, littering the entrance to a narrow path between the mountains, just up ahead. Mounds of Masonian-blue merged with brown leather coats. The rest of the Masonian convoy—a selection of ominous black vans—coughed toxic fumes into the pristine air.

One of the prisoners produced a sharp shriek of terror, and the Rebel on the left took a firm right hook from his guarding Masonian. He collapsed in a flurry of broken noses and blood. Another whack—this time with a Masonian baton.

"They're trying to make him talk," Harrison said grimly.

"We can't let them know about the village," Dan said, sweat beading his brow despite the cold.

A frustrated sigh escaped Harrison's lips. "How many Masonians are left?"

Campbell threw his sight around the immediate area, counted, then ducked. "Nine, from what I can see."

Nine. Not a bad effort from those reckless Rebels, all things considered.

Harrison tucked himself further into the blanket of snow, his index finger poised for instruction. "Right, when I—"

He was abruptly cut off as two more Masonians marched in, shouting and sneering. A woman was between them, kicking wildly, her black hair flying in all directions.

"Get off me, you fucking bastards!"

Campbell would recognise that shrill tone any day. "Ah, shit..."

They peered over the rock, just as Kat's *furious* expression caused a ripple of cruel grins across her captors.

"Oh, fucking Hel!" Harrison bit out. He huffed to the snow beneath his chest. "I'll kill her myself, save Mason the trouble."

Campbell couldn't hide a snicker.

Crouching low and ready to pounce, Harrison cocked his gun. "Alright, on my mark, go in—all guns blazing. Dan and I will target the Masonians around the prisoners. Campbell and Caroline, you take down the rest. And don't—for Odin's sake—let one of them get loose!"

Another quick peek over the rock saw Kat being forced down, beside the Rebel whose face glowed a sinister crimson.

"Okay..." Harrison crouched low, like a wolf. "Three, two... *Now!*"

They burst from behind the rock in a flurry of bullets and cheers. Harrison and Dan ran straight to the prisoners, the shotguns pressed into their shoulders.

Campbell and Caroline ran in the opposite direction, towards the convoy spilling a gaggle of blue coats and long, glinting swords.

Gunshots sounded, echoing through the field of mountains, bouncing off the stone. Campbell responded in kind, finger convulsing against the trigger, and relished the kickback against his shoulder.

Caroline marched forwards, strong and assertive. Revolver held high, her teal coat fluttering above brown boots, long hair flying in waves of rippling gold… An angel worthy of stealing Masonian souls.

Bullets whizzed past Campbell's ears, brutally snatching back reality. Masonians hid behind one of the vans, shielded by the black metal. From its metal belly, the dull, frantic echo of screams seeped out.

The prisoners…

They needed to get them out!

Behind them, Harrison had taken out two of the guarding Masonians. Kat kicked like a wild animal, using her sheer body weight to cause damage. Alice wrestled with a Masonian in the snow, desperate to prize his gun from his hands.

Campbell wrenched his stare forwards and scrambled to Caroline, perched behind a large rock. Bullets continually bashed the surface, spurting bits of gravel and grey dust everywhere. Little shards speckled Caroline's flushed cheeks, resembling small silver freckles.

"We need to get them out of the van," Caroline said, her chest pulsing.

Campbell ducked as another bit of rock blasted apart. "I counted five Masonians behind the van, two on this side, three on the other."

Caroline nodded, her rosy lips parted to release misty breath. "Allfather Guide You," she whispered, and threw herself around the rock.

Close at her tail, Campbell marched towards the van, shooting at one Masonian, then another. One of them lurched back, a bullet in his cranium. Another collapsed, cradling the bloody stump that used to be his hand, and quickly fell silent. Blood stained the snow.

Two down, three to go.

Through the metallic stench of blood, something heavy and bitter remained.

Smoke. Campbell's lungs tightened.

Dangerous light flickered from the front of the van.

"Shit…" Campbell breathed. "We need to get them out of there, *now!*"

Campbell ducked around the van, shielding himself from the flurry of Masonians. He cracked open the shotgun and two smoking cartridges popped out. Reloading, he snapped the shotgun closed and sank to his belly. A series of Masonian feet stared at him, belonging to the unlucky fools on the other side of the van.

Campbell steadied his aim and fired.

Blood-curdling screams punctured the air, red splattered the snow with chunks of leather and gore. Caroline jumped on the fallen Masonian, shrieking and slicing. Warm crimson steamed against the white.

Shouts from across the ice. Campbell scrambled to his feet; the gun lifted high. He deflated when he saw Harrison and Alice, viciously yelling at each other, shoving each other's shoulders before embracing in a relieved, wholesome hug.

"Over here!" Campbell yelled.

Growing flames licked the van's metal skin. Tyres had already caught alight, the entire van buckling beneath softening rubber and pools of bloodied, melted snow.

Inside the van, prisoners kept yelling and banging, throwing their entire bodies against the van's locked doors.

Caroline frantically pulled and shoved, but to no avail.

"Move!" Campbell reloaded and took a direct aim.

Caroline swiftly realised what the plan was. "Everyone, get back!" she shouted, banging her palm on the metal.

Campbell closed one eye and forced his heartbeat to slow. The shot would obliterate the van's locks, but he needed to be precise...

He pulled the trigger.

A dull clink came in response. Campbell's breath stuttered. A *dud? Are you fucking serious?*

With an enraged yell, he dropped the shotgun. With the dud cartridge stuck in the barrel, any shot would just bounce back. The gun was useless!

"Shit!"

As Caroline desperately tried to prize the doors open, Campbell scrambled to the dead Masonians. Most had shortened shotguns, their broad snouts useless for a precise shot. All others had swords.

Heat prickled Campbell's features, the entirety of the van smouldering. Flames licked below the hood as glass cracked and shattered.

A glint of silver. Campbell's panicked breaths faltered as he saw the gun: the *revolver*. The exact size and weight to his father's.

Campbell froze. Light licked his skin, orange heat burned his face, and yet he couldn't move. The weight of that revolver—the feel of the cold, deadly metal in his palm—dragged him back to that night.

He saw himself pointing the revolver inside the crib. He remembered the sound of her cries, the certain finality of his orders weighing on his soul. He recalled how it felt to squeeze the trigger, the wet warmness splattering up his arm...

Nausea bubbled in his stomach. Panic gripped his chest.

He couldn't do it. *He couldn't do this!*

"Campbell!"

Awareness shot back to him. He startled as flames roared. Raging heat prickled his skin...

Adrenaline raced. He ran back to the van, took aim and—

A deafening *bang* echoed.

The locks blew out. Doors swung open. Prisoners flooded from the vans like flour from a spilled sack.

Thirty small bodies—*children*—escaped with nothing but rags and bruises.

Caroline ushered their limping bodies through the snow, away from the fire. Campbell remained behind, still gripping the revolver in cramping fingers, and thought he heard something...

Breath poised, he listened.

"Help!"

Campbell charged into the van. Heat slammed into him, unrelenting, as he searched for the screaming child.

"Where are you?" he yelled. Melting rubber stuck to his boots, sweat ran in thick streams down his face. He pushed on, coughing through the thick smoke.

Eyes burned but he forced them to stay open, willed his feet to keep moving. The van's creaking bones reminded him that he didn't have long, lest they find themselves in an oven.

There, just ahead, he made out a small mound. At first, he thought it was an object. Then, he thought it was dead.

The *thing* coughed out a lungful of smoke.

Campbell charged forwards and picked up the small girl. He ran to the van's entrance but they were sharply tugged back. A metal chain encircled the girl's ankle, leading to a hoop in the floor.

Without thinking—and with none of the hesitation of earlier—Campbell took the revolver and obliterated the loop, and a good portion of the melting floor with it. He plucked the child from the burning rubber and legged it out of the van. The revolver remained behind, already blackening, melding with the sticky floor.

Coughing and spluttering, Campbell burst into the cold, fresh air, and collided straight into Harrison.

"Give her to me!"

Harrison tucked the girl under one arm, supported Campbell with the other, and dragged his shaking, faltering form away from the van. Two steps, then three, then—

The van exploded. A flurry of fire and orange light raced to the stars, melting with the green aurora above. Smoke covered the bloodthirsty glow clinging to the horizon. Fire cast an angry tinge across the mountains.

Standing before this burning bonfire, the surviving Rebels watched with panting breaths, surrounded by the sound of cracking glass, creaking metal, and thirty rejoicing children.

15

———

After Harrison had given the reckless Rebels the bollocking of a lifetime, they put Snow's Breath under complete lockdown. No outside braziers, no unnecessary fires... Everyone hibernated, like the bears that wouldn't see the outside world until the spring.

A day after the incident, they had trudged back up the mountain to dispose of the charred Masonian convoy, and the losses that came with it. Bodies were either burnt, unrecognisable husks, or the local wildlife had been at them. Either way, there was hardly anything to bury, and the fresh layer of snow mercifully covered the spilled blood and blackened stones.

To an outsider, nothing had happened, and the small, isolated town of Snow's Breath remained just as lonely, just as unimportant as it always had been. The only thing that remained was a metal lockbox, completely blackened but otherwise intact. Caroline had made it her duty to get it open, to figure out what was inside. Bets had been made on the contents. *Jewellery* was the firm favourite.

An entire week passed, and Harrison finally conceded they had escaped. No word from Mason, no reprisal for Gainstorn. How had they managed it? Campbell didn't quite know, though he knew better than to test fate. Clearly, the Old Gods were looking out for them. A small smile tickled Campbell's lips, for he'd never really thanked the Old Gods before.

Drunk off mead and the promise of a life without retribution, Snow's Breath developed character. The children from the convoy laughed and played with the Rebels, throwing snowballs and building entire snow-families. Harrison even taught some of the older kids to fire guns, while Caroline added some trusty disarming techniques. When the oldest dedicated their lives to the Rebellion's cause, Harrison grinned, welcoming them with open arms.

And more mead, of course.

But Harrison knew better than to test their luck, especially when it was granted by the Old Gods. Apparently they were fickle creatures.

Just before the *Last Day of the Year*, Harrison declared that he'd organised transport for the children. A one-way ticket to another Rebel camp, far away in the Woodlands. From there, the children would be transported to isolated Rebel outposts across the New World.

They said their goodbyes in the early hours of the *Last Day,* the children hugging everyone in sight, thanking Campbell and Caroline with each grateful squeeze.

Near the trucks that would transport them to the freight train, Harrison embraced Dan in a loving, tender embrace. Although it was just a hug, it seemed far too passionate, far too personal for public eye.

It took a long time for them to part. When they did, Harrison took Dan's face within both hands and kissed him slowly, leisurely, like they were the only two people in the world. Campbell supposed, to each other, they were.

"Tell Isla I love her," Harrison said, when they finally parted. He wiped the thick tear marks from Dan's cheeks with the pads of his thumbs. "Tell her I miss her, tell her I'll be there as soon as I can, tell her—"

"I will, Harrison." Daniel ran soothing fingers through Harrison's matted hair. "I'll tell her everything."

They kissed again, completely lost in each other.

"I love you," Dan whispered against his lips. "Be safe."

Harrison grinned, squeezing more tears out. "You too, Danny."

Mountains moaned as they pulled apart. Slowly, like his feet were made of lead, Dan moved towards the trucks. Harrison watched him and shuffled his feet, unable to stand still. As though he itched to run after him.

When they'd gone, Harrison remained staring at the tyre tracks in the snow, lost in his own thoughts. Leaving him to his privacy, Campbell wandered back to the village. He sighed around the sudden quiet. Snow's Breath seemed far emptier without the children.

He gravitated towards Caroline, who stood before a metal table, wielding a hacksaw. Scraping yellow sparks in every direction, she tried to prize away the back of the lockbox they'd snatched from the convoy's ruins, over a week prior.

"Still trying to get into that thing?" Campbell asked, unable to hide a smirk. Caroline had been trying to crack it open for days now.

"I'm making progress this time!" Her grin that sent those same glowing sparks into Campbell's belly. "Here, look at this."

She pointed to the edge of the lockbox, where the metal had started to peel away. "Slow progress, admittedly," she added.

"Think you'll get it open by tonight?"

Hands on her hips, Caroline arched an eyebrow to her younger sister, who was already stumbling around the immature bonfire. "You mean, before my idiot sister loses her feet entirely?" She chuckled gently beneath her breath. "I kind of envy her, y'know. I mean, I'd die from the hangover alone if I drank as much as she did."

Campbell observed Alice. With more mead down her t-shirt than in her tankard, it was truly a wonder she could stay upright. Although, that might have had something to do with the strong arm around her waist, belonging to a rather dashing young man.

"I think you have more pressing things to worry about." Campbell met Caroline's quizzical stare and nodded towards a very undignified Alice, now sucking off the face of her suitor.

"Ew..." Caroline shuddered.

"Time to step in?"

Caroline observed her younger sister again. Alice pushed the guy away, threw up, then continued kissing him. "Ever the charmer," Caroline muttered.

Campbell inched forwards. "Come on. We'll get her tucked in with a bucket and a mug of chamomile tea."

"Yes..." Caroline sighed, dropping the hacksaw to the table. "Knowing her, she'll be ready to party again as soon as the clocks hit midnight."

* * *

ONCE THEY'D DEALT with Alice, tucking her in with a cold cloth on her brow, Caroline returned to her project and Campbell tucked himself away in the longhouse, cleaning his guns. After a while, Harrison plodded in with a grim expression. He went straight to the lonely bar, poured himself a large drink, and fell into the chair beside Campbell.

"You alright?" Campbell asked, cleaning his shotgun. He'd made quite a mess when removing the dud cartridge.

A large sigh inflated Harrison's chest as he stared into the fire's growing belly. "Dan'll be in the Woodlands by now."

"Ah." Campbell added more grease to the gun, the sharp, cloying scent almost dragging up a gag. "But he'll be back here in a few months, won't he?"

"Yes, thank the Gods." Harrison's face foretold the love he shared with Daniel, for it flickered across his features with the warm light. Campbell smiled at such a sight. In the Rebellion, such bliss was difficult to come across. He was glad his dear friend had found such happiness with Dan. Their love was a pleasure to witness.

"So, why are you so glum?" Campbell asked.

Cheekiness gleamed in a bright jade eye. "Because Kat's gone with him."

That stopped Campbell in his tracks.

Harrison bobbed an agreed eyebrow, stopping to sip on his mead. "She's gone back to Isla."

"Oh?" Campbell unsuccessfully tried to hide his shock. Kat evidently loved her daughter, yet Campbell never considered her to forsake the Rebellion she had dedicated most of her adult life fighting for.

"I believe her most recent dice with death has made her reconsider her life choices," Harrison said, as if reading Campbell's mind. "She's retiring from Rebel life—which is fine, of course—but I didn't expect to be this... *envious*."

Campbell stopped cleaning his gun. Such words coming from Harrison's mouth were akin to blasphemy.

"Don't worry, I'm not going anywhere," Harrison said, with a smile. "I'm just saying that I envy the choices she has. *Stay here* or *go there*... She truly has the freedom to do what she wants, when she wants it." Harrison stared at Campbell's frown with genuine curiosity. "Do you ever feel like that?"

Campbell thought long and hard about his answer. He'd grown up with so little choice, insofar that he was certain his father had decided on Campbell's funeral casket before he was even born. Back then, the only choice he'd ever had was the decision to run back to Harrison, to save him from the bowels of Mason's torture chamber, all those years ago.

That decision had landed him there. It had slipped the mead down his throat and put the shotgun in his hand. Did he regret his decision to join Harrison, to form the Dagger Rebellion?

Gleeful shouts percolated into the longhouse. Clearly, the adults were having their own snowball fight now.

A small smile worked Campbell's lips. No, he didn't regret the decision that day.

He wished he could say the same for all his decisions.

"I regret the choice I made at Gainstorn," he said. He suddenly realised that, in all the months since it happened, he'd never spoken those words out loud.

Harrison parted his lips, as if to speak, but remained silent. In this quiescence, Campbell took a deep, agonising breath.

"You all tell me that I did the right thing at Gainstorn, that I didn't have a choice." Helpless, his eyes filled and spilled tears down chapped cheeks. They disappeared into his thick stubble, as though hiding from the truth. Campbell's chest compressed tightly, painfully—and a weight he never knew was there began to lift, excruciatingly slowly...

"But... I did have a choice," he said, his voice breaking. "And I chose... *wrong.*"

Silence.

Finally, he could breathe.

Deflating into the chair, tears dripped onto his hands, sinking into the calloused skin.

Yet, the words just kept flowing...

"That's why I can't tell Caroline how I feel," he said, admitting the truth he'd kept hidden, even from himself. "I've put it off for all these years, and now it's..."

Campbell took a deep breath. "It's not just the awful, *abhorrent* thing I did… It was that I was *wrong*, that every decision I make from here—about me, about her, about *us*—falls under the crushing weight of the worst decision I've *ever* made, ever *could* make…"

Harrison's throat convulsed on a large, laboured swallow. Tears bobbed precariously against his lashes, threatening to fall at any minute.

Campbell wiped his wrist against his cheek, forcing a hearty sniff. "I have to live with that choice, but I won't allow it to weigh Caroline down, too." A rush of warmth in his belly, both glorious and *excruciating*… "She's worth so much more than that. So much more than me."

Harrison placed his mead on the table with a loud *clunk*. "Jeez mate, is that what you think? That you're a burden to her?"

A despairing laugh, brittle and broken, rattled Campbell's lungs. "I'm a burden to myself, Harrison."

"That's not true. You have *never* been a burden, to her, to me—to *anyone*. And especially not to yourself."

Campbell's throat painfully clogged up. He risked crumbling if he spoke.

Harrison gifted a tender smile, jumping to his feet. "You still got your Pa's old revolver chilling out in your drawer?"

Campbell nodded.

"Wonderful," he said, grinning. "Well, come with me. We're going to have a *Last Day* ritual."

* * *

CAMPBELL COULDN'T BEAR to touch his revolver, or Mason's old sword—which Harrison kept for *sentimental* purposes. Harrison carried both items as he led Campbell through the frivolous atmosphere of Snow's Breath. The sparklers had been brought out, lights fluttering like dancing stars. People laughed and rejoiced, welcoming the upcoming New Year with a sense of renewal and optimism.

That year had been their hardest, by far. Yet, it had also been their most successful. Freed Slaves mingled with the Rebels, sharing mead and beer, drinking to their hearts' content. The very air held a euphoric energy that jumped from one person to another like bolts of lightning.

Harrison was no exception to the sparks of joys, hitting him from all directions. He had a distinct bounce in his step as he hopped up the mountain, Campbell close at his heels.

"Where're we going?" Campbell asked through panting breaths. He'd climbed that damn mountain too many times recently.

Harrison ushered him towards the boundary of the forest, just out of sight from the village. Trees towered above them, encased in thick layers of white. Owls hooted in the distance, the scuttle of nocturnal animals prickling the hairs on the back of Campbell's neck.

They stopped before a large tree that opened out into a clearing. A frozen pool resembled a flat pearl, reflecting the colours from the aurora above. Encased in layers of snow, surrounded by trees and overlooked by heavenly colour and sparkle, the entire clearing was reminiscent of a fairy tale. *Magical.*

A cloud of mist expelled with Harrison's long, laboured sigh. "Two months ago, I brought Dan here and asked him to marry me."

It took a moment for the meaning of such words to hit Campbell. When they did, it felt like he'd been punched with pure starlight.

With an enormous laugh, Campbell jumped forwards and threw his arms around Harrison's broad shoulders. Pulling back with a slap on the arm, he said, "You've been holding this in for *two months?*"

Harrison shrugged a lazy shoulder. "We didn't want word to spread too far, given... potential upcoming events."

Campbell's smile dropped with a loud thud. "So, what's changed?"

Harrison sighed again, slowly revealing the weapons: Campbell's revolver, then Mason's stolen sword.

"Because I think it's time we put Gainstorn behind us. *Both* of us." Blue eyes met jade beneath the glittering Glassland sky. "You are a *good* man, Campbell. A great, honourable man who had the worst decision thrown at him. Gainstorn would have crushed most and yet, here you are, still standing. Still existing."

Harrison lowered himself to his knees. Hands pushed the snow aside, great handfuls at a time, until he revealed the bare earth beneath.

"I think," Harrison said, looking straight into Campbell's eyes—into his *soul*, "that the time has come for you to bury Gainstorn. To stop simply *existing*, but to *live*. *Live* with the knowledge that you saved thirty children only a week ago. And before then, how many others have you saved? How many people have you removed from Mason's clutches just *this year?*"

Campbell forced a swallow, his chest physically aching. He stared at the sky, unwilling to let more tears fall. But they burned, then caught the wind and froze against his eyeballs.

"Bury the past, Campbell," Harrison said. "Like I'm going to."

"Do you think I can?" Campbell's voice was so small, so fragile. A mere echo of what it once was.

Harrison's lips curled. Only slightly, but sincerity cradled each move-ment. "Yes, I do. You deserve to be loved, Campbell. Especially by yourself."

A voice in Campbell's head told him how wrong Harrison was, that he was a monster with a slimy soul and nothing would ever change that.

But as he took great handfuls of cold earth, and as his fingers numbed along with his tears, Campbell pushed away those thoughts. He buried those thoughts with his father's revolver and Mason's sword, cocooning them with black dirt, then with a delicate layer of crisp, white snow.

Not quite rejuvenated, and certainly not forgotten. But healing. Slowly.

On their way back to the village, with Harrison's arm thrown over his shoulders, Campbell said, "I'm going to tell Caroline tonight."

Harrison squeezed his shoulder. "I'm proud of you, mate."

"Good, because I'm terrified."

Laughter tumbled like a raging waterfall. "I'd be scared if you weren't!"

When the village returned into view, with its bonfires and its merriment, the pair sat upon an overlooking rock, just taking in the airs.

It was so quiet, up there in the mountains. Below them, the party roared in full swing. Music, dance, drink—it had everything.

A month ago, they could never imagine a scene like this. They'd be too scared that fate would dance too close to them, brushing them with the cold uncertainty of the future. Given everything, it would have been foolish to light those braziers, or to dance arm-in-arm around them.

But not anymore. Now, as the New Year threatened on the horizon, their joy seemed *right*. It felt... *deserved.*

"So, am I going to be your best man?" Campbell couldn't resist asking when the question popped into his head.

Harrison slapped him on the back, so hard he almost fell down the mountain. "Damn right."

Cheers loudened, preparing for the New Year's arrival. So engrossed in the euphoric sound, they almost missed Caroline's frantic footsteps, racing up behind them.

"*Campbell...*" Her chest almost collapsed from the exertion, her voice strained and guttural. "*Harrison!*"

They turned just as she fell to her knees. Like a pouncing wildcat, Campbell skidded to her side, and helped her onto shaky legs. "What is it? What's happened?"

Pale features, bloodless lips... Pure fear leeched from Caroline, like her very blood had turned to tar. From within her pocket, a trembling hand returned with a piece of paper. A letter, by the barest glance of it.

Gasping all the air on that mountain, she handed it to Harrison. "I-I got the lockbox open and... and found this letter from General Alden... To the leader of the convoy... It-it's dated a day before the convoy passed here..."

Harrison didn't even read the letter. He remained staring at Caroline, the blood slowly dropping from his face.

"What did it say?" he whispered.

Caroline's eyes rapidly filled, her colour draining faster with each second. "It's the Masonian convoy routes for when Mason returns to full strength."

Campbell's heart stopped. "What?"

"The date..." A sob broke loose. "The reason Mason hasn't come after us is because it's not over!"

Silence reigned on that mountainside.

Campbell's mouth grew dry. "What are you saying, Caroline?"

"*She's not born yet!*" she screeched.

16

Just as Caroline's echo dispersed in the chilly air, the ground trembled.

"Did you feel that?"

Breath poised as they listened, *waited*. The world suddenly quietened: the wind slept, the creaking glaciers halted. Even the animals paused beneath the impending breath...

A low rumbling rose around them, like an avalanche's rising roars.

But the noise didn't come from above them. The mountains' snows remained stable, clinging to their rocky mothers as they observed the ominous quiet.

When did they realise the rumbling came, not from above, but from *below*? Only when the screaming began.

"Oh my Gods..." Harrison lunged to the side of the cliff. Campbell and Caroline followed.

The sleepy, isolated town of Snow's Breath shone like a beacon, firelight speckling the dark floor of the valley like burning stars in a black sky.

Illuminated by the aurora's glow, the trio watched—helpless and silent—as the ground cracked. The rumbling grew—a terrible countdown to the fate they all knew was coming—and wolves and animals screeched and howled in the forest. They preluded the sounds of screaming people, echoing through the mountains, bouncing off rock and ice until they scraped Campbell's eardrums again and again...

Chasms rippled through the base of the valley—big black holes in the earth that ate fires, huts, *people.*

"*Alice...*" Caroline breathed. On shaky legs, she stumbled to the path.

Harrison grabbed and pulled her back. His mouth opened to speak, but words had been eroded, sucked into the gaping chasms with the rest of Snow's Breath.

Fires blinked out, one at a time, succumbing to the destruction.

As the dull echo of screams continued to percolate, ice rose. Campbell sank to his knees, the entire valley morphing before his very eyes. Rock punched up, ice followed. Creaks and clangs of moving, shifting ice—*ice that wasn't there before*—sang a dreadful, despairing melody inside his ears. Water rushed in— from *where?* Campbell didn't have time to think, he could just watch.

He watched as the water licked away his friends, his *family.* He stared as the enormous block of jagged ice devoured the valley, sinking into every crack and crevasse until nothing remained.

And he gazed as the entire town of Snow's Breath obliterated before his eyes, until nothing but a new glacier remained.

"Come on..." Harrison choked on the words, pulling a crying Caroline away from the edge. "We need to go."

Panic sank into Campbell. Then terror. Pure, unfiltered *fear* punched into his mind with one, indisputable thought: *Mason was coming for them.*

Engines roared. Black vans tumbled from the south-eastern road. Doors opened, spilling a flood of blue coats and swords into the snow, once pristine and magical, now crushed beneath Masonian boots.

They locked eyes, Rebel to Masonian. Murder threatened.

"Run for the trees," Harrison gasped, faintly. Then he shrieked. "Run, *now!*"

With as much fury as a rolling avalanche, they raced to the forest. Gunshots sounded behind them, a flurry of bullets whizzing past their ears. As they darted between the trees, bark exploded. Caroline shrieked, ducking, her breaths mingling with her audible grief and terror.

A grenade burst with fire and vengeance, thrusting them into the mess of trees and logs. Campbell's spine collided with a trunk on impact, pain radiating up and down his body. He grabbed a teary Caroline as they stumbled to their feet. Harrison staggered not far behind, cradling his hip with a pained grimace.

"Split up!"

They didn't have time to argue. They raced in different directions, dragging a portion of the Masonians with them. Through the abhorrent fear, Campbell's feet slammed against the frozen foliage and sent rough shocks of reality up his legs. They thought they were safe, they thought Mason's retribution would never come. But they were wrong—oh, so wrong...

Of course it was coming, how could it not be? Campbell had been right: Gainstorn could never be buried, it could never be washed away or covered with fresh layers of snow.

That slimy ball of moss would always be there, crushing his soul, following his every moment. As his lungs burned and petrified tears ached to burst, Campbell wanted to scream his apology to the corpses of Snow's Breath: the bodies scraped by stone and immortalised forever beneath the icy bowels of Mason's new glacier.

Bullets continued to fly. The trees almost completely covered the aurora's light. Visibility became strained, the entire forest blanketed in ominous shadow. Yet, Campbell stumbled on, *sprinted* on. For the sake of everything, he had to keep moving!

Another rumbling arose. Birds fluttered from the trees. Branches collapsed, colliding with the frozen ground with defeating thuds. Cracking trunks and breaking branches obliterated the sound of Campbell's blood, roaring past his ears in great torrents of distress.

Earth cracked, then split open. Campbell stopped, gazing helplessly as trees toppled inside the black chasm. Snow and mud rippled down into its deadly depths.

At over ten feet wide, the chasm was far too big to jump.

No... The word floated around his head, unable to escape. He ran further along the chasm, hoping to find a way across. The chasm responded and raced ahead of him, like a living being. More trees creaked and slumped, the entire forest floundering.

Gunshots echoed, louder and closer. Campbell ducked, covering his head, protecting himself from the fate he knew creaked closer with every step...

Harrison appeared. His long brown coat rippled behind him as he fired at his pursuing Masonians.

Campbell screamed and demanded he turn back. There was no way through, no way to traverse the bottomless pit that opened before them...

But it was too late. The chasm liked Harrison's presence. It grew to welcome him into its arms.

Harrison stumbled with a shriek. His eye locked with Campbell's, wide and all too fearful. The chasm morphed around them, eating everything, destroying their freedom before they even had a chance to consider it.

On their other side, Masonians encroached. Closer they came, with evil sneers and revolvers aimed high. Hope dropped from Campbell, tumbling with his heart.

All paths blocked, Masonians stalking closer... Their fate was inevitable.

Campbell shared a knowing look with Harrison. He returned Campbell's teary stare.

Harrison's knuckles whitened around his revolver. "I'll see you on the other side, mate," he whispered.

Harrison raised his gun, its smoking snout gazing hungrily at Campbell before it took its final fill...

Campbell's heart slowed, his mind numbed. He stared at his liberation with a sordid sense of acceptance, and he closed his eyes for the final time...

A gunshot, loud and all too terrifying, ricocheted around the forest. Birds screeched, merging with Harrison's agonised screams.

Campbell's eyes popped open. On his knees, Harrison cradled his bloody hand, staring at the revolver knocked far away, covered in the obliterated remains of Harrison's thumb and index-finger.

Campbell raced forwards. To Harrison? The revolver? He didn't know. He just ran.

Hands grasped him. Batons smashed his torso. Pain shot around every nerve, rippled down every rib... Groaning, Campbell tried to struggle, to rip himself away from those hard, merciless hands.

A brutal *thump* against his stomach had him hunch over. Unable to move, or to breathe, Campbell remained on the forest floor, cradling his throbbing torso.

The world grew dizzy. Lights in the sky, glittering stars... They all mocked the metallic taste in his mouth, and the sight of Harrison being forced to his knees, still cradling his shot, mutilated hand.

Pounding footsteps echoed around them. Campbell's breath stuttered, his mind unwilling to accept the fate, the *future* that came walking towards them, a smoking revolver still gripped tightly...

"Good evening, gentlemen."

Lord Mason snarled at them, his face a terrible mixture of exhilaration and utter, incomprehensible *loathing*...

Campbell mindlessly stared at the Destroyer of the Old World as he struggled to accept what was happening. A few short minutes ago, they had been so content, so happy...

Mason stood before them with gaunt cheeks and grey skin, perusing them with diamond eyes sparkling so vibrantly, so dangerously. Dark bags hung below those hating, *exhausted* eyes, surrounding them in ominous shadow. His matted hair, unkept and falling past his ears, shone as black as a starless night. Clothes hung from his bony shoulders, his once muscular bulk completely eroded. Yes, the echo of a handsome man was still there, but that's all it was: an *echo*. The past nine—*ten*—months had ripped bits of Mason away, turning him into something more monstrous, more vengeful that Campbell could scarcely believe...

I've done this, he solemnly realised. *I've unleashed him on us.*

Raising his nose, Mason granted them a wide, evil grin. "Happy New Year," he said.

Screams—*a woman's screams*—punched the trees. Campbell startled, recognising Caroline's presence before she was dragged in. Bits of leaves and twigs buried in her hair, as though she had been tackled down a bank.

Forced to her knees before Mason, Caroline helplessly struggled against her Masonian captors.

Let her go! Campbell wanted to scream, but words had been forced back inside his gullet, as though hiding.

"Well, aren't you a pretty thing," Mason purred, wandering towards her.

Slowly, he trailed the tip of his finger down her cheek. Caroline instantly stilled, her breaths coming in short, abrupt bursts.

"Don't touch her!" Harrison yelled, his voice strained—with fear or pain?

Mason turned with a sinister grin. "But it's been so, *so* long since I've had a woman, Mr Dagger."

Campbell's breaths faltered. Adrenaline raced through his muscles, his mind entirely focussed on Mason's touch on Caroline's cheek, and the rush of dread that paled her features.

Mason's laugh echoed around the trees. Slowly, like the hungry predator he was, he circled her. "Can you even comprehend the sort of year I've had, my dear? What does a delicate creature like yourself know about pain? *Pure, wretched* pain?"

He stood behind her panting frame and gently kneaded her shoulders, like a lover.

"Alas, I don't expect you to understand. Why should you? You didn't give the order. Neither did you pull the trigger."

Mason's diamond eyes slid into the marrow of Campbell's bones. So much hate lay inside that stare. So much *contempt.*

"I hope you have enjoyed your year of bliss, Mr Anders." Mason gritted his teeth. "Tonight, it ends."

Hands slid from Caroline's shoulders and cradled her head. Long fingers buried in her hair.

Campbell dragged his eyes from Mason's sneer. He couldn't look at him. He couldn't bear to see how much he was enjoying this...

Caroline's Tiger Eye stare blurred in a flurry of tears and panic. Her chest, pulsing furiously, could barely keep up with her breaths. Bloodless lips parted, expecting the inevitable...

"Caroline..." Campbell's voice was small, croaky... But he needed to tell her. Now, as she took those panicking breaths, he *needed* her to know...

I love you.

"Caroline, I-I—"

Her neck twisted with the same sharp *crack* that split Campbell's heart in two. As her body remained held by Mason's hands, Campbell refused to believe it. She wasn't gone...

Breath left Caroline's lungs for the last time.

She isn't gone!

Tiger Eyes rolled up inside her skull. Campbell's heart tumbled to the ground with her. Tears followed, streaming down his cheeks, but he didn't have the energy to cry, or to scream, or to do anything but watch, mindlessly. More *cracks* hung heavily in the air, waiting for their moment.

"Well." Mason smiled again, rubbing his hands together. "Who's next? Hm?"

From the outskirts, a Masonian wandered in, carrying a bloody sack. A smirk on his gaunt face, Mason gathered it and lazily swung it around, spilling thick drops of blood across the snow.

"Do you know how we found you? As you can imagine, I've been a little preoccupied lately, but your Rebel vermin have really been rather secretive." He chuckled to the cold air. "Indeed, I've heard it's been rather difficult to keep consistent tabs on you all. Up until recently, that is."

Mason's cruel smile widened. "Did you think I'd forgotten about you? Left you to live out your days peacefully?" He laughed loudly, madly, to the dancing light above. "Oh, you should know me better than that!"

He marched forwards and grabbed a great chunk of Harrison's hair, forcing their eyes to meet. Blood from the sack dripped around Harrison's knees. "I'd hunt you to the very ends of my world."

Mason threw Harrison away like a used tissue. Wandering the clearing, Mason dug deep in the sack. "So, you can imagine my intrigue when a lone freight train was stopped, just outside the Glasslands. Rather fortuitously, my mate was born in the early hours of this morning. I barely had time to wipe my own filth off my body before I got the call about your little Rebel refugees. And, of course, I just *had* to pay them a visit."

Mason plucked a bloody, hairy lump from the sack and threw it before Harrison. It rolled a few paces, leaking brown blood across the snow.

Kat's severed head, bloody and devoid of eyeballs, gazed with sinister apology.

"If it's any consolation," Mason said, smirking, "she persevered incredibly well. She begged for death long before she gave up your location."

Campbell's chest caved. Every nerve he possessed begged him to scream, to shout, to do *something!*

But he couldn't. Just like Harrison, he remained still, staring at what was left of the woman—the strong, devoted, reckless woman—who they'd once joked about over full tankards of mead.

"Her fate was almost very different," Mason said. A quick whistle to one of his Masonians, who scurried off, out of sight. "When she protected you, Mr Dagger, with such dire determination, I assumed she was your lover." Mason's grin widened. "Oh, how wrong I was."

Masonians arrived with a hooded, trembling body. A man's body.

"No..." Harrison's small voice permeated the air, every hair rising to meet the terror that infested him.

The hooded man was forced to his knees before Mason.

"Of course, Katarina was ever so kind to explain the mix up once I cut out her left eye." Mason ripped the sack of Daniel's head. Dark brown eyes moved frantically around the scene, settling upon Campbell, and then Harrison. Tears and sweat wetted those once flawless cheeks, now full of bloody cuts.

Mason moved behind Dan's kneeling, trembling body. "I do apologise, Harrison. It was wrong of me to presume."

Harrison edged forwards, collapsing onto his bloodied hands.

Mason grinned at his hopelessness, his *horror...* "Are you going to beg me, Mr Dagger?"

From beneath his coat, he brought out a curved knife that shimmered pretty colours from the aurora above. Relishing each movement, Mason curled his fingers in Daniel's hair.

Harrison's glassy eye fell to Daniel's, gazing with a plethora of emotions. *Fear, pain, the dreadful certainty of his future...* All screamed inside his soul, but there was one emotion that Harrison could not miss, that screamed from Daniel with their last ever gaze of adoration.

Please don't beg for me, Daniel's stare relayed. *Don't give him the pleasure.*

Harrison, respecting his beloved's last wish, swallowed the words with a visible shudder.

"Hm," Mason purred. "Shame."

Harrison couldn't bear to look as Mason sliced the knife across Daniel's throat. But they all heard his strained gurgles, and the sickening thump of his falling body. Blood leaked into the snow; a growing pool of crimson that created a sinister contrast against the white. Only when Daniel's body stilled, the life leaving him entirely, did Harrison scream. A strangled noise, full of anguish and hate, that curved his spine and shook his shoulders. Suffering painted his features more than a Masonian baton ever could.

Wandering over with a crooked smile, Mason crouched down. "How does it feel?"

He slipped the warm, bloody knife beneath Harrison's eye patch and sliced it off. It fluttered to the ground in a mocked display of calm, leaving a bloody streak in its path.

"I'm going to hurt you, Mr Dagger," Mason whispered, close to Harrison's shaking body. "You'll beg for death far before the end."

Campbell stared at the spill of blood, marring the snow. Daniel's death carved a deep hole inside his stomach, but Caroline... He couldn't understand why she still wasn't moving. *Why wasn't she moving?*

"Distressing, isn't it? Seeing your family *die*," Mason said, glaring. "I offered you a choice in Gainstorn, Mr Anders. A life, freedom—not just for you but for your whole fucking Rebellion. You could have prevented this day, saved them all."

A grating laugh escaped Mason's lungs. Slowly, he crouched down, until they were at eye-level. Only as Mason's form spoiled his view did Campbell lose himself in those deadly eyes: sparkling, prismatic, utterly heartless. *Sadistic.*

A slow grin materialised on Mason's gaunt face. "I'll ensure you live with that knowledge, to feel the full weight of its burden for the rest of your life."

If he had been capable of talking, Campbell would have told him of the guilt he felt, the *regret* at what he did. He would have explained the layer of moss staining his soul, soaking his blood with a sickly green tinge.

He would have told Mason how *sorry* he was...

But he never said any of that. As they were dragged away from Daniel and Caroline, he didn't say a single word.

17

They threw Campbell out the van.

He collapsed to the snow, cracking the layer of frost on the surface and slicing his hands. Pain shot through his numbing fingers, but he didn't have the energy to feel pain anymore. Not physical pain, at least.

"Have a nice life, rat," his guarding Masonian spat.

The door to the van slid shut and roared across the snow. The south-eastern road, atop the mountains that once overlooked Snow's Breath, became marred with deep, ugly tyre tracks.

Campbell was alone.

He was *so* alone...

A cry—full of hatred and agony and rage—burst from his throat. His entire body shook, his chest collapsing from under him. His ankles, still bruised and battered from the shackles, sent hot rods of pain up and down his legs, so he elected to crawl. Where to?

Home.

He wanted to see his home.

Campbell forced himself to the edge of the cliff. Rock and ice glared back.

Another strangled cry erupted. Hands clawed the rock, carving thin lines of black against the layer of frost. Colourful light danced in the sky, but for the first time, he didn't find it beautiful. It was barbaric. It was sick.

The aurora enjoyed stroking its light upon the glacier, born from the bones of Campbell's family. It liked mocking the happiness they had once felt, the New Year celebrations that now seemed so abhorrent. They'd fallen to their deaths during those celebrations. They'd all plummeted down Mason's black chasms, before he pulled the bloody ice from the ground.

No survivors. Campbell knew there weren't. Mason would have personally picked them off, one by one.

Campbell blinked through his tears, his eyes still sore and burning. His lids, swollen and puffy, were barely able to move. The metal contraption they had forced into his eyes, to hold them open, had nearly blinded him.

"Watch it!" Mason had snapped. "I want him to witness everything."

And he had. With his entire body suspended from the wall of the prison, his eyelids forced up and his head sealed in a metal bracket, Campbell was entirely helpless. He remembered the feel of sweat and blood, burning his eyes with salt and iron. He tried to close them, willed the papery skin to split, so they might fall and shield him from the horrendous sight...

But they didn't. All it did was coax another laugh from Mason's lungs.

Harrison's torture was... *excruciating.* As he dangled by his wrists and blood poured down his naked body, Campbell listened to his horrific, heart-breaking screams, and more of his soul died. Cut clean away, along with Harrison's toes, ears, genitals, skin...

"Open wide, Harrison..." Mason's smile was just as sharp, just as sinister as the curved knife that dripped pearls of Harrison's blood.

Campbell couldn't stop the vomit roaring up his throat. Even those three weeks later, as he watched the aurora's mocking light fall upon that murderous glacier, he could still smell it on himself.

"Please!" Campbell had not recognised the voice that escaped his burning gullet. But Mason had. He'd grinned at Campbell and took sick, perverted pleasure in forcing bloody slices of skin down Harrison's throat.

Mercifully, Harrison passed out a few times. It was during these moments, when his bloodshot, hopeless eye shut away from the world, Campbell hoped he would never wake up. And—for the first time in his life —Campbell prayed to the Old Gods. He begged Odin to take Harrison, to drag him from those awful shackles and cocoon him in a fur-lined blanket. Perhaps Daniel was there too, waiting to kiss Harrison's bloody tears away.

But the Old Gods had stopped listening to Campbell.

Because Harrison woke up. He'd always wake up.

Perhaps the Old Gods had never listened at all.

So Campbell started begging Mason instead. *"I killed her, I was the one who pulled the trigger—why don't you hurt me!"*

Mason forced a metal screwdriver down the bloody hole that used to be Harrison's ear. Through Harrison's grating, strangled screams of utter agony, Mason turned to Campbell with a sick, knowing smile. "I *am* hurting you, Campbell," he'd said.

Time seemed to linger on. Harrison grew wearier with each day, only kept alive by a Doctor who came to deliver antibiotics. They pumped him full of the cruel chemicals just before they forced liquified food up his nose, through a rubber tube. Blood had soaked Harrison's nose and mouth when they ripped the tube out, day after day.

Campbell struggled when the same procedure was done to him, wanting to die of starvation, but also wanting to be spared the pain when they inevitably ripped the tube out.

But lubricant had been on his tube, inserted and removed with tender care. A few moments later, Harrison had screamed and choked on his own blood.

How many days had it been? To Campbell, it felt like an eternity. To Harrison, it must have been infinitely longer.

Despite Harrison's punctured eardrums, Campbell had tried to talk to him, to help him through the horrific nightmare of his reality. As the walls shimmered with frost, and as Harrison's fingers and feet (or what remained of them) turned black with the cold, Campbell still talked to him, reminded him that he wasn't alone, that he would *never* be alone...

The next day, the first thing Mason did was force a gag into Campbell's mouth. The next, he sliced Harrison's tongue clean off.

Days—or weeks, or years, or decades—went by. Harrison grew weaker, his blood thicker. The pool around his body grew, then dried. Screams smeared the walls, Harrison's body shaking ferociously, frantically, as he tried to escape the shackles.

Campbell remained, watching his suffering, his torture, his *death*.

A slow death.

Far too slow.

"Wake him up," Mason snapped to one of his Masonians. He paced the room, his pounding black boots saturated with Harrison's blood, just like his hands.

A bucket of water was thrown over Harrison's pale, mutilated body. Blood rushed to the floor, spilling with the icy water.

Harrison did not stir.

The Masonian marched to him, inspected him, even slapped him a few times.

"I think he's gone, Sir," he said.

Campbell thought his cries had all dried up, just like his eyes. But the relief he had felt, the sheer exhilaration when Mason had examined Harrison's blank eye, and then declared his death, made Campbell's soul rot even more.

The cries came harder, not because Harrison Dagger—the kindest, bravest, most decent man Campbell had ever met—had finally choked on his last breath, but that Campbell was ever so *happy* about it.

If Campbell ever had any doubts that he was a monster, this had sealed the deal.

Harrison's body had bloated with decay. Only then, did Mason finally remove the metal brackets from Campbell's head and eyes.

"Do you wish for death, Campbell?" Mason had asked, softly. "Do you wish to join Harrison in the afterlife? I will not grant you such a mercy. You shall live with your decisions, and these memories. Every day, you shall live knowing that *you* forced my hand to Harrison's throat. *You* pulled the trigger that made Harrison's screams so exquisite to my ears."

Mason bared his teeth in a brutal, evil smile.

"You will leave the Fjordlands before the sun sets, Campbell. For the rest of your life, you shall wander the frozen heart of my world, with nothing but the memories of those you loved, and condemned to death."

Mason leant closer, until his hot breath beat upon Campbell's nose. "Tell me, Campbell, was her death worth all the pain, the suffering? Were her defenceless cries worth mine? Were they worth Harrison's?"

No, they weren't... Campbell cried harder with the truth of that reality. Nothing was worth the screams that scraped down his memories...

"It's all rather hilarious, isn't it?" Mason said, a sensual purr in his voice. "What did you accomplish, hm? Your freed Slaves are buried beneath ice and stone, as is the rest of your Rebellion. Of course, the irony is that Alira still lives. Another body, most certainly. But she exists. She lives on."

Mason rose to his full height, looking down upon Campbell's trembling frame. "I hope you'll remember that, Campbell. For the rest of your days."

Campbell knew he'd remember. He had no doubt of that.

Guilt ate him up, one delicious mouthful at a time. And not just for Gainstorn, but Harrison too. And Caroline, and Daniel, and Alice. All of them—Rebels, freed Slaves, the children on that train—had been slaughtered by Mason because of *him*. *His* actions.

If he hadn't pulled the trigger all this months ago, his friends—his *family*—would still be alive.

Blinking back little shards of glass, Campbell watched the glacier slump down the mountain, and another strangled cry escaped his throat. He wanted to join them. He wanted to hug Harrison's ashes—wherever they were. Mason had ordered Harrison's body to be incinerated. Campbell had begged him to be thrown inside the furnace too, but Mason had just smiled and ordered him to be thrown into the van instead. The bastard didn't even let Campbell say goodbye.

Deep inside his stinking, slimy heart, Campbell knew that Mason was right. Why should Campbell—the monster responsible for all those deaths—be allowed to say goodbye to the man he'd killed.

He'd killed. *Campbell* had killed.

Because although Campbell didn't slice that knife across Harrison's skin, or drag the screams from his throat, *he had killed him*. He'd brought Mason's retribution down on them all. Mason tortured and killed Harrison *because* of Campbell.

He cried even harder.

Seals lounged on the ice rafts at the bottom of the new glacier. Campbell couldn't bear to look at the new species making their home, on the ruins of his.

A retch crunched his stomach, though nothing came up.

Caroline. Visions of those Tiger Eyes flashed. Was Daniel still with her?

Campbell needed to see them. He didn't care if their bodies were decaying, or if animals had torn apart their limbs or snipped their sinew. He needed to see them, to apologise. Maybe their souls would hear him. Maybe he'd finally feel some peace if he covered them with dirt; buried their bodies with the dignity they deserved.

Campbell didn't feel himself walking into the forest until he was already there. Where was he? He didn't know, but he continued on. On and on, through the trees.

Wandering. *Roaming.*

Light morphed above him. Teals and blues changed into greens and pinks. They lit up the forest, as though the very stars were celebrating.

Was it for the New Year, or Mason's retribution? Campbell didn't know the answer, only that the stars must have hated him too.

Hours passed and his limbs ached. Yet, he kept moving. He couldn't stop. If he stopped, he'd hear Harrison's agony, forever rattling around his skull. Boots snapped branches and crunched snow, and he concentrated on those sounds, forced himself to rid the memories that would always plague him, always haunt him.

More hours passed. He kept moving.

He wasn't sure how he found it. Maybe he was subconsciously leading himself there. Maybe the Old Gods just had a sick sense of humour.

Whatever the reason, Campbell gazed at the clearing. As the pearly light of dawn lightened the sky, a lilac hue tinted the frozen pond, the tall trees, the jewel-speckled rocks. Snow glowed silver, and small snowflakes hung in the air, illuminated by the young day's light.

Still magical. Still dragged from a fairy tale.

Campbell sank to his knees.

Harrison had proposed to Daniel there. Harrison had told Campbell to love himself, to bury his demons.

The sound that left Campbell's chest was monstrous, entirely inhuman. Like he was an injured animal.

Perhaps, in a way, he was.

No, *no!* He had no right to that comparison, not when he put Mason's armed hand to Harrison's flesh!

But he hurt so much...

Crawling through the snow, Campbell somehow made it to the tree, where they had clawed through the dirt.

Bury the past, Harrison had said.

Campbell's hands scraped away that same snow, then the dirt beneath. Great handfuls of mud were moved aside, the particles wedging beneath his fingernails, as though they tried to pop the nail from the bed entirely. Hoarse, grating cries worked their rough way up, spewing from his throat like acidic vomit.

Finally, he saw them.

The revolver mocked him, glared at him like an old enemy. The sword—Mason's sword—simply sneered with as much spite as its previous owner.

Both weapons chilled Campbell's muddy hands as he plucked them from the dirt.

Harrison had been wrong. He couldn't bury the past. He could never cover it with layers of dirt and snow and pretend everything was normal. Campbell's soul had been marred, forever. It was mouldy, slimy, merging with the acres of guilt and regret until it resembled something truly horrific.

Harrison didn't see that, and it cost him his life.

And Campbell knew he was responsible for all of it.

* * *

THE REMAINS of Snow's Breath loomed below him. He wasn't entirely sure how he got there, how he moved from the magical clearing to the rock where they had watched everything be destroyed. Campbell almost smelt the blood and blackened coal in the air, and though he knew it was his imagination, he wondered if that's what his soul smelt like. Old and decrepit. Burnt beyond recognition.

The revolver was so heavy in his hand. Orange patches of rust shone in the sunlight that tickled the tops of the mountains.

Light caressed Campbell's gaunt, ashen face, yet he felt none of its warmth, or its comfort. He recalled the sordid, final *crack* of Caroline's neck and thought he might never feel comfort ever again.

With a blind, mindless action, Campbell cocked the revolver. A heartbeat later, the cold metal ring pressed against his temple. His finger poised, ready.

Harrison's face flashed through his mind. Two green eyes gazed at him, beckoned him with laughter and open arms. Campbell wanted to be with him. He didn't want to be alone. He didn't want to feel like a monster anymore.

As the sun smothered the valley with spectacular golden light, Campbell took his final, slow breath.

He pulled the trigger.

No exquisite bang. No sweet finality of death.

Just a dull click, echoing around his skull.

Campbell's eyes popped open.

He pulled the trigger again. Then again. *Again.*

No bullets.

Campbell crumpled. His hand sank like a sack of flour, the revolver clattering against the stone. Great, gut-cramping wails flowed down the mountain, echoing as a choir of pain throughout the valley. Misery rose as a rising flood, and a cacophony of animal sounds joined him in a screaming, howling chorus.

Finally, as his voice grew hoarse and his throat saturated with thousands of tiny needles, Campbell forced himself to quieten.

Silence returned to the valley.

Eyes closed, Campbell listened to his surroundings: the gentle howl of the wind, the creaking slump of glaciers, the distant howl of wolves...

So different to how it used to be. So, so different.

Slowly, like his limbs resembled hunks of lead, Campbell picked up the revolver, lying neglected on the stone. For a while, he just studied it, shocked that it didn't slide through his fingers, like he'd often thought it would do. Next, he studied Mason's sword, counting each sparkling sapphire, each glint of gold and gleam of platinum.

Campbell couldn't change the past. He knew that. He'd known that for months, ever since he shot a screaming baby in her cot.

But how could he go on when his very blood seeped black tar?

You deserved to be loved, Campbell.

More tears trickled down Campbell's cheeks. Faith had left him a long time ago, but Harrison's voice sounded so clear, so *real* inside his head that he could have been sat next to him. Drinking mead, cleaning guns—like they had so often done.

A part of Harrison would always be with him. How could it not? Harrison's soul entwined with the guilt, along with Caroline's, and Dan's, and all the others.

Perhaps Campbell needed to feel that. He needed that guilt, needed to remember why they weren't there. That knowledge —that guilt—began to morph into hatred. Hatred for himself, hatred for Mason.

Hatred for a little girl, whose very existence put vengeful power inside Mason's veins.

Campbell stood on his cut, blistered feet and trembling legs. Mason's sword in one hand, his father's revolver in the other, Campbell knew his future was bleak and empty.

But it glowed with the red, fiery rage of his own justice, his own retribution.

Strong light caressed his features as the sun grew higher in a frost-licked sky.

The Dagger Rebellion had ended. It had died with Harrison's last, wheezing breath. Perhaps even before then, beneath the rainy skies over Gainstorn.

But that didn't mean Campbell had to die with it. And yes, the pain would cripple him and the guilt would eat him, but Campbell had known from a young age to rise up, to smack life in the balls and emerge stronger, more determined than ever.

And he was determined. *So goddamned determined...*

Determined to end Mason. To make *him* scream.

Campbell had already made him scream once. What's to say he couldn't do so again?

Resolve lit bright and forceful inside Campbell's chest, and life finally returned through his numb fingers. He felt their heat as he curled them tightly around the weapons.

Whatever happened, Mason would die. Campbell would ensure it, not just for him, but for Harrison, Caroline—and all the others. The last fight of the Dagger Rebellion, where *Mason's* blood—and not theirs—would stain the snow.

Campbell gazed at the glacier as hate burnt away the slime inside his stomach.

Yes, whatever happened, no matter how much of his monstrous soul he'd have to sell along the way, he'd ensure Mason would die.

"I promise," Campbell whispered to the cold Glassland air. "I swear to you, Harrison, I'll make him pay."

And somehow, *somewhere*, he knew Harrison smiled.

PART 3

18

EAGLES OVERLOOK, YEAR 172

Campbell Anders took another swig.

Amber liquid burned his throat and warmed his chest. Mead expanded his stomach in a dizzying rush, spurring his body's nauseous defiance. *No more*, it begged. Campbell gulped his last mouthful and bashed the tankard on the wooden countertop.

"Another!"

Harald — the innkeeper — raised an annoyed eyebrow. "Haven't you had enough?"

A snide smile spread the cuts on Campbell's chapped lips. "Another."

With a defeated sigh, Harald picked up the mead jug.

Campbell dug deeply in his pocket, fondled his rapidly decreasing collection of gold coins, and threw them on the counter with a loud rattle.

"That'll cover it, right?" He knew it was far below what he owed, especially for the room upstairs, but he'd stopped caring.

Harald raised the scraggy blond eyebrow above his green eye. His other eye (the blue one) narrowed.

"I'll add it to your tab," he said pointedly, and filled the tankard with a disapproving glare. "But it's your last one."

Campbell's stretched lips cracked in a stinging wave. He soothed them with the cold metal tankard and took a long, almost loathsome gulp. Camp-

134

bell replaced the tankard on the counter with a shudder and hunched his shoulders. The leather weapon belt pressed uncomfortably into his belly, digging into his jutting hipbone. Campbell didn't care about *that* either. He wanted to feel the weight of that belt, for it to cut right through him.

Campbell was certain those inanimate weapons — the revolver on one side, the elaborate sword on the other — had tried to kill him over the years. They'd certainly done their best to drown him a few weeks back, when he fell through some thin ice on a lake so frozen, he'd been certain it would hold his meagre weight. That assumption had turned into shocking profanity as he sank chest-deep in black, freezing water, those weapons dragging like lead weights around his hips. Only the promise of hot spiced cider at the nearby town had forced Campbell to claw his way out, but if it were any other day — *if he were sober* — he may have uncurled his grasping fingers until they slid down the ice. He may have allowed the frigid water to caress him, envelop him, to saturate his lungs with the certain finality of his future, however empty it was.

But no, he remained a drunken fool, sipping mead — or beer, cider, whatever he could get his hands on. No whiskey. He couldn't face whiskey.

Even the smell reminded him of—

Memories wrenched Campbell back to that prison, to when they'd forced his eyes open with metal and dried blood, and Mason had cut off piece after piece after piece... Harrison's horrific screams grated his memories into a thousand bloody pieces. Gore blackened his vision.

Campbell chugged down the mead, ignoring the dizziness and nausea, and forced his muscles to relax. The memories receded. Dispersing away, like ripples in a pond. Alcohol allowed that pond to be fluid, carrying away those ripples of hurt and despair before they froze. If Campbell sobered up, that pond would solidify. It would turn into glass and cement those ripples in their terrible, final form.

Campbell didn't want to sober up. For the sake of his very existence, he had to keep that pond liquid. He *had* to keep drinking.

"Another!" Campbell slammed the tankard again, harder this time.

"Really, Campbell? Another?" Harald's glare forced Campbell's aside. "Tell you what: you put down twenty coins — twelve for the room and eight for the mead you already owe — and I'll get you a top-up on the house."

As his face twisted into a scowl, Campbell delved into his pocket again and grabbed every jangling coin. Coins rattled and rolled across the sticky countertop.

Sickness and mead gathered in his gut like a lead balloon, yet Campbell's blank expression came easily as Harald counted the coins.

"Sorry, mate." Nothing about Harald's tone suggested he was in the least bit apologetic. "You're six coins short."

A bitter huff rose from Campbell's throat. "The fuck do I care?"

Returning the spilled coins to his pocket (to buy more booze), he pushed himself from the bar stool. All the mead inside his stomach rushed to his head. The room spun, his eyes rolled inside his skull, and wooden floorboards morphed and tilted beneath his feet. Campbell fell with an almighty slam.

"Bloody hell!" Harald rushed around the bar, shooing ogling customers away. "Nothing to worry about. Please enjoy your evening!"

Campbell's stomach rolled instead of his eyes.

His hip aching from the fall — and from his father's old revolver digging into him — Campbell stumbled to his feet and shook off any helping arm. "I've got it!"

Campbell staggered towards the door. Behind him, the inn resumed its usual vibrant atmosphere: the minstrels sang and relentless chatter permeated the air, only surpassed by the sound of the crackling hearth-fire. With that many guests and a fire that large, the inn must have been stifling, but Campbell felt none of it. He stumbled out into the snowy courtyard of Eagle's Overlook, and a wall of frigid air punched him, grazing the sheens of sweat on his brow and armpits. Even the small of his clammy back chilled to almost unbearable levels. Campbell stumbled on, using what remained of his focus to head towards the balcony at the edge of the courtyard.

The caldera gazed at him, beckoned him. A grand expanse of snow and ice, as flat as a lake, surrounded by a crown of grey, jagged mountains. Stars speckled a sky dancing with ethereal colour, the surviving clouds nothing more than airy wisps carried by the icy breeze.

Campbell stared at the undulating lights above — at each roll of green, each crease of pink — and his stomach lurched.

Campbell Anders, the sole survivor of the infamous Dagger Rebellion, vomited thirty-two coins worth of mead into the prettiest caldera in the New World.

That felt like a new low.

Wiping his mouth on his sleeve, Campbell forced himself upright. Snow and ice taunted him. The entire world was just as hard, just as cold as the heart he had once stabbed when he was a teenager.

That unmarred, pristine blade had been pulled out by its own victim, who had grinned with cruel satisfaction because everyone knew he couldn't be killed...

When Campbell stared at the ruined remains of his home all those years ago — the spectacular icy marvel known these days as South Seal Glacier — he made a promise to Harrison Dagger: to kill Mason, to spread *his* blood on the pristine snow.

Now, with his future bleak and his stomach acid curdling, the promise pressed on Campbell's shoulders. It seemed impossible, improbable. It felt like an empty threat; a weightless oath whispered with rage in his heart and blood on his fingers.

Campbell stared at his fingers. All that blood... Harrison's, and Caroline's, Alice's, Daniel's... Their blood had coagulated, blackening his fingernails. And though no one could see its brown, mottled lustre, he knew they could smell the guilt on him. His slimy soul hadn't dried up. It had rotted away entirely.

The longer Campbell Roamed the New World — the longer he *survived* — he continued to live with the memories, the nightmares of what that *monster* did to his family. Years wore on, and he'd started to truly understand, with sickening intensity, exactly *what* he had done in Gainstorn.

Yes, he'd shot a baby girl because she was going to end the world — and he would never forgive himself for that — but, by doing so, he'd condemned everyone else to death. He had cut the knife into Harrison's skin and made the blood trickle. Harrison wasn't even responsible for the girl's death; not really, not when he'd escape the blood splatter. And that was the other truth: Harrison Dagger, in all his righteous glory, would *never* have done what Campbell did, and that hurt. Truth was like a rusty dagger, slicing into Campbell's heart, cutting bits of him away, just like Mason did to Harrison all those years ago.

Campbell wanted to join them, up there in the heavens. Surely it was easier? Living up there, seeing Mason's torment but knowing they were safe from retribution, safe from the packs of hungry Masonians just *dying* for a piece of Rebel flesh? Because Campbell was just as helpless down there as he would be anywhere else. Mason couldn't die—Campbell couldn't kill him when he was a teenager, and he couldn't kill him now either. The bastard was indestructible, harder than the diamonds his eyes resembled so perfectly...

But the most agonising truth of them all? *Nothing had changed.*

Mason had been immortal when Campbell stared at the glacier that ate his friends, and yet Campbell had still made the impossible promise to kill him, and for what? *Nothing.*

Absolutely *nothing.*

He'd tethered his soul to the New World for *nothing*, forever wishing for an impossibility.

What was the point in remembering that? What was the point in wishing for another life, forever hoping that Mason would die first? No, it was far easier to let drink numb the pain, to blur the reality of Campbell's pathetic, false promises.

He needed a drink.

Fuelled with despair and desperation, Campbell stumbled back to the courtyard, eating a large handful of snow to wash away the acidic tang of vomit.

The sun had long slept, yet Merchants still haggled their wares behind stalls choked with goods. People weaved in and out of wooden counters decorated with guns, clothes, meats, fine fabrics, and jewellery. A myriad of footprints marred the snow, the day's tangle of people having turned the pristine white into grey slush. Campbell huffed to himself, glad to have missed such raucous mania. Where had he been? Upstairs, in his room, sleeping off his hangover.

Legs numbed with the cold, alcohol, or the sordid truth of his reality, Campbell wandered to the nearest stall: a munitions stall, by pure happenstance.

"What are you buying?" Campbell hoped his slurred words, and the stench of his breath, would not dissuade his potential buyer.

A short, stocky man with greying hair and a judging expression sent cold grey eyes up and down Campbell's ragged exterior. "Don't look like you have much to sell, mate."

Campbell didn't recognise his own hands as they plucked his father's rusty revolver from his belt. It was a wonder the ugly thing didn't drip blood on the counter.

"How much for this?"

Inspecting the gun, the vendor sneered. "This is a relic! Ain't worth the metal it's made from." The vendor slammed the gun into Campbell's chest. "Off with you. I'm closing up now."

"Please..." Campbell rarely allowed himself to beg.

He had begged Mason not to mutilate Harrison. Mason's only response had been a cruel smile. Then he'd cut off Harrison's genitals. Screams of utter, heart-breaking agony rattled inside Campbell's head, dragged to the surface by that one paltry word: *Please.*

Campbell swallowed the memories with a visible shudder. "I just need six coins, that's all."

Six coins, making twenty, could buy Harald's deal and land him a drink on the house. And God, he craved that drink...

The vendor's thin lips curled into a bitter smirk. "You stink of shit. Do yourself a favour and sort yourself out *before* you sell your heirlooms."

Campbell's brow crinkled.

Of course, the sword!

Campbell unsheathed it just as the vendor put away his lockbox — a sure sign his business had concluded for the day. All around them, people dispersed, scuttling through the cold to their hearths and their husbands.

Harrison was going to have a husband.

The vendor moved away. Campbell was running out of time. He rushed to the vendor's side with the pristine sword held horizontally in his hands. Sapphires sparkled beneath the aurora's light. "What about this? It's Mason's sword!"

The vendor snorted. "Course it is."

"No, really — I stabbed him with it, right through the heart!"

Hope ballooned inside Campbell's chest as the vendor stopped, turned, and finally met his eye. "And I fucked Mason's daughter."

Campbell stared back, his brain having trouble. "But Mason doesn't have a daughter."

The vendor rolled his eyes and marched off.

A combination of fresh air and vomiting poured some clarity inside Campbell's skull. With his stomach fighting retches and his eyes struggling to focus, he manoeuvred himself towards the view, his weapons returned to his belt. Leaning both arms against the stone railing, he gazed into Mason's frozen world and wondered how to get those six extra coins.

The courtyard, now sparse of people, finally became quiet. Only a few cackling men remained, smoking their cigarettes near the longhouse.

Perhaps Campbell could barter with them? Exchange his measly weapons for a few coins?

Another milky sigh passed his lips. What would Harrison say if he could see him now — drunk off his own remorse, his own guilt? What would Caroline think?

Tears burned his eyes, then numbed with the cold. Campbell wiped his cheeks before the tears froze completely.

Maybe he didn't have to sell anything. Perhaps he just needed to cause a distraction. Nothing too audacious. Just something to keep Harald's attention long enough for him to swipe something from behind the bar?

Speaking of thievery...

Something — *someone* — was in his jacket pocket, fumbling about. Gold coins clanked together as strange fingers fondled his only chance for another, exquisite drink...

Campbell's fingers snapped around the thief's wrist. They froze, their unusually small hand still buried in Campbell's pocket. Hatred and rage ballooned inside his chest. His fist already curled, anticipating the inevitable strike against a shocked cheekbone...

What did Campbell expect when he turned to the thief? Perhaps a drunkard, like himself, scrambling for any coin he could find. He would've preferred a mirror to slam his fist against. Yes, that would have been ideal.

But that's not what he found.

Instead, he stared at the delicate wrist gripped by his hairy hand, then up the small arm to the young girl.

Campbell didn't notice the blue robes, ripped and muddied. Neither did he see the dried blood on her fingers, or the cuts decorating her round cheeks.

But her eyes... They sparkled wildly beneath the ethereal light and sent sharp rods of terror down his spine.

The last time he'd seen those eyes, it had been over ten years ago, beneath the rainy skies in Gainstorn. He'd put a bullet between them.

Even gripped by alcohol's tight fingers, Campbell knew exactly what – *who* – he was looking at.

"Shit," he breathed.

19

———————

Light fluttered above them: a silent melody of blues and pinks that rippled across the sky. Campbell was vaguely aware of that light skimming across her young, soft features.

He stared at the button nose covered with mud; the rosy cheeks marred with deep cuts and abrasions; the floods of greasy chestnut hair, tangled with twigs and leaves... But, above everything, her eyes enchanted him. Too large, almost like she hadn't grown into them yet, they sparkled with the prismatic lustre of a diamond beneath the sun.

Campbell stared harder, lost in those eyes, and for a shocking moment, he realised he could not pull himself away...

She screamed.

She wrestled with his hold and stamped her fur boots in the slush like a raging bull — despite her small stature.

She shocked sense into Campbell. "Hey! Calm down!"

She didn't listen, or she was too far gone with panic to hear him. The girl's screams intensified until her wails echoed across the caldera. Campbell tugged her closer and tried to calm her, but to no avail. She was an animal caught in a snare. Utterly *wild*.

"*Hey!*" Campbell grabbed both her shoulders and shook. "*Calm down!*"

Those too-large eyes widened into orbs of sparkling terror. She quietened. Small arms trembled beneath her grubby robes.

Campbell lifted his gaze and noticed the group of men staring at them, whispering to each other.

Panic bloated Campbell's chest. What if they saw her? Would they hand her over to Mason and inadvertently cause the destruction of the New World?

Campbell remembered an order he'd received many years ago.

"You must kill her."

Fuelled by drink and desperation, rather than rational sense, Campbell grabbed the girl's upper arm and dragged her from the courtyard. That was his first mistake.

The second was throwing a hairy hand over her squealing mouth.

The men stalked closer.

Campbell rushed to the side of the inn, isolated and far from wandering eyes. Maybe that was his final mistake.

The group of men appeared at his only exit, each with a frown of concern and disgust.

"*Fucking hell,*" Campbell hissed to himself, dragging the girl behind him. To her credit, she stayed still, albeit still trembling.

"Evening, gentlemen," Campbell said through a blinding (entirely fake) smile.

"The fuck are you doing?" one of them asked, and not kindly. He looked around Campbell's shoulders to the frightened creature. "Did he try to hurt you, sweetheart?"

Campbell realised their implication, and how his behaviour must have looked. His heart tumbled. "Fellas, please — there's been a gross misunderstanding."

Campbell yanked the girl back as she tried to escape around his legs. He needed time to think about what he was going to do.

Kill her. Kill her. Kill her!

Campbell shook his head, subtly, desperate to see through the fog of his own drunken ideas, and to avoid the unwavering spit of Svenja Svellec's voice inside his head. Regardless of what Campbell's panic expected him to do, the girl's diamond eyes sparkled with the promise of reward, from crazed gang leaders and Masonians alike, and it was imperative those men discovered neither. Campbell could figure out what to do later, *after* they'd regained anonymity.

"Really?" the man asked, reeking of sarcasm. Dark eyes scanned Campbell with clear disgust. "Well, why don't you take your grubby little paws off of her, then you can tell us all about our *misunderstanding*, hm?"

The weight of Campbell's revolver tugged his bruised hipbone. "I will not hurt her," he said, but the words felt hollow.

Deep inside his grimy soul, Campbell knew the best thing would be to kill her. A hard truth, but the right one. Regardless of the screaming, muddy, innocent form Alira now took, she was still the End of Everything. She needed to die for everyone else to live.

But death differed from pain, and Campbell wouldn't hurt her. If he could give her one parting gift, it would be that.

Gainstorm flashed behind his eyelids. That excruciating bang echoed around his memories, and he remembered the red spatter of blood up his arm... The world spun around him — *from guilt or drink?* — and Campbell struggled to stay focused on the situation he had suddenly stumbled across. The barrels of three revolvers beckoned him closer.

"I'm not taking that risk, mate," the man said, his aim far steadier than Campbell's. "Sorry."

Campbell thought he was anything but, and a small titter broke free.

The man cocked his gun. "Let her go. I won't ask again."

Seeing no way out of this, Campbell surrendered his empty palms.

The man did not lower his aim. "Good. Okay, sweetheart, you can come with us now. We'll get you back to your Tribe."

Tribe?

Campbell absorbed the light blue robes smothered with silver thread, and the little runes carved into bone circles, dripping from her gaping sleeves.

A Herder? She a fucking Herder?

Hiding in the mountains, moving with the snow flurries from one icy peak to another... Well, that would explain why she'd remained hidden for so long. So, what was she doing in Eagle's Overlook — the biggest, busiest town in the Snowlands? What the hell happened to her Tribe for a young girl to be wandering the dangerous New World on her own? Predators lurked in towns as well as forests. Clearly, for that was why a misunderstood Campbell had three revolvers aimed between his eyebrows.

Campbell thought, with no small measure of guilt and regret, what a shame it was, that she had survived this long. Fate could have easily ripped her from this world, but no — she had been lucky. She was a survivor. She'd avoided piercing cold and snapping jaws, and now Campbell had to deal with her. Why was life so unfair?

The girl inched past him, rubbing her wrist. Pines and twigs were embedded in her hair, and she seemed so very thin.

Pity crunched Campbell's heart. *What's happened to her?*

"Okay, sweetheart, you're safe now," one man said.

Perhaps hearing the calm reassurance in his words, the girl raised her head. Diamonds sparkled beneath the aurora's dancing light.

Time stopped. The men stared at those eyes; at each little twinkle...

Campbell assessed them carefully. "Fuck..."

Time kick-started with an abrupt bang.

"*The End of Everything!*" one of them screeched. "*Kill her*! Before she destroys us all!"

They aimed between those diamond eyes. They hesitated with drooping jaws, tears threatening. Campbell saw their determination. He saw their fingers twitching against the triggers—

Bangs erupted throughout the square. Crows squawked; dogs barked.

Silence returned with the thump of three lifeless bodies on the frosty ground.

Campbell lowered his smoking revolver.

He knew they would've shot her. In fact, he was certain of it. Campbell had once been in their shoes, after all.

Metal cooled the invisible blood on his hand, the vibrations still echoing up his arm. Campbell stared blindly at the three corpses. Those men were going to kill her, to wipe away the End of Everything's current incarnation before she had time to destroy the world.

So why, in hell's name, didn't he let them shoot?

Nauseous breaths escaped his lungs as Campbell returned his revolver to his belt. He turned to the little girl, standing stoically. Whatever the reason for his actions, Eagle's Overlook was far too populated — for them *both*. Regardless of what she was, no doubt the residents of such a proud town would not be overly delighted with infanticide.

If he were to figure out what to do (*but he knew what he had to do*), he needed space to think; to get them both away from that blood-soaked court-yard before someone discovered them.

Svenja's voice still taunted him — *"Kill her. Kill her."* — as Campbell knelt before his trembling victim. She'd clearly locked up — physically and mentally — and just stared at the three bodies with the whites of her eyes lighting up like fields of fresh snow.

Blood leaked across the floor as Campbell grasped her frozen, cut cheeks with two hairy hands.

"Hey, look at me," he whispered gently. The men had gained her trust with a calm tone of voice, so Campbell might get through to her if he remained... *kind.*

Kind. The word sounded so alien inside his head.

"Hey," he said, a little louder.

Slowly, like she was swimming through tar, she forced her eyes to meet his. Tears gleamed, adding to their inherent sparkle.

"You're alright," Campbell said softly. "You hear me, girl? You're safe..."

His jaw worked around the lie until he managed to swallow, drawing her gaze to the marble bobbing up and down in his throat. She remained silent, yet still trembled. Had she heard him? Campbell wasn't sure. He noticed the blood staining her fingertips. Just how much had she been through? Had she fended off predators and perverts alike?

Yes, Campbell needed to gain her trust. He needed her to be happy and content when he...

Campbell took a hasty look in both directions and licked the sheen of sweat from his upper lip. Blood glimmered on the stone floor, beside them.

Campbell stared at this girl — the gashes in her cheeks, the twigs in her hair — and couldn't help but realise the truth that had long haunted him.

She's just a child.

An innocent creature, born with no knowledge of her destiny. Did she even know who Mason was? What *she* was?

Tears burned behind his eyes, the memories of Gainstorn somehow becoming more harrowing, more wretched. His future — *their* futures — beckoned with the acidic tang inside his mouth.

Gainstorn had destroyed so many lives, including his own. Could he do it all over again?

That wasn't a fair question. He didn't have a choice.

It wasn't just about *him*, about *his* life — as loathsome as it was. The fate of the New World rested on his shoulders, just as he rested his hands on the thing that would destroy them all.

Svenja knew this. That's why she had given him those inexorable orders ten years ago.

This girl would destroy them all. She would be the ultimate End of Everything. What solution was there? Only the certain finality of a murderous bullet.

And yet, the price on this girl's head reached the stars. Mason had offered immediate social exultation for whomever delivered her blood-stained hands into his. And what of the crazed Drug Lords, the ones who would offer this poor girl's head — to *anyone* — in exchange for little bags of white powder?

If Campbell were in another's shoes, perhaps he would have considered such a deal — because, on paper, it sounded pretty darn good. Money in his pocket, unlimited drink in his stomach... Who *wouldn't* want a life without worry, without want, or the insatiable need to provide? Utter bliss, for the rest of his despicable life.

Of course, that ship had sailed a long time ago. Even if Campbell had wanted to further disgrace his soul, would he sell this girl? The one whose cheeks were so round and pale, and with a small nose that looked like it had been carved from soft butter?

No, he mustn't think like that. Not when fate had already etched her name on a bullet inside his revolver.

Campbell had already killed her once. His soul had already rotted down into something monstrous and unrecognisable. He'd already paid the ultimate price for his actions. What else did he have to lose?

Campbell licked his dry lips. "I'm going to take you somewhere safe, where no one can find us, okay?" He suddenly realised how his words must have sounded to outside ears, and immediately dropped his hands from her face. The girl winced and recoiled, perhaps feeling the chill return to her cheeks.

Campbell stood on two shaky legs and noticed a small water pump positioned over a stone basin. Drink still fogged his rational thoughts, and while he knew some inebriation would help with his ultimate task, he didn't trust his conscience. The three bodies of those would-be child-murderers proved he wasn't acting with full mental capacity.

He needed to sober up. Fast.

Without hesitation, he staggered to the pump. Water sloshed with delightful eagerness and filled the basin in no time at all.

With a deep breath, Campbell submerged his head into the water. Coldness gripped him and his lungs ached to suck in a startled breath. Thousands of needles bit his skin, his eyes numbing inside their sockets as the cold radiated deep inside his brain.

When he'd endured as much as he could, Campbell snapped his head up, coughing and spluttering. Clarity stuttered, like it was playing on an old, dusty record player.

The world came back into focus, and he dived again.

When he reappeared a second time, the girl had moved to his side and buried her face beneath the water's slick surface. Small hands gripped the sides of the basin, those bloodied nails scraping stone. Her entire body seemed to mould around the rock as she gulped down mouthfuls of water.

She erupted for two seconds, took a gasping breath, then dived again.

The girl finally stopped drinking, shivered, and threw her head over the side with a massive, gut-heaving retch. She vomited most of the water onto the frosted stone.

Campbell cursed to himself. He tentatively took her upper arm and forced her to look at him. Bloodshot eyes stared sadly as she wiped her mouth on a dirty sleeve, donned with hanging charms and mud.

That ball of pity grew inside Campbell's chest, threatening to burst.

"What's your name, girl?"

He didn't know why he asked it. He shouldn't have done. Doing so would only cause attachment and more pain for them both.

The girl didn't reply. She simply stared at him with those wide, doleful eyes.

Campbell slowly pointed to himself. "Campbell," he said, his lingering Aristocratic accent floating around each syllable. He wondered, spitefully, if Ms Emilia Eynesbury would be proud of such enunciation.

The girl alternated blank stares between his eyes and his finger, now pointing to her.

She remained silent.

Campbell exhaled a defeated breath and stood to his feet. He nodded towards the courtyard, across the corpses cooling in the cold air. They needed to leave before they roused attention.

"Come on," he said, though he didn't know why. The girl clearly didn't understand him.

He took a gentle hold of her arm and immediately felt her stiffen. She started trembling. At first, he thought she was afraid.

Pure, angry heat radiated through her heavy sleeves.

Campbell followed her gaze. "Shit!"

Three Masonians loomed ahead. Blue coats — a darker, richer blue than the girl's Herder robes — stood out in ominous colour against the white and grey. They perused the area with naught a care in the world, and yet their mere presence descended a violent shadow across the once vibrant town.

"Okay, back up." Campbell's breaths came in short bursts. "We need to get out of here, we–"

He was too late. Anger pulsed from her in sharp, almost lyrical beats. She ripped her arm from Campbell's.

With a deafening screech, the End of Everything charged.

20

____

Campbell couldn't stop her.

She raced ahead, her fur boots slipping and sliding. Campbell lunged after her, but the sudden movement caused the world to spin. His eyes rotated in his skull as the entire courtyard tipped…

Campbell collapsed, nauseous dread churning.

The girl's sharp shrieks could scrape snow from the walls of that courtyard. No doubt the Masonians were looking at her by now, laughing at her, mocking those beautiful robes and scratched cheeks, then celebrating with shocked glee at the loud twinkle inside her eyes.

The girl punched the Masonian's shoulder. He laughed, just as Campbell expected him to, and just threw her aside like a rag doll. She hit the stone with a loud thump and more mockery.

"Come on, you little Herder bitch, is that all you've got?"

The girl's grating scream pretended she understood them. Was it just their tone that angered her, or their mere existence?

Whatever the reason for her fury, Campbell knew there was precious time left to get her out of there.

With an audible groan and a crippling wave of sickness, Campbell staggered to his feet. His head spun, and he could no longer focus on the girl, springing up like a feuding hare and slamming her fists into the Masonian's open palms.

Panic replaced the nausea. For the sake of everything — all his sacrifices, the ones he'd loved and lost — he mustn't let them have her! They'd only deliver her to Mason, and so what would've been the point of *everything* Campbell had endured?

Harrison's voice rang inside his head: *On your feet, Anders!*

Raging determination — the desire to do *something*, after all those years of numbness — filled Campbell's chest.

He stuck two fingers down his throat. He gagged once, twice, and flooded the stone with the remaining alcohol inside his stomach.

With a final spit, Campbell fought through the dull throbbing inside his temple and placed one foot in front of the other. Eagle's Overlook gradually came into focus: the stables; the town hall with the ornate clock tower that chimed on every hour; the little girl, screaming with tales of unknown anguish until a Masonian brute whacked her across the cheek.

Fiery heat built inside Campbell. "Hey!"

The girl stumbled and fell, clearly dazed, two thick lines of blood dribbling from her nose. The sight fanned Campbell's fire hotter, brighter.

"*Hey!*"

He thrust his trembling body between the Masonians and the girl, still plastered to the floor and staring vacantly ahead.

The Masonian curled his lips into a vicious smile. Campbell's stomach shuddered at each blackened, cracked tooth.

"This little whore tried to bite me." The Masonian skulked closer, until his rancid breath fluttered across Campbell's nose.

Campbell snarled, "I don't care what she did to you. You touch her again, and I'll open your fucking skull to the crows."

Oh, how *good* that felt! Campbell's belly ballooned with that long-forgotten vengeance, the desire to *finally* fulfil the promise he made all those years ago. His fingers twitched, eager to accept Masonian blood...

Masonian blood?

Campbell's eyes narrowed at the three men. Thick coats flashed dark navy in the brazier's light, as did the circle of fur upon their heads and the dual weapons hanging from their hips. All Masonian items.

But the clothes *beneath* the uniforms? The scruffy brown jumpers, ripped jeans, and scuffed brown leather shoes? They were certainly *not* Masonian.

Campbell noticed the Masonian's dilated pupils; the bruised eyes; the misshapen, almost pinched look to his nose... He remembered one of his father's customers, known throughout Aristocratic circles for his excessive cocaine use. Campbell remembered how his nose had looked: the same as the one before him, so sunken and pinched. That Aristocratic bastard had eventually hidden his problems beneath a scalpel and a hefty medical bill.

Campbell's attention drifted to the other two Masonians, stood stoically, both with sunken eyes and pallid, almost death-like expressions.

These men aren't...

Campbell's realisation hit with a great thump. The lead Masonian laughed manically, his breath reeking of marijuana as he boasted a set of cracked, blackened teeth.

Mason's tightly-clenched fist around drugs would never allow Masonians to have such prolific, damaging use of them. In fact, Campbell only knew of one organisation who had such abundant, exclusive access to the substances that had morphed these men's once handsome features.

No, these men were not Masonians. They weren't nestled in Mason's pocket.

They lived in *Mike the Mulch's*.

Gang members.

Campbell focussed on the girl behind him, stumbling to her feet and wiping her bloody nose on her sleeve. Next came the undeniable fact that these vile men were just as — if not *more* — dangerous than Mason's stooges.

To them, the girl was just fodder. Money. Drugs. The promise of a good sale.

Who would they sell her to? *Anyone.* Absolutely *anyone.*

Cold revulsion slithered up and down Campbell's spine. Mason was undoubtedly a monster — an abhorrent stain on reality — but even *he* had his limits when it came to children.

Those same limits weren't ubiquitous across the New World.

Campbell's orders to kill were promptly smothered beneath fresh panic. He needed to get her the hell out of there. *Fast.*

"You hear me?" The man with the blackened teeth shoved Campbell's shoulder.

"What?"

The man snarled with peeling lips, pure rage swirling around huge, gaping pupils. "I *said* you and your little slut are going to pay for threatening a Masonian."

Masonian, huh? Campbell bit his tongue.

"My apologies," Campbell said, though it pained him to do it. He reached back and gently grasped the girl's upper arm. She tensed beneath his touch, though this time he felt no guilt, only the unrelenting desire to save her from the horrific fate these men promised. "We shall just be on our way, no harm—"

The girl ripped Campbell's revolver from his belt. Howling, she aimed it blindly at the men. They cursed, throwing themselves to the ground in a spill of stolen coats and fur hats.

"Girl, *no!*"

The bang shook the entire courtyard. Snow shivered from thatched roofs. Dogs barked, birds fluttered, and the revolver dropped from the startled girl's hand with a calamitous clank.

Reality slammed with a chorus of alarm. Campbell lunged for his gun, his sword clattering beneath him as he slid across the ground. Fingers curled around the warm barrel — as did the druggie's. Campbell stared blindly into his revolver's smoking depths, and ten long, torturous years galloped by in a flood of failure and sorrow.

Ten years.

He'd been running from his guilt for *ten* years.

Repulsion and glee merged in the druggie's dilated eyes. Stained fingers curled around the trigger. "Nice try, Aristocrat."

The girl leapt onto his back, shrieking like a wild animal. Dirty nails clawed beneath his hat until she ripped it off, along with chunks of his greasy hair. As if Campbell was watching some drink-induced dream, distant wolves howled in rejoicing chorus as this small, hurting girl bared a set of pristine white teeth, and buried them into the man's ear cartilage. His scream ricocheted around the courtyard and bounced across the caldera. Perhaps this was a good thing — perhaps the residents would come to see what all the ruckus was about and help them!

But as the girl ripped her bloody teeth away, along with a hefty chunk of the man's ear, Campbell reluctantly realised any resident would not be on their side.

Why would they help a rabid child? A violent creature? *A wild one*?

The two others dragged the girl off, kicking and screaming. Her soaked teeth glimmered like flawless rubies.

The bleeding druggie jumped to his feet and snatched the revolver from Campbell's grasp. Blood poured down the druggie's face and soaked his stolen uniform as he marched towards the snarling girl. She didn't care, for she was wrapped too tightly in hatred to see the fear that skulked closer, or the end that slept inside Campbell's revolver...

"You're *dead!*" the druggie spat. He raised the gun.

Campbell's selfish mind told itself this was a good thing — that the druggie would do the job he couldn't. And yet, his treacherous heart screamed in panic, and pushed pleas of mercy up his throat. Campbell didn't understand why he begged for the life he would soon end.

None of it mattered anyway. They weren't listening.

They're going to kill her...

He tried to see the good side — that *her* death meant *his* salvation. But such thoughts felt stale and decrepit. Perhaps it was weakness, or just the lingering dribbles of drink, but Campbell's heart dropped at his failure. He thought of the girl and his ignored pleas for her life, then Harrison's life, Caroline's, and all the other lives he'd swore to avenge, to protect, but were now nothing but fading whispers blown away by the breeze...

The aurora brightened. Colour fluttered above them, like delicate bits of ribbon. Beneath the heavenly celebration, diamond eyes sparked a prism of dancing light.

"Holy shit..."

Campbell didn't know who'd spoken, but they made his heart stutter back to life. *Now* was his chance to get her away, to save them both! The tip of his boot pressed to gain traction as he leapt...

But, just as Campbell had often thought, the New World evidently hated him.

As he lunged, his boot slid across the frost. He fell in a calamitous heap at the feet of the bloody gang lackey, who looked at him like he was a dying dog in the mud.

"Going somewhere, mate?" he said, smiling with those hideous teeth. Dilated eyes flicked to the girl, whose reality finally punched through. Colour drained from her face as she realised the depth of the shit she'd buried herself in. Those large diamond eyes found Campbell, and he thought he saw an apology swirling within the flecks of reflected colour.

No doubt Campbell shared her expression. He hoped she'd see his apologies, too. *All of them.*

Unable to move, frozen with pain and trembling limbs, Campbell was helpless as the man crouched down, both elbows on his knees, still cradling Campbell's revolver. "I think our boss will want a word with you two, don't you think, boys?"

The revolver slammed into Campbell's head, and he saw blackness.

21

———

The first thing Campbell noticed was the pain in his skull. He groaned around the throbbing ache, a fresh wave of nausea rising.

As he moved to caress his head, he touched the ground: stiff and fibrous, covered in grit. Campbell paused, eyes still closed, and inhaled the air thick with damp and shit.

With a stuttering heart, Campbell took a careful, blind note of his surroundings: the chilling bite in the air, the cloying stench, the faint flutters of screams that seeped through the walls...

Memories surfaced, hard and unforgiving. Campbell cringed around their certainty; that icy knot of truth that clung to visions of Harrison Dagger, suspended by his wrists, pain twisting his features as Mason smiled and *sliced*...

Panic gripped Campbell's chest and tightened his lungs. Suffocated him. He couldn't bear to open his eyes, to risk the images behind his eyelids becoming a reality.

But they already were a reality. Those visions had already happened.

It was *done*. It was *over*.

Such knowledge sank into Campbell's veins, forcing his breaths to slow, his muscles to relax. Gradually, even as his stomach clenched and cramped, he could breathe a little easier.

Those haunting ripples, skimming across his pond of memories, flowed away, merging into his subconscious, where they'd always remain. Waiting.

With a pained grimace, Campbell opened his eyes, sore and dry, like they'd been forced open again. Even then, when he knew Harrison's torture had long since ended, he could not separate those feelings of hopelessness, and fear, and despair. They merged and congealed, pouring liquid weight into his bones, thickening his movements. Yet, he pushed himself up and cast aching eyes around his cell.

His cell.

He remembered another cell he'd woken up in, long ago, when he was a teenager. Harrison had kicked his bare foot against the wall of the neighbouring cell. Caroline had been there too, thrown with Alice in a flurry of golden hair and cries. The ache in Campbell's stomach moved to his heart. He missed her. He missed her smile, her warmth, her comfort.

If only Campbell had told her how he felt, not just that fateful night, but during the years before Gainstorn. What memories they might have shared, the experiences that would have ballooned Campbell's already jumping heart. Perhaps Caroline would have looked at Campbell like Daniel had looked at Harrison. Maybe Campbell would have also dropped to one knee in that magical clearing. What would have happened if Caroline had said *yes*? What if they'd lived happily ever after? What if the Dagger Rebellion had escaped Mason's retribution?

What if?

Campbell hated those words.

He clicked his tongue around his mouth, cringing at the acidic tang that lingered there. He noticed the painful emptiness inside his stomach.

Albeit banging like a pickaxe, his head was completely empty and irrefutably sober. For the first time in... A while.

"And just when I was getting lonely."

Campbell spun around to the young, almost whimsical voice behind him; at the man curled up in the cell's corner, smothered in shadow despite the silver moonlight shining through the tiny, barred window. Still night. Good, he mustn't have been unconscious for that long.

Or he'd been knocked out for a very, *very* long time.

Large diamond eyes, laden with fear and unspoken apology, flashed behind his retina. Anxiety riddled his gut, rooting itself with ominous foreboding. *Where was she?*

A delicate chuckle quivered the air. "You look like absolute shit, mate."

Campbell's head hurt too much to scowl. "Where are we?"

The man stretched out long legs, swamped in an unflattering mix of corduroy and denim. "Dunno."

"Well, that's very helpful, thank you." Campbell huffed out his sarcasm through long, controlled breaths. "How long have I been out?"

"Few hours, I think."

Campbell deflated with sudden, almost crippling waves of relief. *The same night.*

"Did you see anyone with me? A young girl. Blue robes — not dark blue, like the Masonians', but a light, almost silvery blue." Jeez, why was Campbell so hung up over the colour of her robes?

"Didn't see anyone." The man linked long-fingered hands in his lap. "But she's around. Heard someone say that your '*wild little bitch*' was worth a small fortune to the right buyer."

"Shit!" Campbell paced before the bars, fingers running wild through his hair. Death would be a welcome reprieve compared to what those *buyers* had in store for her young, delicate frame.

Despite being hidden by shadow, Campbell felt the man's calculating stare. It settled on his skin in a flurry of feverish heat, then bored down. Like an ulcer.

"Who is she?" the man asked. "The Mulch doesn't come all the way down from the Icelands for nothing."

A dead weight fell in Campbell's stomach. "What? He's *here*?"

The stranger didn't seemed concerned; he just admired his nails. "Yep, he came in not so long ago, checking if you were conscious."

The Mike the Mulch had ogled Campbell's unconscious body? He shuddered at the thought. Pulling his arms around his chest, Campbell paced the cell at a faster rate. Thoughts raced inside his head, without answer or reprieve. How was he going to get out? How would he get *her* out? Where *was* she, anyway?

Stranded in shadow, the stranger silently watched.

"Do you know how to get out of here?" Campbell asked when the silence became crippling.

The man chuckled. "Ain't no way out of here, mate."

"Have you even tried?" Campbell asked, unable to hide his anger. This man — whoever he was — was getting on his nerves. His cockiness, his blatant disregard for freedom... It hit a painful nail deep inside Campbell's chest, reminding him that escape wasn't always an option — and that was a truth he dared not accept. Not again.

"What d'you want me to do?" the man asked. "We're safer in here. Hell, they'd dismember us outright if they found us wandering about, and I'd rather face my fate with both legs still attached."

"So, you've given up." It wasn't a question. The man clearly had no desire to break free, to prise the bars open with both hands, in the minute hope he'd squeeze through. He'd given up. Could Campbell blame him? He wasn't sure yet. Such defeat was hard to stomach, but there had to be something said for avoiding reckless behaviour, and the consequences that inevitably came with it.

"No, I've not given up," the man said, with no small amount of derision. "But I value my life, clearly more than you do."

That was a hard pill to swallow. It caught in Campbell's throat, so he swallowed again and said, "I value the life of the girl brought in with me. I... I have to save her."

No one would ever understand how painfully incorrect those words were to utter.

Campbell sank to his haunches, sliding down the bars. Cold snaked through his faded leather jacket, covered in spots of grey mud and vomit.

The stranger scooted forward. "Who is she? Some runaway Aristocrat?"

"What, like me?" Campbell's raised eyebrow had the stranger skulk back to the shadows.

"I meant no offence."

Campbell sighed. "She's a Herder. Something happened to her Tribe and..."

In the silence, the stranger crawled into the rays of moonlight. Silver caressed his face, highlighting his high, prominent cheekbones. Shadows glistened in the hollows below, skipping across a fresh face covered in patchy stubble. Indeed, this man was hardly a *man* at all. Late teens, or so Campbell assumed.

Youth poured through his eyes — an incredibly light, cloudy shade of green — that shone brightly, deviously, in the moonlight. Mischievous and cunning. Frightfully intelligent.

"Who is she?" he asked, staring at Campbell with those bright, seafoam-green eyes. "Why is she so valuable?"

Campbell sighed again, his face twisting. A part of him wanted to keep her a secret, to pretend that she was just a normal girl with a normal life — a victim of some perverted goods haul, and not the destined end of the world. Perhaps if Campbell ignored the truth, he wouldn't have to end her short, painful life before it had barely begun.

But as the loneliness — the immeasurable weight of truth — clawed into Campbell's brain, it constricted and curled down his tense shoulders, burying into his heavy heart. Its weight was crushing, and he wasn't strong enough to lift it by himself.

Sometimes, the truth was too heavy to carry alone. If Gainstorn had taught him anything, it was that.

Campbell spoke as if Mason himself lingered within the frosted, glistening walls... "She's the End of Everything."

Words ripped away. Retorts, jibes, commiserations... The man had nothing.

Sensing the man's doubt, Campbell nodded. "Her eyes sparkle like a jeweller's fucking display window. There's no doubt. You'd recognise her as soon as she looked at you."

The man's perfectly shaped eyebrows furrowed far down his face. "Wait, how old is she?"

Staring at his scuffed kneecaps, Campbell thought about that fateful New Year's Eve. Screams of dying Rebels punctured his memories. "She's nine years old," he whispered.

"Most *Aliras* are killed when they're infants," he said, and Campbell tried his best not to wince. "How the hell has she remained hidden — or *alive* — for *nine* years?"

"She's a Herder. They're constantly on the move — the ultimate Roamers.

Her parents too, they..." Campbell remembered her ghostly, vacant expression, and the blood soaking those delicate fingertips... "It's no secret that the End of Everything has diamond eyes. Her parents would have known who she is, and no doubt tried to keep her hidden. And a Herder Tribe that *wants* to stay off-the-grid? It'd be impossible to find them."

"But someone did," the man said. "Find them, I mean."

Defeat slithered out with Campbell's breath. "Yes. They did."

What horrors had that girl seen? What had happened to her parents, her Tribe? Perhaps it wasn't too late. Perhaps her parents were still alive, sharpening their spears and arrowheads, readying themselves to march into civilisation and pluck their beloved daughter out of danger.

Campbell almost hoped they were dead. At least then, there'd be no one to miss her once Campbell buried her shrouded corpse.

"How did you find her?" the man asked.

Campbell's lips curled upwards — an involuntary movement. Entirely unexpected. "Little wretch tried to pickpocket me."

Metal clanged. Boots pounded and echoed around the cells, thrusting Campbell and his cellmate to his feet.

"Good morning, sweethearts." The druggie who'd hit Campbell smiled with those hideously blackened teeth. No longer dressed in that Masonian coat, the man's belts of ammunition and knives clearly spoke of his gang affiliations. Still, Campbell couldn't hide a smirk at the bloodied band of material wrapped around his head. "Boy, she really took a chunk out of you, didn't she?"

The smile dropped heavily, stamped beneath muddied black boots. "That diamond-eyed bitch will get what's coming to her soon enough."

Fists clenched at Campbell's side, his knuckles whitening with the fiery, irrepressible urge to knock out what remained of his teeth. "*Where is she?*"

"That's nothing you need to know, Aristocrat."

He produced a jangling set of keys and hastily opened the cell. Campbell fought the urge to charge like a raging avalanche and burst inside every cell he could find. A familiar black revolver stopped him in his tracks, pointing between his eyes. Campbell knew with grim, agonising experience that—at that close range—that old revolver would blow his skull clean off.

Campbell could practically hear his father's grating laugh, as though it was *his* stained fingers that fondled the trigger.

The druggie waved the gun. "Come on, boys. The Mulch wants a word."

22

———————

Campbell had heard many things about the infamous *Mike the Mulch*. Evidently a tough son-of-a-bitch, as those born and raised in the Icelands often were, Mike the Mulch possessed a special, almost rare type of viciousness. Mix such a trait with a complete lack of empathy and a penchant for home-brewed chemicals, and you had a recipe for the notorious Drug Lord who plagued the New World's northern Territories. Occasionally, Masonians would overwhelm his control and cut away the disease from Mason's land.

But the gang grew back. Like a cancer.

A never-ending supply of chemical goods passed from one hand to another: a stolen Masonian shipment here, or a busted drug-den there... Drugs — the *true* currency of the New World — continuously shifted from Mason's control to Mike's. And whilst Mason always held the upper hand, Mike's reputation was undoubtedly warranted.

Crazy, most people called him. Campbell couldn't comment on that from rumour alone. Yet, bound at his wrists before the infamous leader of the Mulch Gang, Campbell instantly felt the pitiless, almost death-like chill seeping from his body, and couldn't help but consider such hearsay. Campbell stared at the scarred, horrific face of Mike the Mulch and felt his knees tremble.

A lit cigarette hung from Mike's mouth, glowing a bright, ominous orange with each inhale. "Evening, Aristocrat."

His low, gravelly voice instantly dominated the small room, flowing around the small table, the chair, and the open metal lockbox. Bags of white powder nestled within.

Free of alcohol's numbness, Campbell felt fear. Chilling, icy fear that froze his legs. But courage also prevailed. It warmed his chest, then his throat, and Campbell finally felt free and focussed enough to demand answers. Even from the crazed leader of the Mulch Gang.

"Where the *fuck* is she?"

Puffing up broad shoulders, Mike pinched the cigarette between his curving lips. "She's safe. Worth far too much to allow any harm to come to her."

Mike moved around the table, sucking on his cigarette. A long scar carved diagonally from temple to jaw, cutting through his once cerulean eye, now milky white, as it narrowed at Campbell. "But your concern for her welfare intrigues me, Mr Anders."

Campbell's breath stuttered. Mike noticed the bait had caught well and smiled. Stained teeth peeked from cracked lips.

"Oh yes, I know who you are: Campbell Anders, son of Maelstrom's most prolific Slave trader, now exiled from the Fjordlands. Founder of the Dagger Rebellion — and its only survivor."

Bound beside Campbell, the young man took a sharp inhale. "Jeez, you never told me that."

Mike flicked away the glowing remains of his cigarette. "As for you, Joe Matheson, I've yet to decide how much trouble you're really worth."

Joe Matheson choked on his own breath. "With my skill-set? I'm offended."

Campbell glared at Mike. "How do you know me?"

"Your reputation precedes you. A man of your age, accent, and clear... *calibre* had me suspect, but..."

Mike picked up a heavy leather belt from behind the table and slammed it down. Tangled up in the leather, a familiar sword gleamed beneath the bare lightbulb.

"Few steal Mason's personal possessions and live to tell the tale." Cracked lips curled. "A parting gift, perhaps? After he destroyed your rebellion?"

Campbell's tongue twitched and begged to scream. Mason's sword had nothing to do with the Rebellion — Campbell stabbed the immortal bastard over twelve years before Gainstorn ever happened!

Mike's smile grew. "Whatever the reason he let you live, I'm rather surprised you're now helping him."

"*Helping him*?" Campbell almost threw up again. "Why the hell would you say that?"

"The girl." Mike looked down his crooked nose. "You evidently want to protect her, keep her safe. Why else would she still be alive?"

Because Campbell was a drunken fool, and a coward, and no manner of badgering from Svenja Svellec's ghost would make his job easier.

Mike the Mulch smiled. "I must admit, it rather surprised me to hear she's still alive and kicking. I expected a vengeful man like yourself would have no qualms about shooting her between the eyes."

His choice of words was a complete coincidence — *they had to be* — yet they still hit painfully close to home. Gainstorn flashed behind Campbell's eyes: the rain, Mason's desperate pleas, her blue lips, the excruciating bang...

The visions grew, threatening Campbell's grip on reality. Air burst from his chest, panic threatened to take a hold and—

It's okay, I've got you...

Harrison's phantom hold slipped around his shoulders, supporting him until the worst had passed. Once the white dots stopped speckling his vision, Campbell puffed up his shoulders and snapped, "Perhaps I'm just uncomfortable with infanticide." And he was. The slime on his soul screamed it.

Mike hummed to himself and plucked a fresh cigarette from his inside pocket. Silence prevailed as he lit it between his teeth, his scarred face glowing orange. The room choked with tension.

"Regardless," he said, finally, on a smoky breath. "I'm sure you understand I cannot let such merchandise slide. She's incredibly valuable to the right buyer."

"She's a *child*!"

A hoarse laugh burst from Mike's lungs. "She's an instrument of destruction. Nothing more, nothing less." Another suck of smoke. "She's also a walking coin purse. Yes, I could kill her — or let *others* kill her," he added, staring pointedly at Campbell. "But then I'd lose the most lucrative sale of the decade. Why should I allow such a lovely, young opportunity to go to waste? Oh, and don't worry, I'll ensure her owner finishes her off once they're done with her."

Campbell's stomach lurched so hard he almost keeled over. "You're a sick fuck, you know that?"

Mike chuckled around his fag. "I'm not the one who stinks of their own piss. What happened? Survivor's guilt grating a little hard on you, Aristocrat?"

Campbell grit his teeth until his jaw ached.

"Whatever your reason for keeping her alive, I trust you understand that I can't just let the girl walk out of here. I can get a lot of money from a piece as lovely as she, whilst also denying Mason the pleasure of her company." He formed a grin that was as repulsive as it was arrogant. "It's a win-win situation, really."

"Not for her," Campbell said. "You're condemning her to torture and death."

Mike the Mulch glared. "Don't expect me to put the End of Everything's life above mine."

A snarky, evil little huff spat from Campbell's throat. "Oh, I wouldn't dare."

One lackey marched in with a piece of paper held like some precious jewel. "Ben, we have a bite on her."

Campbell's brow scrunched. *Ben? Who the hell is Ben?*

Mike the Mulch studied the parchment and his lips twisted around the cigarette. "Boys, take our good Mr Anders back to his cell." Cold eyes slid to a rigid Joe Matheson. "You and I need to have a chat about Masonian border controls..."

Hands gripped Campbell's arms. He fought against them, all the anger and frustration — not just at Mike the Mulch but at all those years of numbness — erupted from his muscles, his glare, his *throat.*

"You heartless bastard!"

Even as they dragged Campbell, yelling and cursing, from the room, Mike the Mulch didn't even flinch.

* * *

Campbell paced inside his cell. For a while, he did it to keep warm, until–

Until he realised that's exactly what his fifteen-year-old self had done. Probably the same time Mason cut out Harrison's eye.

Instead, Campbell elected to sit against the wall, his ankles crossed and both knees pressed tightly to his chest. Rocking back and forth, he contemplated the conversation he'd had with the most dangerous Drug Lord in the New World.

Bastard.

The more Campbell stewed, the angrier he became. How dare he? How fucking *dare* he?

Tension coiled down the back of his neck, so tight that no amount of shoulder rolling could loosen the dread. With a despairing sigh, he stared at the entrance to the cell. He had scoured every bar, every crack in the stone slabs, yet the place was impenetrable. The only thing to leave that cell was the odd rat, casually strolling between the bars.

Campbell never thought he'd envy a rat.

Doors slammed in the shadows. A figure strolled to the cell.

Campbell's ears perked up. Was it danger, or prey?

Definitely prey.

"You're a sight for sore eyes, mate." Joe Matheson produced a cocky grin. "You're pleased to see me, right?"

If Campbell were a rat, he wouldn't have to suffice such waffle. "The hell are you doing here?"

A dramatic swirl of his fingers and Joe seemed to pluck a ring of keys from thin air. "Thought you might need these," he said, unlocking the cell.

Campbell shot to his feet, aching to burst free. Joe hopped inside and locked them in before he had the chance. Honing his inner wolf, Campbell barely bit back a growl.

"Now, now," Joe said, grinning with blinding white teeth. "You and I need to have a chat."

"Don't be wasting my time now," Campbell said, calm as honey, bitter as lemon. "In case you haven't noticed, I'm running against the clock here."

Joe raised apologetic palms, the large ring of keys dangling from his fingers. "I know, but I'm here to help you. I swear it."

Campbell raised a doubtful eyebrow.

"Okay, look…" Joe sighed, tucking both thumbs in his belt loops. "I don't want that girl to be sold either – I mean, that's a hell of a way to go, innit?"

"You mean tortured, abused, and slaughtered like livestock?" Entire glaciers spat from Campbell's glare. "Yeah, as death sentences go, I suppose that's a real shit straw."

Joe awkwardly cleared his throat. "What I mean is that…" The weight of the world suddenly appeared on Joe's shoulders, ripping away the playfulness of his personality. "You want to keep her alive, don't you?"

"Yes," he said automatically, because he knew it was the right answer to give. And though his heart wanted to rejoice, his rational mind gave a defiant roar.

You must kill her. You must kill her.

Joe scowled. "Y'see, this is where I'm having trouble. A man in your dire position — err, no offence — would roll in a shitload of coin if you were to deliver her to Mason."

"What are you saying?"

With an impatient grunt, Joe glimpsed over his shoulder and took a brave step closer.

"I'd bet he'd pay a lot for her, and not just money, but social… *niceties*. Heck, he might allow you back into the Fjordlands if you— "

Campbell shoved Joe's shoulders so hard he slammed into the bars with a calamitous rattle. "You think I *want* to go back there? I want Maelstrom to burn in its own filth, for all those enslavers, paedophiles, and rapists to drown in their own shit!" Campbell edged closer to Joe, until he breathed stale breath upon his nose. "The Fjordlands are dead to me, and I'll be dead right alongside them should I *ever* deliver her to that *monster!*"

Campbell stormed to the other side of the cell, his chest furiously pulsing.

Slowly, with more care than when he'd first entered the cell, Joe edged forwards. "So, what are you planning to do, then? Wander the wilds with her?"

Campbell hadn't considered that. What would happen if he didn't kill her? If he just kept her… *safe*?

Given Campbell's track record of keeping people *safe*, he'd probably screw up and get her killed. Or raped. Or kidnapped and sold to Mason.

"I don't know what I'd do with her," Campbell admitted. "But like hell am I going to let Mason *or* Mike the Mulch hurt her."

"Delivering her to Mason would mean the end of her reincarnation. No more *Aliras*, no more *End of Everythings*."

Campbell barked out a laugh. Of course, this man thought the same as everyone else did: that Mason wanted to kill Alira to nullify the prophecy. Such an incorrect, prolific rumour had Mason written all over it. He'd probably planted those seeds in the New World's soil decades before Campbell was even born.

One had to admire Mason's ingenuity with such a blatant lie. What better way to convince the population to gift him the End of Everything? For they'd assume he was the only one who could stop her destiny. None would realise the folly in their actions, or that they'd just helped initiate the very prophecy they'd tried to stop.

Not that Campbell knew how or why Mason's child would be the doom of them all. Svenja had always avoided that topic.

Joe licked his lips. "You know what she is. Forgive me, but I don't understand why you *wouldn't* want Mason to neutralise the threat."

"Because I'm not a monster." He tried — oh, he tried — to believe those words. "But, now you mention it, what's stopping *you* from selling her to him? Just like me, you know who she is. The price on Alira's head must be rather appealing, your loyalty to the Mulch Gang notwithstanding."

"My loyalty to Mike the Mulch is entirely circumstantial," he snapped. "Besides, child trafficking isn't something I'd like to add to my resumé."

"And what about selling her to Mason?" Campbell asked pointedly.

Joe's grin showed far too many teeth. Gone was the cocky boy. This was something far more sinister. Calculating. "Selling her to Mason would be her death warrant, and I'm no child-killer."

Campbell suppressed his wince. It wasn't impossible that Joe knew about Gainstorn, but it was highly unlikely. Campbell must remember that, lest those painful ripples solidify.

"At any rate," Joe said. "You've no choice but to believe me."

"Oh?"

Joe wiggled the ring of clinking keys. "I'm the only one who can get you out of here."

Hope and excitement flashed inside Campbell, making his heart race. "Don't mess with me, kid."

"Oh, I wouldn't dare. I am, in fact, being entirely truthful."

"But why?" Campbell didn't understand this man — this cocky, infuriating teenager. Why would he risk his life for a disgraced Aristocratic drunkard, and a girl who would end the world?

"Perhaps I just like to keep my options open," Joe said. There it was again — that little twinkle of mischief, of scheming calculation.

Campbell had absolutely no doubt Joe was hiding his true motives, but the clock ticked loudly and a little girl's future wouldn't wait. Neither would her imminent sale. Regardless of Campbell's own reservations, he didn't have time to argue or beat the truth out of Joe Matheson.

"Fine, let me out of here, and I'll get the girl out, too."

Campbell didn't dwell on the named bullet inside his revolver. Maybe Joe would put a bullet through *his* skull if he discovered Campbell's true motives for getting her out of there. In all honestly, Campbell would welcome it.

Joe's grin reformed anew. He padded to the cell door, keys jangling away. "Oh, if you get caught, we never had this conversation, you hear me?"

"I nicked the keys from your pocket and got out of this cell alone, and with no help from you."

"Knew I could trust you." With a flourish of those rusty keys, Joe hopped to the bars. Doors opened with a loud, welcoming creak. "Well, after you, my good Sir."

Campbell sauntered out. "Oh, Joe?"

Joe turned with a soft, relaxed expression, and choked out a garbled scream as Campbell grabbed him by his scruffy collar and thrust him to the bars with a loud rattle. He growled in his face, "You even consider shipping her off to Mason, and you and I are going to have some serious trouble. Do you understand?"

Joe spluttered around the fist at his throat. "Yes, yes — I understand!"

Campbell released him but said nothing.

Rearranging his collar, as well as his dignity, Joe walked quickly on. "Jeez, you can take the man out of Maelstrom…"

"Oh, shut up," Campbell growled, close at his heels.

23

———

The Gang's hideout was just as Campbell expected it to be: dark, dank, and choked with a thick layer of smoke. Moonlight snaked along walls glimmering with frost, but the windows were nothing more than small slits, revealing a group of mountains that could have been anywhere in the Snowlands.

He'd sort out *that* problem later.

First, Campbell needed to find the girl and get her out before Mike the Mulch realised—

Voices up ahead.

Joe stumbled as Campbell grabbed his jacket and pulled him into the shadows on the wall. Ahead of them, in the adjoining corridor, Mike the Mulch's voice growled through the cold air, "I want her price in *coin*."

"Yes, boss."

"None of that stuff he paid with last time — cut with fucking baby powder."

Last time, he'd said. Campbell shuddered.

"What if he refuses to pay up at the exchange?"

Mike and one of his lackeys — the druggie the girl had chewed at — appeared in the corridor, directly below a flickering lightbulb. It framed the smoke lifting from between Mike's lips.

"Then use your imagination," Mike snarled. "I'll be back in the morning, Sigurd, and I expect to see a great big sack of gold on my desk."

Mike grabbed the cuff of Sigurd's mud-flaked jacket and dragged him close enough for his lit cigarette to singe his eyebrows. "Otherwise, I'll sell *you* instead, and I bet I can find many desperate Aristocrats who'd be willing to have a crack at you, mate."

Sigurd's throat bobbed. "I won't let you down, boss."

"Spectacular." Throwing Sigurd to the wall, Mike marched off. Sigurd straightened his jacket, smoothed his eyebrows, and disappeared into the shadows.

Mike's going somewhere. This was good. Very good. It would be easier to get the girl out when Mike's rancid breath wasn't breathing down his neck.

Joe clearly had the same idea. "He won't go too far," he whispered at Campbell's shoulder. "With cargo like—"

"She's not *cargo*."

"She is to him, mate," Joe said icily. "Ain't no denying that, and he'll do all he can to ensure this sale goes smoothly."

Campbell huffed profanity. How Mike the Mulch slept at night, he'd never know.

"At any rate, it won't help anyone if her eyes keep sparkling."

"Then what the hell do you suggest? Cutting her eyes out?" Campbell gave a look that suggested Joe would lose a lot more than an eye if he even tried.

"I know a guy. I mean, I've done business with him in the past — stuff to do with Mike. I can get something to hide her."

"What?"

Joe winked. "Meet me in Ursa's Leap in five days, and I'll show you myself."

Campbell didn't trust Joe — not on his life — but he'd just broken Campbell out of the cell. If there was even a *slight* chance Joe could get something to hide Alira's infamous eyes, then Campbell, in his continued pretence of being Alira's saviour, would be a fool not to take it. Campbell doubted Joe would sell him out — to Mike, at least. But to *Mason*?

Mason was another story. Would Joe fetch Masonians instead of help?

"If you sell me out, kid—"

Joe's eyes widened. "*Me*? Please, I'm insulted by such an accusation." But behind his genuine smile, something sinister peeked. Another plan, perhaps?

Regardless of Joe's hidden motives, there'd be no reason to meet Joe in five days. Not when the girl was already dead by Campbell's hand, and Campbell himself nestled deep in a tankard in some godforsaken corner of the map.

Campbell could already picture his future self: drooling over his last few coins, his soul twisted and defiled beyond recognition. How many tankards would it take to put Campbell into an early grave? He knew he'd soon find out.

The thought was... hollow and unwelcome. Not the thought of death, but the fleeting glimpse of another life. One where he *clanked* tankards, rather than drowned himself in them.

Campbell's performance grew harder by the minute: his offered hand felt like a dead weight. "Ursa's Leap. See you there."

They slapped sweaty palms.

"Good luck." Joe skulked away like a fox, leaving nothing but the memories of those bright green eyes.

Wiping clammy hands on his jeans, Campbell prowled down the corridor, pushed on by the howling wind. The light faded, swallowed up by the cold and the lingering aura of smoke. Darkness remained, clinging to his clogged pores.

Where the hell is she?

Sigurd appeared in a cloud of smoke from the spliff hanging from his mouth. He'd clearly gone for a hit before he checked on Mike's *merchandise*. As he followed Sigurd through the empty corridors, Campbell thanked whatever Gods were up there for such herbal hobbies. If Sigurd hadn't craved that spliff, Campbell wouldn't have a direct route to the girl. Small mercies, admittedly, but after a decade spent crouching in rotting depression, Campbell would take any help he could get.

Fate rarely helped Campbell. *Why now?*

Sigurd opened a creaky door with a wide grin. "You in here, sweetheart?"

The door closed slowly, obviously on some sort of mechanism to prevent it from slamming—a strange thing to see in a drug-den. Perhaps Mike's men had commandeered this place, whatever it was. An old Masonian fort, perhaps? But surely Masonians wouldn't care for a softly shutting door, either?

Whatever the reason for the odd contraption, Campbell took full advantage. He easily slipped into the cell before the door softly clicked shut.

Dark stone walls cushioned two cells, separated by bars, each with a bucket and a small wooden stool. Bare lightbulbs shone above the cells — one above each — and highlighted everything: the slender wisps of spiderweb, the glistening frost, the scraps of mouldy food and muddy threads of hay...

They also highlighted the small being, doused in those blue robes, hiding in the cell's corner. Knees to her chest, head to her knees, she'd wrapped herself into the smallest ball possible. Like she'd tried to disappear into the wall behind her.

Hidden in the shadows, Campbell observed the small creature, then the state of the cells, and the row of small metal loops in the ceiling above Sigurd.

Breath stuttered at the back of Campbell's throat. He thought that strange contraption to shut the door had been a little too... *Aristocratic* for a man like Mike the Mulch. But these cells and the goddamned *curtain-rail* before them left little doubt.

This wasn't a Masonian fort. It wasn't even a prison.

It was a viewing parlour.

Campbell's despicable father had run a similar place, down in the Fjordlands. Slaves, recently plucked from freedom, were kept in those cells, hungry and hopeless. As those red velvet curtains parted, revealing the room of Aristocrats keen for their new merchandise, there was nowhere to hide, and no hope left. The only alternative? Shipped down to the Fjordlands, to bulk up the Bolton Square Slave Auctions. Which option was better?

Such establishments were rare across the New World. They were deemed too insecure and far too remote. How dare high-ranking Aristocrats traipse miles across the mountains? Why view Slaves in the depths of a murky, damp fort in the middle of a mountain range, when they could view them in

Bolton Square instead, then return to their comfy drawing rooms and bottles of pink champagne?

The depravity of Aristocrats never ceased to amaze. Or disgust.

Campbell thought such places had been demolished — or at least, they had in the Fjordlands. But in the remotest regions of the New World, those seedy places became... forgotten. Abandoned. Perfect for illegal activities, and for selling human beings.

Yes, they were particularly useful for the purpose they were originally built for.

Campbell crept forwards. He melded into the shadows, his faded black leather jacket seeping into the crevasses like he and the stone structure had the same origins. He supposed, in a way, they did.

Sigurd moved further into the cell. "You're about to meet someone very special, sweetheart. I'm not to touch a pretty hair on your head—all for the promise of a good sale. Even if you did bite my ear off. Then again, I suppose what the buyer can't see won't hurt him now, will it? How shall you repay me, huh?"

The girl didn't even flinch. Sigurd cocked his head to one side and scratched beneath the bloodstained bandage.

"You don't understand a word I'm saying, do you?" He huffed to himself. "Shame, really. Half the fun is in the taunt."

He edged closer. Footsteps echoed around the parlour. Sigurd plucked a hunting knife from the holster on his thigh, the blade longer than his hand and shining with sinister clarity. "Come on now, sweetheart." Sigurd twirled the knife, the metal winking. "Let's see if I can unblock your ears..."

Campbell lunged. He landed on Sigurd's back and dug his elbow in his spine with sharp, relentless punches. Sigurd reared up with an unnatural screech and threw himself against the bars, trapping Campbell between them. Sigurd slammed back again and again, the bars rattling, until a pained shriek tore from Campbell's throat and his grip loosened.

Sigurd drove his elbow into Campbell's belly, knocking him off entirely. Campbell fell in a panting heap and found the winking blade inches from his lips.

"You'll drown in your own blood, Aristocrat!"

A shadow of wild hair and teeth leapt on Sigurd's shoulders with far more dexterity than Campbell. Sigurd lurched back, the knife flying from his hands and rattling against the bars. The girl clung to Sigurd like her life depended on it, those grubby fingers digging into the bloodied bandage around his head until his scream echoed against the stone. Anguish and hate laced Sigurd's throat, but not fear. A dangerous animal — a *predator* — fighting against the assault of prey as he tried to get the first bite.

Free of panic's choking hold, Campbell searched for the dropped knife, desperate to spot that winking blade. One corner, then the next, then—

There!

It rested just outside the bars, marred with pieces of black dust.

Campbell scrambled across the floor. Sigurd flung himself from one side to the next. Dust speckled the air, clinging to Campbell's throat until he coughed and spluttered.

The knife!

Sigurd stumbled and his foot slammed into Campbell's reaching fingers. Hot pain lurched up Campbell's hand, bones grinding beneath the solid tread of Sigurd's boots. Sigurd stumbled, then toppled. His foot twisted — a full agonising circle — atop Campbell's hand and his skin ripped open, dragged beneath the dirty rubber. Campbell choked on his own scream, his blood spreading in a thick pool of scarlet. Skin burned with the force of a million scalding pokers, his fingers unable to curl even if he'd wanted them to.

Sigurd fell to the hay-stained floor. He slammed hard enough for the girl's hold to loosen. Sigurd howled and finally shoved her off. The girl fell and cracked her head against the hard floor. She lay there, motionless.

"Girl?" Campbell had no control over his throat — *girl* or screams were all he could manage.

Cradling his bleeding hand, Campbell stared at the pliant, limp girl on the floor. A large sheen of crimson spread from her temple, trickling into her greasy hairline.

Dead?

Campbell should have been relieved. Motionless on the cold stone, blood cooling around her, the girl's life was now out of his hands. He didn't need to kill her, like the ghost inside his head begged him to. He didn't even need to save her. Fate had wiped Campbell's name from the signposts of destiny and maybe — *maybe* — Campbell could finally get out of there, alone, and have his fucking drink.

So why — *oh, why* — did he feel so—

He's killed her...

—empty and alone and so utterly distraught and—

He's fucking killed her!

Panic and pain morphed. A cauldron of hate boiled Campbell's heart, his agony disappearing beneath fresh, delicious adrenaline.

She's dead!

That realisation hit Campbell with as much power as a steam train. The smouldering fire in that train's belly ignited inside his own, and Campbell felt more than he had done in ten long years.

And, despite every action, every truth he had avoided, and succumbed to, he wished with the entirety of his mouldy, rotted soul that he could breathe some life back into that little, innocent girl.

Because she did not deserve to die.

Not by Sigurd's hand. Not by Campbell's.

That little girl — *surviving, coping, fighting* — deserved better than Sigurd, and Mike the Mulch, and Campbell. She deserved to live and laugh, not to lie on a freezing floor, so broken and scared and *dead*.

She deserved better than Gainstorn.

"You fucking *killed* her!"

Campbell leapt on a stunned Sigurd. One knee pressed against each jutting hipbone, Campbell clenched Sigurd's shirt with his injured hand and pummelled the fucker.

"You. Fucking. Killed. Her!"

Each word was a curse, spat from the depths of Campbell's being — the dark parts of himself that he'd allowed to grow and consume him, withering and decaying each atom, each poisoned sinew of his body until only a husk of the man Harrison had known — the man he'd called *brother* — remained. Anger and hatred poured through Campbell's knuckles and spread blood across Sigurd's breaking face, and through the shattered cartilage and torn skin, Campbell saw his own reflection gaping back at him.

Campbell roared — all the feeling he'd been denying himself for so long erupting as a keening wail. He needed to destroy the memories of himself, the part that had so willingly held a smoking barrel above a blood-stained crib. He destroyed the sorry excuse of a man who'd followed those perverse orders without fully considering the consequences, who'd helped paint the blood of his friends — *his family* — across the New World mountains, and who'd spent the better part of a decade hiding at the bottom of a tankard because of it.

As Sigurd's final breath stuttered between Campbell's knuckles, the Aristocrat who had considered murdering *another* innocent child lay pulverised beneath his hands.

Campbell's screams turned to cries, then to sobs, and when Sigurd's battered face held no more resemblance to his, imagined or otherwise, his strength finally ebbed. He collapsed beside Sigurd's bloody, unrecognisable corpse and sucked in stale, damp air in quick bursts. Lungs burned, as hot and bright as his muscles, and his hands ached with fresh pain, but Campbell's shoulders felt lighter, freer, than they had done in ten years.

Would it last? Campbell didn't care. He savoured that moment: the glorious sense of justice and deliverance.

But then he remembered.

"Girl!"

Campbell crawled on his knees and elbows, his hands far too mangled to be of any use, and perched beside the girl. He debated cradling her cheeks, to see if any warmth still lingered there, but he didn't want to mar her smooth, rosy skin.

Rosy?

Campbell frowned. He inspected her wound closely. A shallow gash at her temple released a surprising amount of blood, but the wound itself was superficial.

Hope tried to glow, but Campbell dared not acknowledge it. Not now, not when it had been so cruelly ripped away so many times before.

But he needed to see whether that hope could solidify, if it had any chance of gluing his heart back together, piece by shattered piece.

Campbell grabbed Sigurd's discarded hunting knife from outside the cell and wiped the dirtied blade on his sleeve, and held the pristine blade beneath the girl's nose. A few precious seconds felt like an eternity, but the blade clouded.

Campbell's breath escaped as he saw hers.

Alive! She's alive!

Campbell's lips curled into an unfamiliar shape. *Happiness*, Campbell realised. He'd forgotten how it felt.

Distant clanks and creaks rippled like the surface of a pond. The Mulch Gang weren't far. Or the girl's buyer, for that matter.

"Shit!" Campbell suppressed a wince as he touched the girl's shoulders. "Come on, *wake up!*"

She groaned softly, her face twisting, and Campbell's heart jumped with glee.

"Hey, girl," he whispered through a smile.

She tenderly felt the back of her head and grimaced around what was, undoubtedly, a very big bump. Diamonds sparkled as those enormous eyes peeked open. She blinked furiously, as if trying to remember what had happened. Though, given their current predicament, amnesia was probably a good thing.

Campbell eased her up until she sat cradling her sore head. Noise — slamming doors and barking commands — wiped the easy smile from Campbell's face, and he was suddenly very aware of the sweat beading his brow and the burning fog of pain rippling up both wrists.

"Here." He didn't question why he gave her Sigurd's hunting knife. Neither did she question the gift. She tucked the knife in Sigurd's leather knife holster, which she strapped around (and around) her small thigh while Campbell bandaged his battered hands with torn rags from Sigurd's shirt.

"Come on," Campbell said, and gestured her to follow. She did without question. Like a lamb to slaughter — if Campbell still held that butchering knife.

But he didn't hold it. He'd thrown it into the furthest, deepest ditch he could find.

Kill her! You must kill her!

"Fuck you, Svenja," Campbell hissed to himself. The voice immediately quietened.

24

———

They continued in silence, careful where to place their feet. The girl followed obediently in Campbell's shadow, pausing occasionally to lean against the wall and caress her head. A nasty bruise already shaded her temple.

Hopping from one empty room to another, Campbell dragged them away from searching eyes. From somewhere ahead, Mike's enraged shouts catapulted Campbell's heart up his throat.

"Find them!" That gravelly voice lingered long after its owner had disappeared.

Huddling in a tiny room choked with confiscated artefacts, Campbell watched the rush of bodies undulate down the corridor. They were lessening now, following the rumours they'd been seen on the other side of the complex. Joe's doing, Campbell surmised.

Hm, perhaps he is honourable.

Honourable or not, Campbell needed to rethink his plan to meet Joe. Campbell didn't know what he was going to do with the life now inexorably tied to his own, but her eyes were the first enormous bullseye they'd need to deal with. First hide her eyes, then hide *her*. It was simple, really.

If Joe claimed he could get something to conceal them, then maybe Campbell should go to—

A tug on the back of his jacket caught his attention. The girl stood behind him, smiling sheepishly. Her hands sparkled with metal and sapphires.

"Holy shit…"

His weapons: Mason's sword and his father's revolver. She'd remembered them? Campbell cast a fleeting glance around the room, at the layers of junk that stuffed every crack and crevice. How she found them amid all that crap was anyone's guess, but the true miracle was how Campbell could touch his father's old revolver without shivering.

Campbell nodded a sincere word of thanks and strapped the weapons around his hips.

They crept further through the bowels of Mike's lair.

A rush of frigid air tingled Campbell's chapped cheeks. He inhaled deeply, relishing the taste of air freed from weed and damp.

Must be this way. He grabbed the girl's hand and tugged her along. She didn't object or even flinch. She just trotted along behind him like a dutiful pet.

It was a harsh likeness to make, but Campbell had bigger things to worry about. As long as she remained glued to his heels, neither of them should care exactly what metaphor Campbell used.

Perhaps in a few days, I'll think of something nicer.

Days. Campbell fought down the choking rush of panic.

What the hell were they going to do? They had no money, no food, no shelter. At this rate, they wouldn't survive a day out in the wilderness, never mind several—

Voices skittered through the air.

They ducked into an opened store cupboard. The girl clamped both hands across her mouth, her eyes squeezed shut.

She looked so frightened and fragile. Like a moth. A gust of wind could blow her over, rip those silvery wings straight off and cast her helpless off a mountainside. To see her like that, so scared and… *alone.* Campbell's heart ached, the weight of her past and future flowing from her shoulders and onto his. Would he be strong enough to carry them both? To shield her from that gust of wind so she could fly free?

The voices quietened and moved further up the corridor. Campbell edged out of the cupboard. No movement, other than the fire's shadows.

Ahead, a wide-open door teased the expanse of virgin snow and a night's sky painted with teal light.

"Come on." He felt her at his tail as he rushed across the stone. One step, five — a few more paces and they'd be—

Footsteps pounded. Campbell turned. Too late.

A freight car full of lead slammed into his side — or at least that's what it felt like. Campbell grunted as he hit the floor with almost two-hundred-pounds of muscle pressing him down.

"Found you!"

Dizziness flooded Campbell's vision, the world spinning and convulsing before his eyes. Adrenaline, fear, pain — he felt it all. His hipbone, already bruised and bloodied from those damned weapons, almost cut straight through the skin as his holstered gun screamed for his touch.

The brute astride him clung to his jacket and hoisted him up. Rancid, hot breath beat down on Campbell's forehead. "Just where are you going with my property?"

Oh, fuck.

The buyer. A pot-marked face sneered with yellowed teeth, beneath a nose so full of blackheads, it almost matched the scruff of stubble on his chin. *Chins*, plural. The man was a tank sculpted from the icy wind itself — wretched bite and all.

This was the man Mike had lined up to buy the girl? If Campbell could move any part of his upper body, he would have shuddered at the thought.

"I'll deal with you first," he said, grey eyes sitting like two cold pebbles in his face. "Then, I'll take what's mine and leave you for the wolves. They'll rip the flesh clean off those brittle bones of yours."

Campbell bent his knee, readying himself. "Yours first, mate."

His knee hit home like a sledgehammer. The buyer's breath *oomph*ed out of him in a stale rush as his grip loosened. Campbell scooted back, just far enough out of reach to pluck his gun from its holster. He cocked the gun with a satisfying click and—

With a roar fit for legends, the brute threw himself over Campbell. The revolver ripped from Campbell's aching fingers, sticky from blood and lacking the strength Campbell could've *sworn* they'd once had. The gun clattered far out of Campbell's reach, tickling the boundary of snow that Campbell was so desperate to sink his painful limbs into.

"I'll cut you up myself, you Aristocratic maggot!"

Campbell tried to argue, to coax his Aristocratic tongue into some rather colourful insults of its own, but thick hands swiftly wrapped around his throat. The squeeze was instant, unyielding. His tongue felt like it was being pushed out of his mouth, those sausage-like fingers digging unmercifully into his skin. One more ounce of pressure and Campbell's larynx would surely crack like charred wood. Campbell struggled for air, his mouth open and his tongue hanging limp, but his lungs refused to work. His vision blurred as white spots began speckling.

A lithe lump of blue threw itself against the brute, whacking the shoulders that were almost as wide as the girl's height. Through Campbell's blurring vision, the girl pummelled his gigantic frame, much like Campbell had done to Sigurd, but the brute barely noticed the assault. To him, they were nothing but moth wings fluttering against the breeze.

But those sharp teeth bared into a snarl, and Campbell suddenly remembered that she wasn't a moth at all.

She was a wolf.

The man writhed; she clung on tightly. They remained locked in a violent dance – *a vicious waltz* – and Harrison's words fluttered across Campbell's memories...

If you decide to waltz with wolves, you're likely to be bitten.

The man howled a dangerous, entirely satisfying sound of pain as she dug her sharp, unassuming canines into the fleshy part of his shoulder. Blood spilled down her chin and oozed against his brown leather suspenders. He tried to shake her off, but she'd clamped on too tightly.

Those huge hands released Campbell, who gasped down all the air he could, his lungs on fire and his throat raw, like he'd swallowed sandpaper. Lines sharpened, his vision clearing to spot the brute's unfiltered rage.

With little more than a wave, the brute slapped the girl from his shoulder. She fell in a heap, another crimson cut adding to her collection.

"*Run...*" Campbell tried to speak, but the words refused to come. He groaned stupidly, fire ants rushing up his throat and eating any sound that tried to break free.

The brute wiped the gushing blood from his neck like it was nothing more than a mosquito bite. "Wait your turn, bitch."

The brute was back on Campbell with a flash of white stars, hands the size of small mountains crushing the life out of him one agonising breath at a time. That familiar fog of death penetrated Campbell's vision, and he knew with undeniable certainty that his end was near. Harrison breathed down his neck, holding his hand through the fresh rush of fear.

It'll be over soon, mate.

But Campbell didn't want it to be over. Crushed beyond rational thought, Campbell finally understood that his life did not end ten years ago. It had simply changed course. Gainstorn had sent him down a different path — one littered with torturous pain and guilt — but one also flooded with the brilliant light of *purpose*. Finally, after all those years, he had a true, *achievable* purpose.

And he needed that purpose far, *far* more than she needed him. He craved such a purpose — one not built on death and destruction, but of life and perseverance.

Of survival.

And now, just when he'd found it — found *her* — this despicable mother*fucker* was about to rip it all away. To crush whatever was left of Campbell's soul into a carpet of leaf litter, never to grow again, or even evolve into something different. It would remain forever mouldy, forever trapped in that damp, stinking pile of rotting goo — and Campbell didn't deserve that.

Once, maybe. But not now.

This was not a promise whispered with rage in his heart and desperation in his cries, but one born of tenderness. Of doing the *right* thing. Not made from the deaths of those he loved — slain by a hand that felt like his but looked like Mason's — but from a time he saved a bleeding Harrison from a tyrant's clutches, or unlocked the door of Caroline and Alice's cell, or ran back into a burning Masonian truck to save the last of thirty children.

His purpose hadn't always been to kill. Once, a long time ago, it had been to save, to *protect...*

That was the *true* purpose of the Dagger Rebellion. How could he ever forget?

All the times Campbell wished for death rushed down a raging waterfall, into a bottomless past that could never be changed. But in his pale future was a life Campbell craved. That he wanted to experience.

That he wanted to live for.

On your feet, Anders — Campbell's voice, not Harrison's. But the meaning had not changed.

With his last ounce of breath — of life and determination and the warm, sobering glow of *purpose* — Campbell thrust his sticky, bloody thumbs into the oozing wound on the brute's shoulder, and dug in.

Wet warmth trickled over his fingernails, then up to his knuckles. He dug deeper, stretching the skin, clawing at flesh, dragging a scream so inhuman from the brute's mouth that wolves' howls rejoiced across the mountains.

The brute lurched back. Glorious air stabbed Campbell's lungs, fresh blood rushed into his thumping head. Adrenaline curled his hand into a numb ball, and he struck. Teeth flew like flying brown pearls.

Campbell punched again and again.

The brute lost his balance. Campbell struck with his knee again — not to maim, but to startle. It worked: the brute almost toppled. Campbell didn't stop there: he stabbed his thumb into the brute's eye. He curled back like a screaming babe, his shoulders hunched. Campbell reached for the sword, eager for a curtain of steaming blood to decorate the brute's bulbous belly.

The brute swiped his foot beneath Campbell's. He hit the stone with a resounding slam, his injured hand caught beneath his hip and his weapon. Tears itched Campbell's eyes with the stinging pain, his entire body panting, sucking in that glorious air to numb his breaking body.

The brute stood to his full height — a towering giant of a man that could've walked straight out of a Herdinese legend. *Jötun,* Campbell realised. *Definitely a Jötun.*

He stalked closer, one of his huge sausage-like fingers pressed on his bleeding eye socket, the other already grasping for Campbell's throat. The man could and *would* kill him with one hand.

My revolver!

Campbell's fingers played with the empty holster. His heart sank, freezing to the floor beneath his shoes. He'd always known those fucking weapons were trying to kill him. Now, they might just succeed.

Campbell didn't like his chances, but he still stood before this *Jötun* of a man with his fists and head held high.

"After you, my good Sir," Campbell spat.

The words struck as the intended insult. The brute charged, his mouth twisted into a feral snarl and —

A calamitous bang shook the snow-slicked mountains.

Campbell stopped. The brute stopped. They just looked at each other, listening to the bang's echo.

The man's paling lips parted with a gurgle of blood. Grey eyes turned distant and rolled back inside his skull. He fell in a heap of muscle, bone, and a lone bullet, shot straight between his shoulder blades.

Sitting against the wall, clinging to it, a trembling girl held Campbell's smoking revolver with both hands.

Campbell stared mindlessly at the gun, remembering a similar scenario ten years ago. Only now, their positions had been reversed.

Campbell edged out of her line of sight. She didn't move. The gun remained high, aimed down the empty corridor. Vacant eyes caught the fire-light and resembled orange garnets, sparkling wildly with unshed tears.

Both palms raised in surrender, Campbell cautiously knelt at her side. "Hey," he whispered. She didn't appear to hear him.

Licking his lips, he wrapped his fingers around the warm barrel. The scent of gunpowder and gun oil assaulted his nose — a scent he'd nearly forgotten. It made him nauseous.

The girl startled and finally met his stare. She dropped the gun, like its very existence burned her. Campbell knew the feeling well. Campbell nestled his father's old revolver in his lap and tried not to dwell on the thematic ramifications of what she'd done for him.

That she had saved him.

She'd saved him from that brute of a man, and certain death. But Campbell couldn't shake the feeling that she had saved him in an entirely different way, too — one she could never know about. Campbell didn't like to delve too deeply, but he could have sworn his soul felt a little cleaner. Only a little. Like the plague of rot had winced at the sound of that bullet, shot by a little girl with diamond eyes.

"Thank you," Campbell said.

The girl looked at him. *Really* looked at him. Campbell met her stare for as long as he dared, given its fatal intensity, but just when he was about to break first, the girl lunged for him.

If he hadn't been nearly strangled to death — *twice* — less than ten minutes ago, Campbell would have been prepared for such an attack. As it happens, he was completely unprotected as the girl threw her arms around him, squeezing him like her very salvation nestled within the seams of Campbell's faded leather jacket.

And — again, he thought, because his brain still lacked oxygen — Campbell's arms curved around *her* slight frame, too. Her body trembled with suppressed cries, so he held her closer, harder. Warmth flooded his chest — and not just from the girl. As his soul healed, that field of rot still screamed for death, for murder, in a voice that very much sounded like Svenja Svellec's, but Campbell ignored it easily. Nothing mattered now, except for the little girl crying in his arms, wordlessly begging for comfort and safety. *For protection.*

And Lord above, Campbell wanted to protect her. With every fibre of his being.

25

———

They left Mike's hideout just as the sun bled young light across the world. The mountains rejoiced in a field of orange, the sky marred by fiery streaks. Birds sang and criss-crossed above, as Campbell and the girl trudged through the snow.

It took them the better part of the day to climb down the mountain, and a few hours more to reach the forest. Towering trees protected them from the scarlet sunset, and any wandering eyes, and Campbell breathed a sigh of relief. His feet ached — as did the rest of him — and the girl was undoubtedly suffering from her nasty bang on the head. She never complained, or tugged on his coat to ask him to slow down or take a break. To Campbell's knowledge, she hadn't even snuck off to relieve herself — a fact Campbell was suddenly very aware of. He rushed them to a nearby stream and offered it to her, hoping she'd use it to assuage her obvious dehydration.

The girl looked at Campbell, frowning. Campbell scooped up the cold, clear water in his bandaged palm and eagerly slurped. He gestured her to do the same. A sheepish smile tricked her delicate, bruised features, and she shook her head.

Huh. Maybe she wasn't dehydrated? Obviously nine-year-olds were capable of hydrating themselves.

"Suit yourself." Campbell drank anyway, shivering as cold drops traced his chest. His hands, shrouded in blood-soaked bandages, ached ferociously in the stream and he winced.

With a newfound bravery — *or was it trust?* — the girl took his hand and slowly unwrapped his makeshift bandages. Campbell tried to tug his hand away, but he couldn't. He'd frozen – a statue beneath her touch.

Campbell's mangled hand shone a deep, ruby red in the light from the setting sun. He swallowed at the angry, hot puffiness developing around the tears of flesh. God knows what had been stuck beneath Sigurd's boot.

The girl examined the wound. She appeared no stranger to blood or injuries — or the first raging signs of infection.

Campbell's frown grew as she scurried off, kicking over logs and crawling through idle shrubs and weeds. When she returned with her selection of plants, Campbell remembered a similar scenario, many years ago, when Caroline asked him to gather herbs to soothe Harrison's mutilated face. Emotion threatened to ball in his throat, the echoes so fresh — the déjà vu so strong — as the girl prepared the plants and rubbed the sweet-smelling goo into his hand. A hiss of pain erupted between his teeth. The girl looked up with placating eyes, an apology swirling within them.

As they continued their trek, Campbell flexed his hand. Sore, but no longer burning. Clearly, the girl knew her way around the wilderness.

Campbell shook his head incredulously. Obviously she did: she was a Herder, after all. Those nomadic, shy people fit on the New World like the leaves on their *Yggdrasil* World Tree.

The girl trotted ahead, skipping over rocks and swinging from overhanging branches. She watched the world around her with fitting a sense of childlike wonder, but Campbell knew this bewilderment went farther, deeper than her age. She was born from Mason's hold over the New World, so the New World flowed in her blood. It only made sense that she would exist in it with a similar sense of symbiosis.

Perhaps that was why this incarnation of Alira had survived so successfully as a Herder. The Herdinese Culture was the baking tin that held the End of Everything's batter, and the New World was the oven that caused it to swell, to rise into a fluffy cake.

Campbell's stomach grumbled.

Regardless of how well-suited this girl was to the New World, the truth of her destiny would always follow her, yapping at her heels like a hungry wolf pup. If Mason found her, it would be game over for them all. Mason would use her to kill everyone.

Campbell's heart crunched — not for the destruction of the New World, but what Mason would *do* to achieve it.

Caroline had once said the events of Gainstorn had been a mercy to Alira. That, if Mason had taken her away, he'd shroud her in a black veil of despair. Perhaps, if Mason found Alira early enough, if he had enough time to groom and seduce her, she wouldn't consider it rape. Perhaps Alira would fall willingly into Mason's arms, even if it meant the destruction of them all.

Perhaps held an awful weight.

It wasn't Campbell's job to consider what would happen if Mason found her, for his entire purpose in this bright new life was to ensure that Mason *didn't*.

Some poetic justice lay deep in the knowledge that Campbell would starve Mason of the mate he so desperately craved, and Campbell couldn't deny himself the thrill such knowledge brought. But that was only part of it.

Atonement felt right. He wanted to make amends for his past and build a future where he could be proud of his actions.

But it would take work and patience — from them both. She clearly knew more about Roaming than he did. She was a prowling wolf in the undergrowth. He was a fat tabby cat who'd spent too long lounging before a wood burner.

Yes, he had a lot to learn.

* * *

Ursa's Leap was a small, quaint little town. Tucked away at the base of a stark cliff face, the isolated town was Masonian-free and yet accessible, and popular, enough to sport a cosy inn, just by the protected remains of Ursa — the huge bear said to have taken a nosedive off the cliff.

No one knew why that massive bear fell. Some claimed the bear had fallen accidentally, either evading or hunting, or had unluckily stepped on a loose piece of rock. Others claimed the enormous bear was a biological mistake, and its unnatural size had driven it mad.

Personally, Campbell didn't give two shits why the bear had ended up at the base of that mountain, but its fate clearly entranced the girl. She stared at the monstrous skull with sadness and wonder in her eyes, as if trying to understand what drove the legendary Ursa to leap.

Campbell pulled her away from the rope barricades and ignored the small tear trickling down her cheek. She wiped it away quickly, as if hoping he hadn't noticed.

Leaving her in a secluded bush at the side of the inn, Campbell puffed up his shoulders and entered the stuffy, choked establishment with his head held high. Tables littered scuffed wooden floors, sticky with mead. Wolfhounds meandered the tables and cleaned up any spilled food from the floor, or even from the tables themselves, their long, grasping tongues far too fleeting for any drunk guest to notice.

Sweat beaded the back of Campbell's neck as he walked to the bar. "I need a room."

The innkeeper seemed a respectful gentleman with smooth skin and clothes unmarked by time or moths. "You got the coin?"

"Of course." A smiling Campbell dropped a fat purse on the counter. Dogs' tongues weren't the only things these drunk guests would miss looting their tables.

Less than five minutes later, Campbell dragged the girl through his room's open window. Campbell smiled at the way the girl's eyes widened, her attention scouring the room like she expected the very walls to twist and jump on her.

"Seen nothing like this before, huh?" Campbell muttered to himself. Of course, the girl remained silent, but the amazed *hmm* in her throat suggested she'd gotten the gist.

Campbell stared at the cosy fireplace, bordered with granite, and the four-posted bed layered with red velvet cushions and quilts. He'd decided to sleep on the floor that night anyway, but the girl's utter glee as she jumped on the bed told all that she'd already staked her claim.

"Glad you're comfy here, girl."

"*Maya.*"

Campbell startled. Limbs froze, solidified by the faint, croaky, and highly accented voice. He gazed with evident confusion at the girl sitting cross-legged on the bed. "What?"

A beautiful, glorious smile worked across the girl's mouth. It lifted everything in the room, Campbell especially.

She pointed to him. "*Campbell.*" She turned the finger to herself. "*Maya.*"

Her name. She'd told Campbell her name.

Names were important. Names held trust and friendship.

Did she consider him her friend?

Campbell swallowed thickly, his throat burning. He tested the name on his tongue. "*Maya.*"

It fit her perfectly. Sweet and delicate, but full of power.

Not Alira, he realised. *Alira* wasn't her name. *Alira* was the girl who haunted his dreams, who would destroy the world and everything in it.

Maya was just a lost little girl who'd been dealt a real shit hand in life. Maya had grown up on a mountain beneath the stars, who had somehow survived bears and bullets, and who'd sank into that cheap feather bed like it was the greatest thing in the world.

Campbell had killed *Alira,* but had saved *Maya.* Just like *Maya* had saved *him.*

"Maya," Campbell said again, and he smiled.

He offered his hand. She took it, though she clearly didn't know why. "Nice to meet you," he said.

Campbell Anders shook Maya's hand.

* * *

Campbell showed Maya the tub tucked behind the wooden screen, meanly filled but steaming, and left her to bathe. Downstairs at a corner table, away from prying eyes, Campbell sipped his tankard of tepid water. He could have stolen more money for mead, if he'd wanted to, but the thought of any alcohol had grown stale inside his mouth. No, water was best.

Hours passed. The inn emptied as the rabble dispersed, leaving the dogs and a few lone maids to clear up the mess. Campbell convinced the barmaid to leave him the scraps from forgotten plates, and he ate to settle the growling ache in his stomach. He flexed his injured hand as it gripped the gnawed leg of lamb, surprised by the lack of pain. The girl — *Maya* — clearly knew her stuff.

Clean and safe — for the first time in God-knows how long — Maya was tucked between layers of duck feathers and blankets, snoring her little head off. Campbell had placed some scraps of food on the bedside table and left her to dream. No doubt they'd get used to each other's company, but for now, he felt uncomfortable being in the same room as a sleeping child.

Instead, he watched the dogs downstairs and waited for Joe Matheson. He half expected the bastard wouldn't come, or he'd bring half the Snowland Masonians along with him. Campbell would deal with *that* problem later, but Joe had promised his aid and help was a fleeting concept in the New World, and not something to be ignored.

Still, something about Joe's blind offer of aid didn't sit well with Campbell. Defences were easily built and even harder to break, and Joe needed to give a damn good reason to cross into Campbell's heavily-guarded fort.

Nearing midnight, Campbell dozing in the corner, the door opened. A flurry of snow-licked air burst into the inn. Even the fire shivered.

Campbell startled and placed a cautious hand on his revolver.

"Ah, there you are, mate!" Joe Matheson's gleaming white teeth shone like pearly beacons. "I'm glad you made it here and aren't dead an' all."

Campbell's aching fingers tightened on his gun. "Are you alone?"

Joe's smile faltered. "Of course. Why wouldn't I be?"

Campbell's scowl told all.

"Oh…" Joe's bitter laugh disagreed with the smile on his face. "Give me a bit of credit, mate. I helped you get out of Mike's lair."

"You got me out of the cell, nothing more."

"I dragged Mike's forces to the other side of the fortress!"

"Not all of them. We had to contend with the girl's buyer, who had — in case you hadn't noticed — walked straight out of a Herdinese legend!"

Joe huffed and slouched in his chair. "Well, forgive my ignorance when it comes to the New World's paedophiles."

This was getting them nowhere. Campbell licked his chapped lips and whispered, "Give me one reason I can trust you."

Joe looked like he'd march off out of spite, but he finally wiped away his scowl and dived into his enormous rucksack. "Here."

He placed a black velvet case on the table. Nearly threw it, in fact, but swiftly decided against it — like he'd remembered the contents were extremely delicate.

Delicate, indeed. Campbell stared at the three pairs of coloured contact lenses: amber, blue, and green. "Where did you get these?"

Joe folded his arm defiantly. "I told you: I have *contacts.*"

Did Joe understand the value in those lenses? That each pair of coloured glass allowed them — allowed *Maya* — more freedom than Campbell could ever offer?

"Thank you," Campbell said sincerely.

Tension rolled down Joe's shoulders. "You're welcome." With a defeated sigh, he nodded to his rucksack. "I scrounged up some clothes for her, too. Even if you hide her eyes, those Herder robes are going to attract unwanted attention. Your clothes..." A snide smirk formed. "You'll manage."

"I..." There had to be a catch... "I can't pay you."

"Never expected you to, mate." Joe awkwardly fished around in his pocket. "That reminds me..."

The thrown object clanked loudly against the wood, the dimming firelight catching the mess of diamonds and sapphires, set in a gold bangle.

Campbell whistled between his teeth. The hefty weight alone screamed its value. "Your contact provided this as well?"

Joe laughed softly. "No. That one, I stole." *Course he did.* "But I figured your purse is a tad empty, and you'll need supplies to Roam. This'll help."

Campbell accepted the gifts, but his suspicion didn't ease. "There's a catch. There *has* to be. Why would you do this?"

Joe leant both elbows on the table. "Because I trade in information, as well as goods. And I reckon you have a buck-load of information."

The penny dropped with a loud bang. "The girl?"

Joe nodded. "Who is she to you, Campbell? Really?"

Surrounded by walls and wolfhounds, Campbell couldn't escape. He could lie easily, but there was no telling Joe would believe him. Intelligence screamed behind those pale green eyes, and Campbell knew the payment had to be juicy enough to keep them both alive, and far from Mike the Mulch.

And Mason.

Campbell imagined the snitching rumours gathering on Joe's tongue, begging to find Mason's ears. Joe would get an awful lot of coin for Alira's whereabouts – far more than Mike the Mulch could offer.

So, what could Campbell offer? What could Campbell possibly say to convince Joe to keep the girl far out of Mason's clutches?

The truth, he realised.

Campbell swiped some imaginary breadcrumbs from the table. "Let me tell you why Alira is the End of Everything, and *why* Mason is so desperate to find her."

Their conversation lasted long into the night. By the time Joe left, pale and trembly, Campbell's defensive walls had formed cracks. No doubt those cracks would widen, in time. Campbell wasn't entirely sure he wanted them to.

But if Joe Matheson continued to help them, he realised he might not have a choice.

26

Eagle's Overlook appeared far busier during the daytime. Campbell wondered when he'd last been awake (or *sober*) enough to appreciate the market's size and bustling atmosphere. A constant river of people meandered between the stalls, the relentless chatter from haggling goods stinging Campbell's senses. Crowds this large unnerved him. His shoulders hunched as he wandered through the mass of people, the noise rattling his eardrums. He suddenly realised why he never went outside during the daytime (or, again, *sober*).

It was worth it, of course. His head felt clearer than it had done in years. Even his blood felt a little thicker — like his entire body had become more solid, more real. He'd stopped being a figment of his own imagination.

Maya skipped ahead, the wondrous delights of this alien scene painting a glorious grin on her face. Her amber eyes scanned the hordes of goods, the dagger strapped over her denim jeans plainly visible should anyone decide to buy *her* instead. Her leather coat, so long it almost reached the frost-licked stone, swayed with each movement as she rushed on.

In their first short week together, Campbell had discovered many things about Maya. She was a keen learner, and a prolific hunter. The girl could catch rabbits with her bare hands — and eat them raw. She loved the aurora and would gaze at those flickering lights with tears in her eyes, and a delicate, almost hopeful smile on her face. What did those lights mean to her? Campbell would ask her, one day.

Sauntering a little way behind her, Campbell made it to the munitions stall. A familiar face sneered from behind the counter. "You again?" The vendor clicked his tongue. "Off with you — and your worthless relics."

Campbell, rather triumphantly, placed a fat handful of coin on the table. The vendor's lower jaw almost fell off.

A new hunting rifle tucked under his arm, Campbell continued to peruse the wares. He passed an antique book stall — a curious thing to see in the New World. The cold, damp climate made book hoarding an expensive occupation, not to mention that vast swathes of people were illiterate, especially that far north.

Perhaps it was that rarity that made Campbell look at the books on offer. So many of them: history and people and dreams condensed into withering piles of paper. It was an impossible reality, to know that many of the authors were already dead, and yet their souls lived on between the pages, tucked between leather and ink.

One book caught Campbell's attention. An incredibly old thing, its stained pages choked with damp and fraying around the edges. Flicking between the hard leather binding, Campbell marvelled at the illustrations: pencil drawings. A children's fantasy, by the barest glance.

"How much for this?" he asked

The vendor — an old woman — narrowed her eyes, almost as withered as the books she sold. "Three coins."

"Three? You sure?" Campbell was sure he'd misheard.

The woman nodded. "Aye. People rarely go for books as old as that these days. Pages are practically falling out of it."

Campbell couldn't argue there. The thing could've rolled straight out of the Old World. "Alright, done."

He found Maya leaning against the balcony, gazing at the caldera. The unblemished blue sky highlighted each little crack and crevice in the rocks far below. Distant glaciers glowed like shiny pearls, only the barest hint of turquoise hinting their inner secrets.

Maya pulled her gaze from the view when Campbell approached. In this light, the amber lenses set her eyes aflame.

Campbell offered her the rifle first. "For you," he said, urging her to take it. The rifle was almost as tall as she was, yet she cradled its lithe structure like she was born for it. Oh yes, a fine piece of hunting kit. She might even shoot them a deer for dinner with those keen eyes of hers — after a lesson or two, of course.

Campbell lowered himself to one knee, the antique book in his upturned palms. Maya's eyes flicked to him, then back to the book. Perhaps she didn't know what to do with it.

She gasped as Campbell showed her the illustrations, her fingertip delicately tracing the faded lines. Oh yes, those she knew. Her smile widened, and Campbell almost smelt her singed hair as she focussed on those printed sketches like a bolt of lightning.

Campbell was determined she'd read it one day. That was why he'd bought the book in the first place: to teach her English, to help her read and write. Perhaps, one day, she'd write her own story between the pages of some long-forgotten book. Perhaps, long after they were both dead, Mason would read it and know that it was *he*, Campbell Anders, who had protected her for all those years.

But, more than anything, he wanted to *talk* to her. She needed to understand *what* he had to say.

Truth was a fickle thing, so easily moulded. Truth depended on the situation. It could be twisted, only slightly, to preserve another truth.

Joe Matheson needed to hear the truth of Alira's destiny to ensure his loyalty, to be absolutely certain he wouldn't knock on Mason's front door.

But Maya? *Maya* wasn't Alira. *Maya* needed another version of Alira's truth. *Maya* needed the fear to take root inside her bones until she viewed Mason as the *enemy*, and not her soulmate. Mason's absurd rumour about killing her — about stopping the End of Everything — could be used against him. Not to drag her name to his door with the promise of riches and the lie of a nullified prophecy, but to keep her far, *far* away.

After all, why would she willingly knock on the door of her supposed murderer?

Campbell smiled, utterly assured, and looked at the ancient book in his hands.

Alice's Adventures in Wonderland, by *Lewis Caroll*.

Fitting, it seemed, for the New World was Maya's wonderland. Who knew what secrets it would hold for her? For them both?

Campbell gazed across the caldera, the sun's warm breath upon his cheeks, and smiled.

I'll keep her safe, Harrison, he thought. *I promise.*

The End

BONUS

WATERMAN'S QUARRY

YEAR 183

P anic never solved anything. Campbell knew that.

But General Alden's knife was pressed to Maya's throat, and panic clawed into Campbell's bones.

Sweat slicked his palms. The burning village seared his skin as the sounds of death roared: the jeering Masonians; the moans of dying citizens; the creaks and cracks of smouldering houses...

Fear scratched up Campbell's throat and begged him to scream with all the fury of a father desperate to save his daughter. Campbell swallowed the urge with a shiver. "Let her go, Alden."

Alden smiled, hideous and wretched: the smile of a man who'd already claimed victory. "Oh, I don't think so. She either comes with us, or I leave her body for the crows. Your choice."

Panic bloated Campbell's lungs, already choked with salty smoke and heat. Maya's throat, reddened from the blade, bobbed gently as she tried to stay calm. Her dying breath skirted reality, and Campbell's urge to scream rushed anew. This time, he couldn't stop it. "Please, she's innocent in all of this!"

Alden's smile widened. "Not for me to decide. I guess time will just have to tell."

Time. Campbell thought they had time. They'd survived for eleven years with nothing but time, basking in each other's company. How had it all gone so terribly wrong?

Alden raised his elbow. Maya's life hung at the precipice as a new dress, made of blood, begged to soak her mud-stained clothes.

Campbell couldn't lose her. Not now, not because of *him*.

He couldn't lose his family again.

"Wait!" The sword spilled through his fingers, like smoke. "I surrender!"

* * *

CAMPBELL HAD NEVER THOUGHT of himself as a *kind* man. Harrison had always taken that label and wore it loudly enough for the both of them.

Instead, Campbell was the rational one. He was the one who considered options, the weight of his wants and desires battling with the combined weight of knowledge, power, and truth. It had always been like that: Campbell's feelings entwining so tumultuously with his rational thoughts.

Gainstorn occurred because Campbell knew the consequences for them all, should Mason have left with that baby.

And now, soaked by the relentless rain in the Masonian Barracks, Campbell knew that he would do anything — *anything at all* — to keep Maya from falling into Mason's clutches.

Slavery was the only sure way she'd leave that place. A hard fact, but one Campbell clung onto.

Maya's tears merged with the rain. "But he'll kill you," she said.

Campbell did not want to see her cry, even if the rain hid her tears. "I know he will, but I signed my death warrant to Mason a long time ago. You, on the other hand, did not, and I will die with a smile upon my face knowing that you're somewhere far away from him."

"But I won't leave you here to be butchered!"

And I won't leave you here with Mason, Campbell wanted to say, but he held his tongue. Masonian ears were tricky, sly things, and even innocuous comments wriggled to their master.

But God, he wished he could tell her. He wanted to scream his apology to her, to the mountains, the stars — even to the Old Gods themselves. Campbell wasn't a fool, he knew the life he was subjecting her to, but Maya was strong, so much stronger than he was. She'd survived this far. She — his reckless, headstrong, resourceful girl — would survive this.

His heart ached. So fucking much.

Campbell wished he could wrap his arms around her and explain it all. Eleven years of lies swelled between them, and yet he still couldn't explain his actions. He couldn't tell the person he cared for the most that this ridiculous deal was, in fact, the kindest thing he'd ever done.

As the Masonians dragged them apart, the seams stitching Campbell's soul started to unravel, one loop at a time. His legs begged to crumble as they threw Maya back on the train, and his chest ripped open as her screams of anguish echoed inside her metal prison.

Campbell used the rain to wipe away his tears.

General Alden led him further into the Barracks, towards his ultimate fate. Maya's screams stayed with him: a new stain upon his soul.

* * *

CAMPBELL HAD NEVER BEEN afraid of death. The thought of an eternity in darkness had never unsettled him, as it had done to so many others. Instead, Campbell was afraid of what he'd *miss*. Of those he'd leave behind, of the tears shed in his memory — should anyone be alive to shed them. He was afraid of the experiences stolen from him, of the marvellous sights, smells, and tastes denied because he'd been ripped from the world and thrust to an ethereal plain he doubted even existed. All the emotions people felt when they expected to ascend to heaven — joy, hope, serenity — none of it mattered to Campbell, because what was the point? It didn't matter if Campbell danced with flames in hell, or drank mead with his lost family in heaven, because the end result was still unchanged: he was gone. Whose shoulder would Maya cry on if not Campbell's?

Such thoughts sent waves of profound loss through Campbell, though he daren't show it. Standing in a large interrogation chamber, his hands shackled and the glaring spotlights biting at his retina, Campbell chewed his tongue with the rippling dread. Maya was likely on her way to Maelstrom by now, readying herself for her abysmal future. Did she blame Campbell?

Did she *hate* him?

Campbell didn't fear death, but *that* scared him shitless.

Fear morphed into anger as pounding footsteps — *terribly familiar* — echoed down the corridor. Oh, how Campbell *longed* to scrape those footsteps from the New World, to bury their owner in a chasm of ice so deep, so dark, no one would *ever* remember his name...

Such hopes were folly. Of course they would remember. They always did.

"Campbell Anders." Mason's smile was wide and cruel, and boasted far too many teeth. "I wondered when we'd cross paths again."

Mason's face had filled out since they'd last met. Campbell dared not think too deeply, or at all, of the last time he'd been that close to the Destroyer of the Old World, for Harrison's torturous screams would follow close behind. Yet, Campbell recalled how gaunt and grey Mason had appeared back then, like his essence had been eaten away.

The man prowling before him was no longer a ghost recovering from Gainstorn's torture; he was a well-built, muscular machine. Power seeped from beneath Mason's uniform, not unlike the shimmering veil that had always poured from Svenja Svellec. And, just like Svenja Svellec, and like many predators, Mason had an alluring quality. He was a monster, using a pretty magnet of charm and seduction to help him capture his prey.

Maya's screams sprinted to Campbell's thoughts, and the fear returned unbridled. Any reservations he had about enslaving her were stomped beneath Mason's polished black boots.

Campbell snarled, his hands trembling with suppressed rage. "You fucking bastard..."

Mason mocked his hurt. "Oh, Campbell... Surely we're past such banal insults?"

Hands clasped behind his back, Mason edged forwards. Slightly taller than Campbell, he effortlessly looked down his nose as he studied Campbell's scarred, dirty features. "Time has not treated you kindly, has it?"

"I'm afraid Roamers don't have the luxury of immortality."

Mason cracked a smirk. "Quite." He turned his back, mildly avoiding knocking Campbell's thigh with his sword. Campbell stared longingly at the polished blade, and wished he could thrust it deep into Mason's heart. Again.

"Why am I here, Mason? I've done all you've asked. I've not stepped foot inside the Fjordlands since..." He couldn't say it.

Mason's smile grew. "Since I tortured and killed Harrison Dagger?"

Breath scraped Campbell's throat like sandpaper. "Why am I here?"

"Because rebellion has once again raised its wretched head in my world." Shadows dropped the smile from Mason's lips. "And I remember who stood at the top of the last rebellion I crushed."

"You believe I'm involved in this?"

Mason raised his eyebrows. "The great *Campbell Anders*? I'd be shocked if you weren't. Aren't discord and disorder your specialties?"

"The Dagger Rebellion was a long time ago. My priorities have changed since then."

"You mean, the *girl?*" Mason's eyes sparkled beneath the clinical light. "She's rather pretty, or so I'm told. I didn't know you liked them as young as I do."

Mason's smile, so similar to the one he'd boasted when he snapped Caroline's neck, crawled over Campbell's skin.

"If you dare touch her —"

"Oh, she's far beyond my reach now," Mason said, and Campbell forced his knees to stay painfully locked as soothing relief shot through them. "It was a clever move, offering her to Slavery. Did you suddenly remember the old Aristocratic etiquette of respecting each other's property?"

Actually, the Aristocratic *anything* had always passed Campbell by. His only wish had been to get Maya as far away as possible. That Mason respected some inhumane, diabolical *etiquette* between Slave Owners was an added bonus.

Mason huffed out an amused — and entirely annoyed — breath and paced the room in slow circles. "Regardless of her fate, I did not do so out of the kindest of my heart—"

"Because you don't have one," Campbell spat.

Mason's tone hardened. "Then you, of all people, should know better than to piss me off."

Maya's fate dangled on frayed thread. It had been less than an hour since she'd left. Had she even been sold yet? Campbell doubted Mason's *etiquette* extended to unowned Slaves.

Tiredness gripped Campbell's muscles. He wished to lie down and decay into a pile of mulch, or be ripped apart by wolves. Anything to get out of this conversation — because Mason was right: a deal was a deal. For Maya's sake, he needed to play fair.

Campbell licked his lips. "Mikael Ashworth. He's this new rebellion's leader, right?"

Mason glared with glistening, icy daggers. "An old friend of the Dagger Family, I take it?"

"I don't know him." Campbell couldn't discern the emotion that peeked through Mason's eyes. Disappointment, or distrust? "I knew his parents," Campbell elaborated. "Not well, but I knew them."

"But not Mikael Ashworth?"

"I don't get on with children." *Except Maya* — but *boy*, did she test him. "He was only four days old when his mother fled. I never saw them again."

"And his father?"

"Killed the day you created South Seal Glacier."

Campbell tried to keep his face neutral, to stop the flood of hate and despair that *begged* to punch Mason's smirking face.

"Beautiful glacier, isn't it?" That didn't deserve a response. "So, what you really have to offer me is an enormous load of *shit* — is that right?"

"*You* kidnapped us, and brought me here based on an *assumption*. Don't you *dare* expect me to be sorry for delivering information that doesn't meet your standards."

Mason laughed: a hearty, bone-chilling guffaw. "Oh, I see that Anders' spunk has finally returned! I thought Harrison's screams had indefinitely sucked it out of you." Mason sneered. "You did beg for his life so sweetly."

Shut up! Campbell wanted to scream at him — or hit him or hurt him or *kill* him! — but he resisted. Rising to the bait would only drive the hook deeper.

Mason edged closer, his lip curling. "Do you dream of my rotting corpse, Campbell?" His smile dissolved. "Because I wish for yours. Every *fucking* day..."

"You had your chance twenty years ago, *mate*." Campbell relished the fleeting shock on Mason's face. "*You* were the one who cast me into my own hell by living — by *remembering*."

"Evidently your *hell* was far too fleeting. The girl you're so desperate to protect merely proves that."

"Is that what this is? Another attempt to make me suffer? An excuse to bring me in, so I can finally draw my last breath beneath your sword?"

Mason *pffted* through gritted teeth. "Hardly. No, I require information and you — rather coincidentally — seemed the most likely person to possess it. That I can finally, *finally* disembowel you afterwards is what I like to call, an *additional benefit*."

Campbell inflated his chest. Death had welcomed him once before. It would do so again. "Then you better get slicing."

Mason huffed out a laugh and sauntered to the far wall, admiring the silver scars on his knuckles. Funny, Campbell didn't think Mason *could* scar...

"Where is Svenja Svellec, Campbell?"

Svenja Svellec. That was a name Campbell hadn't heard in a while. "No idea."

"Are quite certain of that?" Mason narrowed his eyes. "I recall she was always whispering in your ear."

"Yes, well, Gainstorn ruined that friendship pretty quickly."

"Gainstorn ruined *all* your friendships."

Campbell's fists clenched, blood pumping in fiery streams through his bruised, bound wrists. "A consequence of your mate's brains splattering up my arm."

Mason's fist shot like a bolt of lightning.

Pain exploded across Campbell's left cheek. His head snapped to the side, his neck and shoulders barking in protest, and his knees finally gave out. They slammed to the floor, sending rough shocks of pain up Campbell's entire body. Campbell admired how the white marble floor gloriously contrasted the long string of red swaying from his split lip.

Mason's chest pulsed furiously, his teeth bared in a ferocious snarl. "You dare speak of my mate again, and you'll lose far more than a tongue."

Campbell deserved that punch, and the threat that came with it. The memory of his cruel words left a bitter, acidic aftertaste, along with the heady tang of copper. Campbell's memories of Gainstorn were tarnished with horror, and he'd never expect, nor accept forgiveness — not from anyone. Not Mason, and especially not Maya. Nevertheless, words held power, and he'd wanted to give Mason a blow he'd be unable to heal from.

Campbell spat out a mouthful of blood, wincing as his back-left molar flew out with it.

"I don't know where Svenja Svellec is," he said roughly around his aching jaw and swelling lip. "She was smart and disappeared immediately after Gainstorn. No one knew where, and like hell was she going to tell us with you on our tail."

Mason hummed bitterly. "You're a seemingly endless barrel of information."

"Lose the sarcasm." With twisting grimace and a rush of nausea, Campbell heaved himself up. "I told you: we have nothing to do with this new rebellion."

Campbell noticed the swirl of amusement in Mason's eyes. Indeed, if Mason truly expected Campbell to hold anything of value, he would promptly send him to the next torture chamber. That Campbell was still standing and still (relatively) unharmed suggested another reason entirely for his visit.

"But you know that, don't you?" Campbell said. Mason lifted his nose, his eyes ever so slightly narrowed as a smug smile tried to form. "You know I'm innocent — that I have nothing to do with any of this. You just wanted an excuse to drag me here, to — what? Kill me? Delayed revenge — is that what this is all about?"

Mason contemplated for a moment. "Not entirely. Yes, I was curious to see just how much you know, and your death will please me greatly — I'm a man of simple pleasures, after all." Mason stepped closer, until his hot, whiskey-infused breath singed Campbell's nose. "But, more than anything, I want to see the look on your face when you realise you've failed." A blinding grin tricked anyone into thinking Mason was handsome. "I've found her."

Her. There was only one *her* Mason could possibly be referring to.

"*Alira...*" Campbell whispered.

She's not Maya. She's not Maya...

Mason had found *Alira*. He hadn't found *Maya*.

The bastard obviously assumed Campbell's agitation was from the knowledge he'd just shared; and not about how the *real* End of Everything was on her way to the Bolton Square Slave Auctions.

"Alira is a stunning young woman, and ever so eager to complete her destiny. Once she Comes of Age, I'll be *more* than happy to oblige her with that."

Mason's wink landed in Campbell's stomach and he almost threw up. God save that stupid woman's soul when the truth of her deception inevitably shone.

"So, you see, Gainstorn did nothing. It added, what? Twenty years to my search?" Mason's throaty laugh rattled the bloody gap in Campbell's gum. "Before Gainstorn, I'd already waited over a hundred-and-fifty years. Twenty is *nothing*."

Campbell knew where Mason's spiel was heading. He tried to prepare himself for the inevitable blow, but truth always had a knack of hitting Campbell where it most hurt.

"Harrison Dagger died—rather needlessly, I might add — for *twenty* years?" He tutted to himself. "If I'd known *that* was all Gainstorn was going to add, I wouldn't have bothered to torture him in the first place."

Mason noticed Campbell's fists, clenched into two white balls, and he grinned. "Who knows? Perhaps, to show I possess no ill-feelings towards the unfortunate Mr Dagger, I shall name my Firstborn *Harrison*?"

Campbell cracked. He shot forward, teeth bared and ready to snap and snarl and *bite* — just like Maya. Bound fists raised and readied to smash, but two Masonians grabbed him. Wooden batons — hard as lead — swung at his abdomen. His stomach crumpled with the force, but Campbell's anger was too bright, too blinding for him to stay down for long. The Masonians dragged him, kicking and screaming, towards the door — to the last cell he would ever set foot in.

"*I'll kill you, Mason!*" he screeched. "*I'm going to fucking kill you!*"

Behind him, watching his efforts, Mason laughed.

* * *

WEEKS WENT BY. Campbell could tell by the change in light coming in through the window — no wider than a finger — that allowed a solitary slither of sunlight. A part of him resented the fact that he counted the days, for only then did he know how long Maya had been enslaved, but he was desperate to keep track of them. He needed to know how long he remained in that cell, because each day *there* meant that Maya was still hidden. Campbell had absolutely no doubt that Mason would spit Maya's *true* identity in his face, should he ever discover it.

So, Campbell counted those hours with a hopeless pain lodged deep inside his heart. He'd never felt so useless, so helpless. He'd already looked for cracks in the walls, or nicks in the cell's locks, but it was fruitless. They'd taken his shoelaces, and they'd even checked his pockets to make sure he didn't have a spare. Campbell blinked back tears and tried not to think of the last time he visited those cells.

When pounding footsteps thundered through the walls, Campbell had been imprisoned for twenty-six days.

An excruciatingly long time.

And far too short.

Campbell didn't bother getting up when Mason prowled before the bars, but it did shock him to see Mason dressed in a tuxedo. The black tails of his bowtie spread over his collarbones, bordering the opened collar of his white shirt. He'd clearly been partying — and drinking, if the strong waft was anything to go by.

For the first time in eleven years, Campbell craved hard liquor.

Mason leant on the wall opposite Campbell's cell, his arms and ankles crossed, and looked ever so pleased with himself. "You look like you've seen better days."

Sprawled on the floor and nestled between fat rat droppings, Campbell didn't give a flying fuck about his appearance. "What do you want?"

"Only to say that your little *Wild One* is rather captivating."

Campbell's heart stuttered, even as he schooled a calm, confused expression. Mason, clearly tipsy, bought it far too easily.

"That's what my Masonians call her: *Wild One*." Mason shrugged a lazy shoulder. "I didn't really see why — she's hardly the first unwilling Slave to cause a scene in Bolton Square."

Atta girl, Maya... Campbell would have to ask Maya how many noses she broke when he'd *inevitably* see her again.

Mason's stare turned contemplative. "Then, to my utmost surprise, I found her trying to make a run for it."

Campbell's heart skipped a beat — or maybe it raced like thunderous hooves. He met Mason's infamous stare and the evil, calculating satisfaction that swirled within.

"I'll admit, she's a brave young woman. She barely flinched when she realised the Theatre wasn't empty — or whom, exactly, she had stumbled across." Mason clicked his tongue at the dusty air. "Brave, but foolish. To think she would have escaped at all..." He shook his head, that calculating smirk growing. "Such impulsiveness could get a Slave killed."

Campbell's blood pretended to be molasses, trying to drag him down as he stumbled to his feet. Mason followed his sluggish movements with glowing eyes. "Fortunately, I can think of many, *many* ways I'd rather use that impulsiveness of hers." His grin slithered down Campbell's spine. "Did I already mention that she's a very attractive young woman?"

Campbell outstretched a placating hand, the *begs* aching in his throat. "She's of no consequence, she's —"

Mason swatted away his pleas like buzzing flies. "Save it. If she were of no consequence, we wouldn't be having this conversation. Which begs the question, what is she to *you*? Not a lover, I don't think. The bond between you is not romantic love, but more... *familial?*" Mason cocked his head, studying. "Such as the love between a father and his daughter. Tell me, Campbell — am I close?"

Campbell prayed to Maya's Old Gods and tried, *begged*, his treacherous body to remain numb. For his knees to stop trembling, for his fists to stop clenching... But, after everything, how could he stop the tears flooding his eyes?

Mason's grin widened. Impossibly so. "How very interesting."

Mason pushed himself from the wall and sauntered closer to Campbell's cell. If he was anyone else, Campbell would thrust his hands through the bars and strangle the fucker. But Mason would just smile at his poor efforts, swat away his hands, and pat away the creases in his suit. Campbell's fleeting moment of satisfaction would not be worth the taunts.

"You are to be executed in Bolton Square tomorrow," Mason said. "Hanged from the neck until dead."

Campbell huffed out a laugh, despite it all. "The noose? Seems rather... *off-hand*, for you."

"As I last said you to: Gainstorn isn't really worth the effort anymore." Mason smile dropped with his arms. "I'm washing my hands of you."

There was a day Campbell would rejoice for the noose. Truth be told, it wasn't a bad way to go, considering Mason's bloodthirsty proclivities. Perhaps Campbell should succumb to his fate. Maybe he should finally put down his weapons and be gone from that fucking world for good.

"Oh," Mason said, on his way out. "I'll be sure to keep an eye on your little *Wild One* in your absence. Perhaps Emilia will even succeed in transforming her into a decent Slave."

As Mason's pounding footsteps merged with the distant screams, Campbell pushed aside thoughts of the gallows and focussed on the snippets of information Mason had told him.

Emilia Eynesbury has Maya. Did she buy her at the Bolton Square Slave Auctions? Whatever for? A sophisticated woman such as Ms Eynesbury didn't seem the type to buy *Wild Ones*.

Regardless, that Maya was *still* Maya and not *Alira* filled Campbell's shrinking, shrivelling heart with glee. A laugh broke free — then another, and another — and before Campbell could pull himself together, his bony, narrow chest was being whacked by waves of ridiculous laughter. He keeled over, unsure if the tears running down his cheeks were from despair or madness, and curled himself into the tightest ball possible.

There, he remained, bathing in a sliver of moonlight — the last he'd ever see.

* * *

Bolton Square. Campbell hated the place. Well, actually, he despised all of Maelstrom, but Bolton Square held its head high as the epicentre of Maelstrom's greed and cruelty.

It had changed little over the course of his exile. Only a few new shops in the area seemed unfamiliar to him — including the gargantuan department store, *Harrisons*. Campbell was certain they'd moved premises sometime over the past thirty years, no doubt to profit from the bustling city centre, but he couldn't recall if the place had *always* been called *Harrisons*, or if that was also a new addition. The store had been in the Addington Family for years, so surely it had always been called that? Campbell couldn't imagine a new store willingly having any connotation, intentional or otherwise, with the infamous leader of the Dagger Rebellion.

Yes, the name must have been a complete coincidence, but one Campbell couldn't stop staring at. It filled him with calm, he supposed, to have a reminder of his dear friend blinking at him in polished, gold letters. A final reminder that Campbell wasn't alone, even in his final moments.

Masonians hurled him to the gallows. Wood creaked and groaned beneath his boots as Campbell stared at the crowd.

Campbell seemed so high up. He enjoyed looking down on them and he even spat on some Aristocrat's top-hat. Campbell grinned, madly, despite the scolding *whack* of a nearby baton.

People jeered for death — *his*, especially. Was Mason in the crowd? Probably. Campbell refused to indulge the bastard and made a point not to look at the crowd again.

Instead, he gazed at the sky. Bleak and grey, as most Fjordland skies were. To most, those damp, dirty skies would be miserable. Not to Campbell. To him, they felt like freedom. They felt like the promise of something *more*. Something above the clouds, dancing with those colourful lights and hiding the stars from the debauchery that lay below. Those clouds were a protective blanket over the heavens.

Campbell closed his eyes as the first cool raindrops fell. They trickled down his temple and over his jutting throat. Water, fresh and freeing, sank into his pores and buried in his skin. He could still feel those merciful droplets as the black hood was thrown over his head. As the stench of sweat and stale breath rolled through him, Campbell imagined the world beyond those fluffy silver clouds, and he smiled through the tightening noose around his throat.

Campbell didn't believe in heaven or hell, but he'd watch Maya from behind her beloved aurora. Even in death, he'd ensure he'd watch over her.

The wooden planks trembled. Campbell's air *whoosh*ed out his lungs for the very last time and —

He fell.

Towards death but—

His feet hit something.

Campbell startled as he stood on something... *solid?*

"For the Free People!"

A cacophony of squeals and shouts burst Campbell's eardrums. Breath rushed down his throat at an impossible rate, the box — or whatever it was — beneath his feet close to toppling as Campbell tried desperately to maintain balance.

Cold air and noise burst around him as the hood was ripped off, his hands and feet tingling as someone unbound his wrists and ankles. A young man, not much older than Maya, stood grinning with a spare gun.

"Well, come on, then," he said.

Campbell didn't waste time asking questions. Borrowed gun in hand, he roared into the streets of Maelstrom with a flurry of bitter bullets. God, he *hated* that fucking city.

A flood of screaming Aristocrats carried them down the streets. Campbell took a frantic look around and suddenly realised where they headed. "No, wait! Stop, we're going the wrong way!"

Cushioned from all sides by Rebels, he had no choice but to be carried in the rush, away from the Eynesbury Residence.

Away from *Maya.*

Campbell tugged the closest rebel to a stop. "We *have* to go back!"

"Are you crazy? Masonians are everywhere — we'd be killed in minutes!"

The man shook himself free and resumed the sprint. Campbell tried to stop them several more times, but no one would listen. Desperation ruling, he tugged himself away from the crowd and ducked into a nearby alley. If no one would help him, then he'd do it himself. But the young man who'd saved him remained close at his heels.

"Bad idea, mate," he said, his soaked sandy-blond hair stuck to his scalp. "You'd be shot in seconds."

Campbell stared at the streets. The rush of Aristocrats had already started to slow, the excitement of the morning being brushed away and hidden beneath a fresh china tea set.

Nevertheless, Masonians prowled the city like rabid dogs, and Campbell's face was a flashing bullseye.

But I can't leave Maya...

"I need to save someone. She's at Eynesbury's, on the other side of the city. If we could just —"

"There's no time, I'm sorry." Was the man's apology sincere? Difficult to tell. "*The Eynesbury* isn't a sadist like the rest of them. Whoever this girl is, she'll be safe with her."

Safe? There was no such thing in Maelstrom.

But the man spoke truth: Eynesbury wasn't the *worst* Aristocrat, not by a long shot. Maybe Maya would be safe under her roof? *Mason has etiquette,* Campbell reminded himself, his limbs automatically flowing with the flood of escaping Rebels. *Mason won't harm her if she belongs to another. We still have time.*

* * *

Time passed by far too quickly.

Campbell didn't forget about Maya, and he vowed to rescue her from Emilia's clutches, but the rebels were tricky and demanded use of *his* services first.

"We need you to negotiate with the Herders up near Bear's Folly," said the man — who turned out to be *the* Mikael Ashworth. "*Then* we can discuss your adopted daughter's freedom."

Campbell dared not breathe a word about Maya's true identity. There'd been rumours of Svenja Svellec prowling the snowy mountains, after all those years of wintry solitude, and the last thing Campbell or Maya needed was *her* spitting her vitriol. If the truth did happen to get out, Campbell would make damn sure Svenja never touched a single hair on Maya's head.

Weeks gradually morphed into months, and the Free People's Rebellion carved its way into Campbell's every waking thought. They traversed miles: trading weapons, buying information, bribing local innkeepers. Campbell knew he'd slipped into his old role far too easily; he also found he didn't care.

Purpose kept his mind clear and his objectives set. He was doing this for *Maya*, to get her *away* from Mason. If he had to take a Masonian garrison down, or two, to achieve that, then so be it.

Sacrifice. That's all Campbell had ever known. One more wouldn't cause too much ruckus, surely? Not when Maya was safe from Mason's clutches.

Campbell wondered how long this *sacrifice* would be as he stood knee-deep in the snow, the bitter wind blowing up his jacket and making his teeth chatter. Clouds marred the dark night's sky, until only the faintest whisper of moonlight fluttered across the mountains, the burning braziers, and the white-robed Herders, mulling about their fur tents.

"We want more weapons," the lead Herder said. Campbell couldn't remember his name. *Something* Ice-Dancer, at any rate. His Tribe was a modest size, with fifteen Herders of varying ages. Children played with the reindeer, their white robes merging with the snow, as they held hands and sang with squeaky, out-of-tune voices. Campbell's heart ached as he imagined the life Maya could have had, if it weren't for Mason and his Masonians, and he avoided the children at all costs, refusing to even meet their questioning eyes.

"We've given you weapons," Campbell said, turning back to the brute of a man whose face, inked with Herdinese runes, was a stark contrast to his white robes. Campbell tried to ignore the little bone charms, hanging with lilac thread from his gaping sleeves, for they reminded him of Maya's sky-blue robes when she tried to pickpocket him.

"Not enough," Ice-Dancer said, his mouth twisting. He gestured to the wooden box choked with guns and ammunition belts. "This will fight one Masonian garrison, that is all. We need more weapons."

Guilt banged inside Campbell's stomach. He knew the weapons weren't enough, not for the number of frozen Herdinese bodies they kept having to step over. Mason knew the Herders were exchanging information with Ashworth for Rebel weapons, and the Herders needed *more* weapons to protect themselves. They needed more than the Rebellion could possibly provide.

"I'm sorry." Campbell shrugged his broad shoulders. "There's nothing I can do."

Ice-Dancer grimaced, the black ink on his skin convulsing in angry patterns. "We have children here!"

Campbell forced his stare away from the circle of children, and onto the limping figure roaming through the snow. Whoever it was, they had silver hair and a long wooden cane, for they walked with a pronounced and familiar limp.

"Excuse me." Campbell patted Ice-Dancer on the shoulder, ignored his glare, and went towards the figure.

"Hello, Aristocrat." Firelight gleamed across Svenja Svellec's grin. "It's been a while, hasn't it?"

Campbell's fists balled. "What the hell are you doing here, Svenja?"

"Same as you." She cocked her head to the side — the epitome of innocence, pretending she wasn't a snake. "Trading information for goods."

Campbell's eyes narrowed. "And what are you trading? Information, or goods?"

Her grin widened. "A bit of both." She stepped closer. "Rather like your friend, Mr Matheson. Seen him around, lately?"

No. As it happens, all letters to Joe, via the usual bribed innkeeper, had been left unanswered. Campbell already didn't like what she was implying. "Just tell me what you know, Svenja."

Svenja's grin malformed. It turned predatory. Sinister. "Ask yourself who snitched on you to the Masonians. Who knew you'd be at Waterman's Quarry?"

Too shocked to think, Campbell didn't even get to question how *Svenja* knew they'd been at Waterman's Quarry. She just roamed off, the firelight bouncing off her smug smile, and left Campbell with a dire, sinking feeling in his gut.

Joe couldn't have... He wouldn't of...

Oh, but he *would* though, wouldn't he? He'd played this game from the very beginning — didn't he say he traded information? And what better information did he have, than the location of a disgraced Aristocrat? Campbell had allowed his defensive walls to shatter. He'd let Joe wander in, unguarded and unchecked, and now the conniving bastard had set fire to his entire castle.

And Maya's fate? *Collateral damage.*

That's all she was to Joe. Collateral *fucking* damage...

Hate replaced the doubt. He balled his hands, pushing little crimson half-moons into his palms. He'd wring Joe's neck by the time this was all over, of that he was certain.

Campbell stewed over this for days, long after the Herder Tribe had moved on. A few days later, they'd heard the news: the Ice-Dancer Tribe had been decimated, smote on the side of the mountain. Smoke from their burning remains reached high into the sky, visible all across the Snowlands.

"Looks like we should have given them more weapons," Ashworth remarked, staring the grey, convulsing pillar.

And as more crescent moons etched into his palms, Campbell couldn't find the energy to nod.

* * *

The True Alira Found.

Campbell stared at the headline blankly. Like the letters would somehow float away and cease to exist. Maybe it was a joke?

Maya wasn't in Mason's Palace. Maya was at Emilia Eynesbury's. Wasn't she?

"You knew." Ashworth glared at him from across the wooden table. He felt Isla's eyes — *Harrison's eyes* — on his back, too, but Campbell still had trouble facing her. She shared little resemblance to Harrison, but her mother, Kat? Oh, she resembled her strongly. And every time Campbell looked at Isla Dagger, all he saw was her mother's severed head, hanging from Mason's grip. No doubt Isla rebutted Campbell's seemingly unfriendly attitude towards her, but he didn't spare energy to care.

Especially not now, when Mason's smug face blared from the black-and-white page.

"Knew what?" Campbell growled.

"You know *exactly* what. You knew your *Maya* was the End of Everything." Ashworth pushed himself upright and prowled around the room, like a mountain lion waiting to pounce. "Why didn't you kill her when she was a child?"

A bitter laugh rippled up Campbell's gullet. "You make it sound so easy." Campbell forced icy daggers from eyes the colour of glaciers. "Have you ever killed a child, Ashworth? Because believe you me, that's not a mark you want on your soul. It sinks deep, and it's unable to be washed away.

"But regardless of my motives," Campbell said hurriedly, when Ashworth's jaw clenched, "we need to find a way to get her out of there. Now, more than ever, we need to keep her safe and *away from Mason*."

Campbell couldn't think about what that monster was doing to Maya. Campbell knew, with grave certainty, how slow news travelled in the New World. How many days had it been since Mason realised who Maya was? All answers made him sick to his stomach.

Despite Campbell's deception, Ashworth agreed. Plans were made to somehow get Maya out of the Palace, mostly surreptitious agreements with Rebel sympathisers, but nothing ever came to fruition. All their plans were too audacious, or just impossible to pull off. Mason's Palace was a fortress — Mason himself *lived there* — and Campbell's rational brain told him that breaking Maya out of Mason's clawed clutches would not be easy. At the end of the day, the Rebels just did not have the weapons, resources, or manpower to pull off such a stunt.

Campbell's mood, his *hope*, shattered a little more each day, and before anyone knew it, weeks had gone by.

Campbell didn't believe the newspaper headline when Ashworth slammed the thin, crinkled paper on the table.

Pregnant in the Palace!

Campbell's throat worked on a large swallow. Then he laughed.

No, that can't possibly *be right…*

"The hell is this?" Campbell finally choked out.

"It's time for Plan B," Ashworth said. Brown eyes fell on Campbell like balls of molten sand.

If he were to look back on that conversation, perhaps Campbell would have suspected that Ashworth's *Plan B* was, in fact, his *Plan A* all along. But, riddled with numb foreboding and *failure*, fighting the familiar darkness growing on his soul, Campbell was utterly, completely stuck beneath Ashworth's dirty fingernail.

A snide smile spread across Ashworth's thin lips. "Really, Campbell, I should be applauding you. Because of your secrets, we finally have an opportunity to kill Mason."

Campbell's ears perked up at that, Ashworth's declaration like a beam of sunlight, cutting through the hazy fog inside Campbell's head. He met Mikael Ashworth's sharp smile with a cringing stomach. "What are you talking about?"

"The last time I saw her, Svenja Svellec told me a neat little tidbit about

Alira." He sank into the chair opposite Campbell, stretching his long limbs across the scuffed wooden table.

Campbell listened numbly as Ashworth explained what happened if Alira miscarried Mason's child, and how it would open a fleeting window of opportunity that could deliver Mason's killing blow. When silence returned to their little shack, Campbell's head shook violently.

"No, I refuse." He couldn't allow Maya to go through that. The conception was horrific enough, and now *this?* "She's *innocent!*"

"She's the End of Everything," Ashworth said with a huff of disbelief. "If left unchecked, she will kill everybody."

"She's not *Alira*, her name is —"

"She has diamond eyes. That makes her *Alira* in my book."

Campbell wished he had a proper retort — something other than the blind begs that fell of deaf, stubborn ears.

When Campbell's shouts of profanity had stopped echoing, Ashworth puffed up his shoulders. "There's someone I want you to meet…"

The door opened and a man walked in: tall; lanky; dressed in clothes far too big for his slender frame. His eyes were the shade of obsidian, and his hair stole the colour between ivory and snow.

His name was Elliot Trevelyan, and his goal was simple: *infiltrate, poison, kill.*

Campbell couldn't believe the words coming out of their mouths. The sheer callousness of their plans were… *abhorrent.*

The chair creaked as Campbell stood to his full height, fists clenched on the table. "I won't let you do this."

"You don't have a choice." Ashworth leant back and linked his fingers behind his head, elbows jutting out. "We're doing this with or without you."

"I'll stop you."

"How?" Ashworth tilted his head, looking down his thin nose with such pity, Campbell momentarily forget he was just a little older than Maya herself. "You are one man, Campbell. I have the loyalty of the entire Rebellion."

Campbell gritted his teeth. "I'll send word to Mason himself." The words were sharp stones rattling around his mouth. "I'll warn him before this callous twat can even touch her, I'll —"

"Then what did my mother and father die for?"

Campbell cringed at the softly-spoken words, said with as much conviction as Harrison, as much bile as Katarina. Still, he couldn't look at her...

"No, answer me," Isla said, taking small steps forward, her hair falling like sheets of oil across her shoulders. "My parents died because of what you all did at Gainstorn — a necessary evil to delay Mason. But now we have the chance to *kill* him. Not delay him, not make him disappear for a few months... To properly *kill* him. This is what the Dagger Rebellion fought for, the future my *father* believed we'd have. And now you want to destroy us all, to poison what remains of my father's spirit by *warning* Mason of his doom?" If Campbell's stomach was a chalkboard, her words were scraping nails. "How *dare* you sit here and act all morally superior! How *dare* you judge us when you shot a fucking *baby,* just to keep Mason debilitated for a *few months!*" She slid into the chair beside Campbell and gripped his stubby face between his hands. Campbell was helpless as Isla tilted his head to meet hers; he was unable to pull himself free as he sank into those jade-green eyes.

Harrison stared back. Placating. Pleading.

You promised me, mate. Campbell imagined the words but they still spoke truth. *You promised you'd avenge me, Daniel, Caroline, and all the others...*

Yes, he did promise.

He'd promised he'd keep Maya safe, too, but he'd already broken that one. He'd already failed her, and by doing so, he'd failed everyone else in the New World.

Failure infested Campbell's blood, strangling his resolve. Maybe, just maybe, there was one unbroken promise he still had left; one that he wasn't prepared to lose...

"Don't kill her," Campbell breathed, helpless as a single tear trickled down his cheek. "She's a *good* person. She's not like him..."

"We know," Isla said. Her red lips tried not to smile. "And I swear to you, we won't kill her."

But as they made their preparations, Campbell numbly sitting on the outskirts, he couldn't shake the feeling that a little patch of mould had started to regrow, spurting from the scars inside his soul.

* * *

THE PATCH OF MOULD GREW. Slowly, at first, then faster and faster, until he felt its weight with every waking breath. As the days passed, and then the weeks, then months, Campbell poured everything he had into the Rebellion. He had to, for if he stopped and thought about Maya — what Mason was doing to her, what *the Rebels* were planning — Campbell was afraid he'd drown in his guilt and never come up for air.

And he needed to breathe. He needed to be the shoulder Maya could cry on. He needed to hold her, *explain* to her *why* he wouldn't stop Trevelyan.

But the truth of Maya's predicament was a vicious shadow that refused to leave him.

Pregnant in the Palace. Campbell kept staring at the paper and sobbed until his tears caused the ink to merge, until the letters resembled the same dirty mulch that made up Campbell's soul.

Five months had already gone by, and it wasn't long until Elliot Trevelyan would infiltrate the Palace. Campbell still tried convince the Rebels against such drastic action, and suggested other avenues, more ludicrous, perhaps, but safer for them all, and far more merciful. The Rebels had none of it. Every time Campbell brought it up, Isla would take his scarred hand, and remind him of Harrison's sacrifice, of *all* of their sacrifices.

One day, when they were deep inside the Snowlands, they even took a detour and passed South Seal Glacier. Campbell had used Ashworth's sniper to shoot all the seals at the base, and once the ice bled with crimson, Campbell screamed his guilt and pain to the entire mountain range.

He didn't care who saw, or who heard. He needed to release his pain — pain for his soul, suddenly so grimy — and the pain for Maya, the little girl who had put her hand inside his pocket, searching for coins so she could eat.

Did that little girl still exist? She had to.

She wasn't *Alira*. She wasn't *the End of Everything*.

Her name was Maya.

One day, as Campbell still clung to that truth, the ground shook beneath them. Particles of dust rained from the ceiling and tankards spilled across the table.

"What in the name of the Old Gods was *that*?" Isla said once the tremors had ceased, her panting breaths and pale complexion mirroring Ashworth's.

Campbell's heart threatened to rip straight through his chest. He knew exactly what had caused the quake: he'd felt one just like it, the day his entire world shattered.

It wasn't long (by New World standards, at least) until they heard the news, and Campbell's suspicions had been confirmed. Erinton's Cavern was... gone. Obliterated. Smeared with blood and dust at the bottom of a mountain that didn't exist yesterday.

Campbell ground his teeth, his hands scrunched into two tight balls. Mason had scraped more innocent lives from existence. It defied logic: the largest settlement in the Ice Territory had just... ceased to exist.

Erinton Cavern's destruction brought with it a brutal reminder of Mason's power, and that he could wipe them off the map with a single wave of his hand. The Apocalypse grew nearer with each stuttering breath, and Campbell finally understood that towns like Erinton's Cavern were just the beginning, should Mason's child — *Maya's child* — take its first breath.

Campbell cradled his head, tears dripping from his chin, and remained silent as Elliot Trevelyan said his goodbyes. It was uncertain if he would return, but his sacrifice was a willing one — a necessity.

As the screams of murdered civilians moaned with the wind, for the first time, Campbell agreed with Ashworth's plan.

Even if he hated himself for it.

* * *

THE NEWS of Maya's miscarriage sliced off a piece of Campbell's heart. He rarely spoke after that, choosing instead to go hunting. He brought food to the table, and he drank gallons of mead, but he refused to speak about Maya or Trevelyan.

Except, that is, when they heard of Trevelyan's demise.

"They say Alira killed him," Ashworth said, looking down his nose again. Campbell was growing tired of that look. The boy was less than half of Campbell's age, and yet he acted so fucking superior. "It makes sense, given how *excited* she apparently was to give birth and end the world."

"Don't mistake excitement for grief," Campbell said weakly. "She's mourning."

"No, she's having fucking afternoon tea with Emilia Eynesbury," Isla snapped. "She's spending more time shopping in Maelstrom than she is in Mason's Palace!"

Lies, all of it. Or, at least, some half-hearted retelling of the truth. Maya hated Aristocrats. She hated Mason. Hell would freeze over before she'd willingly spend time with them.

Such rumours continued for a few more months. Before long, newspapers referred to Maya as Mason's new *consort.*

"Ridiculous hearsay," Campbell remarked. He gripped his hunting knife, still bloody, and impaled the newspaper to the table with such force, the little tokens scattered across the map. "Maya would *never* be his consort."

Campbell's next argument, after the newspapers had claimed Maya and Mason had been seen together, arm-in-arm: "You can't trust the tabloids. Remember what they said about the Lightlands? That he made them for her as a fucking gift?" Campbell knew this was false because Mason had never gifted anyone *anything*. Mason lacked the capacity for such kindness.

Campbell often exhausted himself with such arguments, and he elected to spend most of his time at the bottom of a tankard, wishing for a simpler time. Time went by, and only when Ashworth declared a planned bomb-attack on Maelstrom did Campbell finally remember he was in a rebellion.

"How?" Campbell asked. He must have had hundreds of discussions with Ashworth about raiding Maelstrom (mostly when he thought Maya was still imprisoned there), and Ashworth had emphatically refused each time. What made *this* any different?

Theodore Addington, an ex-Aristocratic and who, in Campbell's opinion, was a foul excuse for a Rebel, gestured to a tall, dark-haired figure who strolled into the light.

You've got to be kidding me...

A cloud of white smoke seeped from Mike the Mulch's smirking mouth. "Evenin', Aristocrat."

For a few tense moments, Campbell was speechless.

Mike's smile only grew. "Aw, he's missed me."

Campbell ignored the grizzly, scarred face of that appalling human being, and rounded on Ashworth. "What is *he* doing here?"

"Carter has made a deal with us."

"*Carter?*"

With a final puff of smoke, Mike threw his lit cigarette stump to the floor, grounding it into the wooden panels with his boot. "My friends call me Ben Carter."

"I'm not your *friend*," Campbell spat. He turned to Ashworth again and demanded answers.

Truth reminded Campbell that he always had trouble with it, but when he heard — directly from the mountain lion's mouth — that *Ben Carter* was joining the Free People's Rebellion, Campbell was certain he'd been transported to another universe.

"I want the Icelands," Carter said, effortlessly ignoring the string of profanity that left Campbell's mouth five seconds earlier. "And I want them, ideally, before Mason kills any more of its people. I bring men, supplies, and weapons. If you help me get the Icelands, I'll help you kill Mason, and, by extension, help you get Alira."

Alira. Did he remember selling nine-year old Maya to that *Jötun*? Uncertain — Mike, or *Ben,* made no comment on it, but a milky eye glared at Campbell with a knowing hatred.

Campbell cleared his throat and refused to make eye-contact.

Nevertheless, *Ben Carter*'s sudden appearance, and *help*, was the hope Campbell needed. He felt it growing in his chest, stitching the sliced pieces of his heart back together.

We're going to get her out, he thought ecstatically. *We'll put Mason in the ground and then we'll be able to get her out!*

"When?" Campbell asked, fuelled with sudden bloodlust. Perhaps, if Mason was a rotting corpse, Maya's suffering wouldn't sting him quite as much?

"Tomorrow," Ashworth said. "During the executions in Bolton Square. We'll blow Mason into a thousand sticky pieces."

Good. Campbell hoped the entire gallows would crumble to ash, too.

And at least Maya would be nowhere in sight. She'd be safe in Mason's Palace, and soon free of it forever.

The plan, they all thought, was flawless. But there was one circumstance they did not see. "She was pregnant," Isla whispered, her face pale. "She was fucking pregnant."

Campbell didn't have time to dwell on the *was* in that statement.

Equal parts angry and stunned, Campbell replayed what Theodore Addington had just told them: Maya was not safely tucked away in the Palace. Maya was there, in Maelstrom. *With* Mason, *who was still alive.*

Campbell stewed: Mason was in the middle of an explosion, and he was *still alive.*

The failed attempt on Mason's life flooded urgency into the Rebels. Clearly, Mason was just as wretched, just as heartless as Campbell thought he was, for the monster didn't need to mourn Maya's miscarriage. He'd just forced another one into her instead.

Campbell gritted his teeth as a new plan swiftly took shape, filling his heart with thunder. He strapped his usual weapons — stolen from a Masonian shipment of seconded goods, no less — and cursed the way they seemed to follow him everywhere. He couldn't get rid of them, could he? They were attached to his soul with strings of wispy spiderweb.

Maybe this audacious plan would finally clean the grime from his heart, his soul — his very existence.

The plan was set: half the Rebels would bomb Maelstrom (again) and cause a distraction, the other half (including Campbell) would break into Palace, extradite every innocent soul in it, and then blow the damned place to hell.

On the fateful night, just on the outskirts of Mason's Palace, Campbell disembarked the Rebel train and smiled a wolf's grin. Far away bangs punched the air, the dark horizon flashing with orange. Smoke rose in great billows, soon smothered by the growing fog. Campbell and a handful of Rebels waited on the outskirts of Mason's Palace as news of Maelstrom's attack spread. Finally, Mason stormed out, two-dozen Masonians on his heels, with his diamond eyes blazed with anger. The sight only stoked the fire deep inside Campbell's torso.

Two years after Campbell had been forced to enslaved Maya, *this* was what he'd been waiting for. Tonight, as Maelstrom sang with fire and brimstone, he'd finally get her out.

Campbell wasn't sure who screamed first: the Slaves, or the Masonians patrolling the area. Indeed, Mason was a fool to take so many of his forces with him to Maelstrom, for the Palace remained unprotected in his absence. The lines in Mason's logic blurred between foolishness and arrogance.

Gunshots sang in a dreadful (*glorious*) melody that inspired the fires to grow, sparks of heated gunpowder shivering like fireflies. As blood pooled around felled blue coats and swords, smoke swiftly choked the air. Heat prickled Campbell's rough cheeks like a fiery lover's kiss.

Slaves ran heedlessly through the Palace.

"Get them out!" Campbell yelled. "Get them to the train!"

Rebels answered his calls and ushered the Slaves from Mason's burning Palace. The Mulch Gang, however, seemed more interested in causing carnage. They ripped portraits from the walls and smashed priceless objects, the sounds of shattering crystal cutting through the haze of black smoke like a knife through soft butter.

Where's Maya? Campbell checked the rooms, his worry growing. She had to be here — she *had* to be!

He raced up the marble stairs as more *pops* from shattering glass filled his ears. Colourful crystal rained from above as the stained-glass shattered with the rising heat.

Upstairs, where the air was cooler and more breathable, time *ticked* on and bit at Campbell's heels. No doubt Masonian reinforcements would be incoming. Mason, too.

A flash of copper raced passed him. He reached out and caught it — *her*. A Slave — one of Mason's Maids, by the looks of her uniform.

"Where is she?" Campbell barked in her face.

The woman blanched, her porcelain-white skin somehow losing yet more colour. Her eyes shone like balls of blue glass.

"Who?" she gasped.

"*Maya.*" Campbell tried to stay calm but time kept sprinting ahead... "Where's *Maya*?"

Confusion lingered between them, and Campbell was about to rush on without her help, when she suddenly said, "This way." She charged ahead, her vibrant orange hair rippling like the growing flames.

The woman sprinted with admirable speed and finally pointed to a door. Campbell tried the lock. It didn't budge.

Campbell's anger rose into a boiling hot cauldron that threatened to over-flow. *Of course he's locked her in, the bastard!*

Campbell squeezed his old, *trusty* revolver in his sweaty palm and obliterated the lock with an almighty bang.

The door popped open. Campbell rushed in and —

There she was.

Campbell's breath stuttered. His heart, his limbs... All were still. As Mason's Palace crumbled around them, *below* them, Campbell could do nothing but stare at the *woman* — no longer a *girl* — before him.

Her face, thinner and more angular than he remembered, gaped at him.

Campbell inched closer. Her dress was... *too* nice. Her chestnut hair was... *too* styled and *too* glossy. The room was full of luxuries Campbell never expected he'd see in a prison cell, even one built by Mason.

Those *absurd* headlines and news articles flashed across his vision.

Afternoon tea. Arm-in-arm.

Consort.

Her eyes fell to his, and Campbell knew with a certainty that dropped his heart to his filthy shoes, that trickled tears from his eyes and lodged a painful ball at the back of his throat.

For in those eyes, sparkling with the intensity of pain and sorrow, and the colours of shock and warped triumph, Campbell didn't see *Maya*. *Maya* didn't exist anymore. She had been erased from reality, as though the *Connection* Mason formed with her had... *changed* her, on a fundamental level that Campbell could never, *ever* comprehend.

And with that realisation came another: if this woman was not Maya, then there was only one person she could be.

Campbell remembered the impossible choice he made at Gainstorn. He remembered *why* he did such an awful thing; *why* he chose the fate of one life if it meant the survival of everyone else.

Svenja Svellec's voice floated across Campbell's mind, like a whisper of music playing in another room: a song one could never quite distinguish, but you'd recognise the tune anywhere.

Kill her, it said.

Maya was dead. *Alira* stood before him.

"Hey, girl," he said.

The End

THANK YOU FOR READING!

Have you signed up to my newsletter? You'll receive exclusive stories, a free map of the New World, and get first dibs on all my future releases. If I've (hopefully!) convinced you, scan the QR code below to sign up and receive your free PDF Map of the New World, created by the incredible Andrés Aguirre Jurado (@aaguirreart).

If you've enjoyed The Waltz of Wolves, please consider leaving a review on Amazon and/or Goodreads, as these are incredibly important for all authors, but especially for indie authors. Not only do reviews help more people find my books, but reviews also provide valuable feedback for me, too!

ALSO BY ESME CARMICHAEL

The Connection Series: Book 1

The End of Everything

Welcome to the New World. Try not to get killed.

It's been 183 years since Mason destroyed the Old World, terraforming it into a beautiful, frozen land which he claims with tyrannical sovereignty.

Alira is a wanted woman. Prophesied to destroy the New World, hunted by those wishing to prevent her destiny, she has a deadly price on her head. Feisty and dangerous, Alira does all she can to survive. Her plan? Stay hidden. Her very life depends on it. But when Alira meets Mason, she can't deny the strange connection that sings between them. A connection that terrifies her more than his infamous, deadly stare...

For there is only one rule in the New World. *Never* look Mason in the eye.

Download *The End of Everything* now:

ALSO BY ESME CARMICHAEL

The Connection Series: Book 2

The Mover of Mountains

Welcome to the Palace. Try to survive.

Maya is gone. Now, imprisoned in the bowels of Mason's Palace, Alira must find the strength to survive. But as destiny sings louder with each passing day, Alira can't understand why Mason wants to destroy the world he so lovingly created. What secrets is he hiding about his past, about *her* future?

As unexpected alliances are formed and enemies lurk around every corner, Alira wonders if she will ever find happiness. And, most importantly, what part of her humanity is she prepared to sacrifice in exchange for a future?

Download *The Mover of Mountains*:

ALSO BY ESME CARMICHAEL

The Connection Series: Book 3

The Sound of Silence

Welcome to the Rebellion. Ready to fight?

Alira has escaped. Now, thrown amongst the Rebels and under the command of the ruthless Mikael Ashworth, the horrors of Mason's Palace refuse to abate. Haunted by her past, terrified for her future, Alira must decide where she stands in the upcoming war.

Tensions rise, betrayals sting, and Alira's trust starts to spread thin. But how can she hope to trust others if she can't yet trust herself?

As mountains crumble and music screams, the Family waits. And the clock is ticking.

Download *The Sound of Silence*:

ALSO BY ESME CARMICHAEL

The Connection Series: Book 4

The Bonds of Blood

Welcome to the End of Everything. Try to escape your destiny.

<u>Coming soon</u>

Preorder now:

CONTENT WARNINGS

- Sustained threat
- Foul language
- Violence
- Torture
- Child abuse
- Gaslighting
- Suicidal thoughts
- Depression
- Infanticide
- Death
- Grief
- Alcoholism
- Slavery
- Sexual assault (implied only)
- Emotional abuse / manipulation
- Pregnancy through rape (implied only)
- Miscarriage (implied only)
- Forced abortion (implied only)

ABOUT THE AUTHOR

Esme Carmichael is a UK independent author and published her debut novel, *The End of Everything*, in January 2021. Most of her stories have vivid worlds, dark and dystopian themes, and characters you'll love-to-hate, and hate-to-love.

Esme co-hosts the live-streamed Steam Queens podcast, is an ambassador for #TheWriterCommunity, works full time as an ocean scientist, and refuses to believe her TBR-pile is out of control.